"Move under that stree— P9-CQB-210 She gave the shovel a shake. "And put your hands in the air."

"Yes, ma'am."

Cool as a cucumber, the stranger did as he was told. Grace estimated that he was between thirty-five and forty, with dark hair, eyes that watched her with undisguised amusement, and a little lopsided smile that, at any other time, would have made her want to smile back. Not this time.

"Maybe you should put your weapon down before it misfires—"

"And maybe you should stop cracking jokes and take this situation a little more seriously."

"Sorry."

"Are you aware that breaking and entering is a crime?" Resting the shovel on her shoulders and holding it with one hand, she used the other to take her cell phone out of her bag.

"I wasn't breaking and entering."

"You did last night. I have the bump to prove it."

"I'm sorry about the bump. *And* the concussion, but the man who inflicted those injuries wasn't me."

Her finger above the nine key, she stopped. "How do you know about the concussion?"

"My father told me." When she frowned, he added, "I'm Matt Baxter."

The phone almost dropped out of her hand. Matt Baxter. The FBI agent.

Also by CHRISTIANE HEGGAN

CHRISTIANE HEGGAN

WHERE TRUTH LIES

MIRA

ISBN-13: 978-0-7783-2337-2
ISBN-10:   0-7783-2337-4

WHERE TRUTH LIES

www.MIRABooks.com

Printed in U.S.A.

To Gerd and Maria, for their warm
and wonderful hospitality.

To Anne and Jerry for persuading us
to accompany them to Austria.

And to Bob, who turns every vacation
into an unforgettable adventure.

Prologue

Point Pleasant, Pennsylvania
June 13, 1986

"What do you mean, she's dead?"

The two men stood under the moonless night sky. They were in their early twenties, solidly built, with the speaker only an inch or so shorter than his friend. Both had been celebrating, and while they had drunk more than their share, they were sobering up fast.

"I don't know what happened." The other man's voice shook as he ran his hand through his hair. "One minute she was fine and the next she stopped breathing."

"Don't give me that crap! You were having sex

with her, for God's sake! You have to know what happened." He kept stealing quick, frightened glances toward the car, but made no move to approach it. "What did you do to her?"

"Nothing! I slapped her a little when she started hitting me, not hard, just enough to shut her up, and..." He took a shallow breath. "She hit the back of her head on the door."

"Jesus Christ."

"I didn't mean to kill her, I swear."

"Maybe she's not dead." Finally gathering the courage to take some kind of action, the shorter man walked toward the old Chevy Impala parked off the road, and peered inside. At the sight of the lifeless body sprawled on the backseat, one arm dangling, he swallowed. Fighting off a wave of nausea, he opened the door.

"What are you doing?"

"Checking to see if she's dead." He leaned over the body and pressed two fingers to the girl's throat, waiting to feel a pulse.

"Well?"

"She's dead. And we're in deep shit." He sat on the ground and took his head between his hands. "I told you this was a bad idea, but you wouldn't listen."

"Hey, I didn't hear you complain once we got

underway, did I? You were just as anxious to screw her as I was, standing there, waiting your turn."

"Shut up."

"It's the truth. You're in this just as deep as I am."

"You're the one who killed her."

"And you're the one who forced her into the car."

"I'm going to be sick." He wrapped his arms around his midriff, and started rocking back and forth. "What are we going to do?" he moaned.

"First things first."

"Meaning what?"

"We have to get rid of the body."

The man on the ground looked around him. "Where?"

"The river?"

"Are you crazy? That's the first place the cops will look. And once they find the body, there will be evidence, you can be sure of that."

"Then *you* think of something, Einstein."

There was a short silence before the man on the ground stood up. "She was hitchhiking, which means that anybody could have picked her up, right?"

"Right."

"And everyone in town knows that she has a history of running away, once when she was fifteen, and another time when she was seventeen. She ended up in Tennessee that time, and stayed there for a whole week before she called her folks to say she was all right."

"What are you getting at?"

"Nobody's going to be surprised to hear that she did it again. If you remember, Chief Baxter was pretty pissed off the last time. His entire police department and more than a hundred volunteers combed the countryside for days, looking for her."

"So?"

"So they're not going to bust their asses looking for her now. Sure, they'll go through the motions, but after a few days, they'll assume that she took off again, and this time she intends to stay away."

His friend finally got it. "And all we have to do is bury her someplace where they won't find her."

"That part isn't so easy."

"Yes, it is. I know a place."

One

Boston, Massachusetts
October 9, 2006

"Oooh, and don't forget *this* baby." Angie Viero took the black dress out of Grace's bedroom closet and held it at arm's length. "No vacation is complete without a sexy little number like this one." She was a short, compact woman of thirty-five with a lovely, expressive face and thick, curly black hair everyone loved except Angie.

Grace McKenzie snapped the dress from her friend's hand and hung it back on the rack. "I'm going to Napa Valley to visit my father, not to audition for an X-rated movie."

"How will you ever find a man if you don't advertise?" Angie lamented. "You've got a great body, girl. Show it off."

Grace took two pairs of blue jeans, both faded and soft as silk, and tossed them on the bed. "I swore off men, remember?"

"It's been two whole months since you broke up with what's his name."

"Preston."

Angie made a face. "The name alone should have been a red flag. Anyway, just because *Preston* was a world-class jerk doesn't mean that all men are created equal. Look at me. I found Mr. Right. So will you."

"I'm not interested in finding Mr. Right."

"Girlfriend, you're about to change your mind."

Grace let out a groan as Angie took a photograph out of her pants pocket and dangled it in front of Grace's nose. "What do you think of *that?* Is he a dreamboat or what?"

Grace glanced at the photograph of a good-looking man in tight shorts and a T-shirt that emphasized his impressive torso. "Where did you find that one?"

"On the Internet. There are dozens—hundreds— of dating services out there, did you know that? No, of course you don't. You don't want to make the effort, Grace. That's your problem."

"My problem is that when it comes to choosing

men, I suck. And I'm not talking just about Preston. There have been other fiascos. It's enough to make me want to become a nun."

"No need to do anything so drastic, not when you have *me* to act as your screener. What do you say? From now on, no more losers for Grace McKenzie."

"What do you think of this silk blouse? To wear with the jeans?" Grace held the garment against her chest.

"Good men don't fall out of trees, you know."

"Or maybe the white pants? No. Too New England."

Angie held the hunk's photograph in front of Grace's nose. "His name is Chuck. Now that's a man's name. He's a marathon runner, likes to kayak, and plans to climb Mount Everest. Oh, and he cooks. You need a man who cooks, Grace."

"I noticed that you left out his IQ. Wasn't that listed in his résumé?"

"He graduated from college. Isn't that enough?" She wiggled the picture. "Tempting, isn't he? Come on, would you take another look?"

Grace put the white pants back and opted for a navy jogging suit instead. "No, I won't. Your brand-new career as my official matchmaker has just ended."

"You didn't give me a chance!"

"That's because finding myself a man is not what I want. End of discussion. And before you tell me that the clock is ticking, I'll remind you that I'm only thirty-four."

"And the world is full of twenty-year-olds."

Grace laughed and tweaked her friend's cheek. "Stop worrying about my love life."

"Someone has to."

Although some people might have found Angie's concern for her friend's love life intrusive, Grace didn't. Born and raised in the United States, Angie came from a family with strong, if somewhat outdated, Italian values and traditions. In the Viero household, family came first, and career second—at least for the women.

Angie and Grace had met four years ago when Grace had become the new curator at the Griff Museum of Modern Art where Angie worked as an archivist. Sharing a passion for art, cannolis and old movies, they had become instant friends.

Grace's foray through her closet was interrupted by the sound of the buzzer. She walked over to the bedroom intercom and pressed a button. "Yes, Sam?"

The lobby attendant answered right away. "You have a visitor, Miss McKenzie. A Mrs. Sarah Hatfield?"

Grace heard Angie gasp and had a difficult time containing her own shock. Ten years ago, Sarah Hatfield had been a breath away from becoming her mother-in-law.

"What could the mighty Sarah possibly want with you after all these years?" Angie whispered.

"I have no idea. I wasn't aware that she knew where I lived."

Angie made a spooky face. "Sarah knows all. Me? I'm outta here."

"You're not going to leave me alone with her."

"Sorry, kiddo. You're on your own. I can't stand the woman."

"You've never met her!"

"Her reputation precedes her." She gave Grace a peck on the cheek, whispered a quick, "stay cool," and was gone.

"Miss McKenzie?" Sam sounded concerned. "Should I send her up?"

Peeking from behind the silk screen that separated the bedroom from the rest of the apartment, Grace threw a quick look at the living area. Two empty mugs sat on the glass coffee table beside a half-eaten bagel, several pages of *The Boston Globe* were scattered on the floor and yesterday's unread mail was still on the sofa where she had tossed it last night. The place was a mess. When was the last time she had dusted?

"Miss McKenzie, should I tell her this is a bad time?"

Yes, Sam, you do that. In fact, tell her that I moved and didn't leave a forwarding address. Tell her that I've died. She took a deep breath. "It's all right, Sam. You can send her up."

She released the intercom button and ran back to the living room, grabbing items at random and throwing them behind the silk screen. Sarah hated clutter. It was one of the things, among many, that she had despised about her future daughter-in-law— the clutter. Grace, on the other hand, couldn't live without it. "It's an artistic thing," she had told Sarah. The older woman's reply had been a haughty lift of her right eyebrow, an expression that had once sent chills down Grace's spine.

The front doorbell rang, cutting short her anxieties.

Forcing herself to remain calm, she walked over to the door and opened it. The years had been kind to Steven's mother. Although she must now be close to seventy and was completely gray, the short stylish haircut made her look years younger. Her hazel eyes were still as sharp as ever, although Grace detected something else in them, something she couldn't quite identify.

"Hello, Grace." Sarah inspected her from head to toe, taking in the slender figure, the short, tousled blond hair, the Number 12 football jersey with the name Tom Brady on the front, and the blue jeans, ripped at the knees.

Grace gave an awkward nod. Even now that she no longer had to please her, being in the same room with this bastion of Philadelphia society still made her uncomfortable. "Sarah." She cleared her throat. "This is quite a surprise."

"I'm sure." Then, because Grace still hadn't invited her in, she added, "Have I caught you at a bad time?"

"Sort of, but it's all right. Come on in, and don't mind the mess."

Once inside, the inspection continued, moving from the chintz sofa and matching chairs to the authentic Tiffany lamp and the bright throw rugs scattered over the hardwood floor. Her gaze stopped on the stale bagel. "Did I interrupt your lunch?"

"That was breakfast. Cold pizza is on the menu for lunch. If you care to stay."

Sarah's sense of humor was practically nonexistent, but a corner of her mouth curved a little, mimicking a smile. "I won't stay long."

Grace removed an art magazine from one of the chintz chairs and set it on the coffee table. "Please, sit down. Can I get you anything?"

"No, thank you." Only then did she notice the suitcase Grace had taken down from the living room closet earlier. "Are you going somewhere?"

"Napa Valley, to visit my dad."

"He lives in California now?"

"He finally gave in to a lifelong dream of becoming a winemaker. He moved out west a few years ago."

"Please tell him I wish him well."

"I will." Why all this civility? Grace wondered. And why hadn't Steven warned her that his mother was planning on paying her a visit? Unless he didn't know. Sarah loved catching people off guard.

"Grace." Sarah removed her black leather gloves, one finger at a time. "I need your help in a little matter."

That was another surprise. Sarah had a slew of people who took care of her "little matters"—attorneys, close friends, servants. And even if she didn't, Grace would be the last person she'd come to. From the moment Steven had brought her to meet his mother, Sarah had made it clear that she didn't approve of his choice for a wife. Grace was a working girl, a commoner, and as such, she would never understand what it took to be a Hatfield, to stand by her man, to keep a perfect home, to give lavish parties and to sit on the board of half a dozen organizations.

But it wasn't until Steven had announced that he wanted to become an artist and not a politician like his father and grandfather before him, that Sarah's wrath had come to full bloom. Angry at her son's decision to break a century-old family tradition, she had cut off all financial support and told him not to bother sending her a wedding invitation.

Grace would never know whether or not the wedding would have taken place. Just as she was beginning to have serious doubts about marrying into a family that would probably never accept her, she had learned of Steven's affair with a young artist. Almost relieved, Grace had broken the engagement, and never saw Sarah again. Until today.

"Does this little matter have anything to do with art?" Grace asked, wondering why Sarah was taking such a long time to come to the point. "Because if it does, I'm sure Steven could help you better than—"

"No, he can't." For the first time, Sarah's gaze faltered. "Steven is dead."

Two

For a moment, Grace was incapable of a reaction. Dropping onto the couch, she just sat there, numbed by the news. When she found her voice again, it was barely audible. "Dead? Steven? How?"

"He was murdered. Shot at point-blank range in his gallery."

Grace's head was spinning. *Murdered. Shot.* Those weren't words she could easily associate with Steven, who had always been a peaceful, happy-go-lucky kind of guy. What could he possibly have done to arouse such wrath?

The answer came to her in the next second. "Was a woman involved?" she asked.

"A *married* woman," Sarah replied. "Her name is Denise Baxter. Apparently, her husband found out about the affair, went to look for Steven and shot him in the heart."

Grace covered her mouth with both hands. "Oh, God, Sarah, how awful. How truly awful. I'm so sorry."

"I warned him that someday his antics would bring him more trouble than he'd be able to handle. He didn't listen. He never listened."

"When did this happen?"

"A week ago."

Grace's back went rigid. "And you didn't let me know?"

"Why would I? You and Steven broke up more than ten years ago."

"But we remained friends, and we kept in touch. In fact, I talked to him less than a month ago."

"I wasn't aware of that," Sarah said stiffly.

"Why are you telling me now?"

"Because of the will."

The surprises just kept on coming. "I'm mentioned in Steven's will?"

"He left you the gallery."

This time Grace fell back against the cushions, too stunned to say anything.

Sarah reached into her black alligator bag, extracted a sheaf of paper, folded in three, and handed it to her. "This is a copy of the will. You may want to look at page four."

Grace took the will from Sarah's hand, flipped to the fourth page and read. It was just as Sarah had said, written in legalese but quite clear. Steven had left her the Hatfield Gallery in New Hope, Pennsylvania. After she read the paragraph again, she shook her head. "I can't accept it."

"He thought you'd say that. Please read on."

Grace read the next paragraph. "In the event that Grace McKenzie turns down my bequest, I ask that she spend one week at the gallery before making her final decision. If, after that time, her position remains unchanged, the gallery shall go to my mother, Sarah Hatfield."

"Have you seen the gallery?" Sarah asked as Grace slowly refolded the document.

"No. Steven had invited me to the grand opening, but the museum was preparing for an important exhibition at the time and I couldn't get away." Actually, she hadn't wanted to run into Sarah. "I had made plans to drive down the following year, but didn't."

"A pity. You would like it."

"I'm sure of it. Steven was very proud of it." She handed the will back, but Sarah made no move to take it. "I wish you had called," Grace said. "I would have saved you a trip."

"It's clear that Steven thought very highly of you, as a person and as an art expert."

She almost sounded sincere. "I have a job, Sarah. A job I love."

"But isn't the Griff closed for renovations until after Thanksgiving?"

She had done her homework. "My father is expecting me. I have airplane tickets. I'm practically packed." Why was she giving so many explanations when a simple no was enough?

"From what I could see, in the couple of days that I was there," Sarah continued, "New Hope is a peaceful, closely-knit community that thrives on art and tourism. Naturally, Steven's murder has left the residents shaken. The only other incident that caused as much emotion happened more than twenty years ago, when a local girl disappeared and was never found."

"Sarah—"

"Just one week, Grace, that's all he's asking. You said the two of you had remained friends. If that's true, won't you grant a friend his last wish?"

"Please don't do that."

But Sarah was relentless. "I'm sure your father would understand."

Grace felt herself weakening. Damn that woman. She was right about one thing, though—Grace's father would understand. And she would still have three whole weeks with him. "I might be able to arrange it."

"Splendid," Sarah said, her voice more confident now. "You have carte blanche to reopen the gallery for business and run it any way you wish. Some paintings are there permanently, others are on consignment. The majority are from local artists, and selling quite well, I must add.

"And in case you're skittish, I hired a cleaning crew to scrub the place from top to bottom. You wouldn't know a murder was committed." She spoke fast and earnestly, sounding almost like a real estate agent anxious to make a sale. "The police impounded Steven's Porsche before releasing it. I had a driver take it back to Philadelphia. They also took his cell phone and laptop. I understand that's standard procedure in a murder case."

It was much more than Grace wanted to know, but she didn't interrupt her. People dealt with their grief differently, and if this was Sarah's way to deal with hers, who was she to question it?

"The only item I brought back," Sarah continued, "is his Rolex, because it's quite valuable. I left his clothes in his cottage for the time being. I may give them to a local charity later. All pertinent paperwork—client contracts, show schedules, commercial invoices, etc.—can be found in the desk at the gallery. Oh, and you'll need the code for the burglar alarm. I didn't write it down, for safety reasons, but you shouldn't have any difficulty remembering it."

"I'm terrible with figures."

"Not this one. The code is your birthday, month and year, and the password, should the alarm go off accidentally, is Madame Bovary. I don't get it, but perhaps you will."

She did. *Madame Bovary* was Grace's favorite book. She had read it a number of times and had insisted that Steven read it, too. After much protest, he had agreed to give the book a try, and had hated it. "You realize that my decision won't change. I won't accept the inheritance."

"I understand that."

Grace looked at the will again. It was difficult to be mad at Steven for putting her in such a situation. He had always been an impulsive person, and often drove her crazy with his last-minute decisions. Nor could she be upset with Sarah for wanting to make sure that her son's wishes were respected. She may have been angry with him, but her love had remained just as strong.

"Are you all right with Steven's decision to leave me the gallery?" she asked. "I'm sure you weren't expecting that."

"I never doubted your talents as an art expert, Grace."

That didn't exactly answer her question, but Grace didn't push it. "All right. I'll go to New Hope, for one week. Not a minute more."

"Those are the terms." She reached into her handbag again. This time she retrieved a thick envelope. "In here you'll find everything you'll need—the address of the gallery, as well as Steven's cottage, where you'll be staying, the keys to both, a notarized letter from Steven's attorney in Philadelphia, in case anyone questions your presence."

"You think someone will?"

"I doubt it. While I was in New Hope, making arrangements to have Steven's body sent home, I spoke with Josh Nader, the chief of police there. He was very accommodating. I told him about the will, although I did not mention the special stipulation should you turn the inheritance down. As far as he and everyone else in town is concerned, you are the new owner of Hatfield Gallery. Chief Nader said to call on him if you need anything."

"Were you that sure that I would agree to go?"

Sarah didn't answer the question, but pointed at the envelope in Grace's hands. "I also included five thousand dollars to cover your expenses—"

"I won't take it." Before Sarah could protest, Grace opened the envelope, took out the money and handed it to the older woman, whose mouth opened in surprise.

"But why not? You will be incurring expenses."

"Please put your money away before I change my mind."

"Is your airplane ticket refundable?"

"I don't know. It doesn't matter. Put your money away."

Unaccustomed to taking orders, Sarah's defiant gaze held hers for a while. When Grace didn't flinch, Sarah let out a soft laugh. "I should have taken time to know you better, Grace. I might have liked you."

Three

FBI Special Agent Matt Baxter stopped to catch his breath and turned to check on his two buddies, Austrian police officers Stefan Birsner and Ernst Verlag. Both were in superb shape, but at this altitude, the steep climb up the Hintertux glacier was a challenge for even the most experienced climbers.

The lift had dropped them off at the Gefrorene Wand Summit and they'd had to walk the rest of the way to the cabin, where, hopefully, the yearlong chase would end. Stefan raised his hand in acknowledgment, and Matt nodded before resuming his walk. They were lucky, first to have found someone who would operate the lift, and second, that at this early morning hour, the trails were empty. The last thing they needed, should the plan backfire, was an audience.

Matt looked up. The cabin wasn't much farther. It looked desolate, surrounded by all that snow, and unoccupied, which concerned him. The last report he'd received from the Vienna office was that Basim Rashad, one of the most wanted terrorists in the world, had rented the cabin for the week.

Based on the information, Matt had enlisted the help of the Austrian police, and had mapped out their route. He had turned down an offer to use a police helicopter. The sound of a chopper would alert Rashad, and who knew what that maniac was capable of if he found himself cornered? Matt had no intention of returning to Vienna with the ashes of another martyr who had died for his cause. His mission was to bring the Iranian back alive so he could face trial for masterminding a deadly bombing of the U.S. Embassy in Indonesia.

Matt stopped and surveyed the cabin, hoping that Rashad was still in bed and not watching the mountain through his window. But why would he? So far, his plans had gone off without a hitch. After playing cat and mouse with the FBI for the last year,

Rashad had vanished into thin air somewhere between Bangkok and Rangoon.

Alerted that the terrorist might have sneaked into Austria—more precisely, the Mayrhofen Resort in the Ziller Valley—Matt had immediately reserved a room at the luxurious Innertalerhof Hotel in nearby Gerlos, where he had waited to hear from the Vienna office.

That was a week ago. Rashad had to be feeling pretty invincible by now.

Matt took a pair of binoculars from his backpack and focused on the cabin. It remained dark, with no sign of life, not even a trail of smoke coming from the chimney.

Either Rashad was fond of subzero temperatures, or someone had tipped him off and he was long gone.

He heard a low whistle and turned around. Stefan was pointing at the side door where a pair of skis was propped against a utility fence.

Relieved, Matt gestured for the two men to cover the back of the house. He would take the front.

He hadn't taken the first step when all hell broke loose.

The front door slammed open and a fully-dressed man, on skis, jumped out and started down the slope.

"Shit!"

Matt made a "let's go" gesture and took off after him.

The "Tux" as the locals called it, was a skier's dream. Due to the height and freezing temperatures of the glacier, the Tux was open for skiing all year round and had guaranteed powder as early as October. Matt had skied the glacier's many trails often, always for pleasure, but at this moment, his mind was only on two things—catching the bastard and staying alive.

As the slope got steeper, an almost-vertical drop from the top, Matt realized that Rashad, a risk-taker, was as skilled on skis as he was behind the wheel of an all-terrain vehicle or a twin-engine plane. Catching him wouldn't be easy.

Matt now had a pretty good idea of where the Iranian was going—the car park eleven kilometers down. Always prepared, Rashad had probably left a car in the parking lot in order to facilitate his escape, should that become necessary.

"Sorry, Rashad," Matt muttered. "Not this time."

As Rashad raced downhill, he glanced over his shoulder, grinned and raised his left pole in a salute.

"You little shit." In response, Matt let off the brakes. Leaning forward, knees bent, his poles tucked under his arms, he tore down the mountain like a speed demon. Behind him, one of the Austrians yelled a warning. Matt ignored him.

He passed the fleeing man at high speed, waiting until he was well ahead before snapping into a smart stop.

Rashad tried to veer off to the right, but Ernst had already moved into position, while Stefan kept to the left. Trapped, Basim kept on skiing, coming straight at Matt.

What the hell was that fool doing?

Matt braced himself for a collision, then at the last possible moment, Rashad stopped, sending a plume of powder up in the air.

Matt was on him in an instant.

"You have great courage, Agent Baxter." Rashad spoke with a thick middle-eastern accent. "I admire that in a man."

"Save it, Basim," Matt said, calling him by his first name as was the Arab custom. "It's all over for you."

"It doesn't have to be. You let me go and I'll make it worth your while."

"You think I want your blood money, Basim?"

"Money is money. Just think of all it can buy you. Retirement, perhaps? Wouldn't you like that? Or would you rather die from an assassin's bullet? Because that's what's waiting for you, my friend. You put me away and you sign your death sentence."

The threat didn't faze Matt. He'd heard worse.

"You're the only one with a death sentence in his future, Basim."

The two Austrians, young, tall and blond, moved forward. A pair of handcuffs dangled from Stefan's hand as he approached the Iranian.

As Rashad was being cuffed, Matt called his superior at the Sacher Hotel in Vienna. "We got him," he said, watching Basim shoot him a murderous look. "Is that chopper on the way? I've seen enough snow to last me for a lifetime."

"It should arrive any moment," Roger Fairfax replied. "And by the way, that was good work, Matt. I'll buy you a beer when you get back in town."

In the distance, the sound of a helicopter engine grew closer. "They're here," Matt said. "See you soon, Roger."

The helicopter was just overhead now. As the pilot started to lower the cable that would lift Basim into the chopper, Matt's cell phone rang. "Hello?" He covered his other ear with his hand to shield off the noise of the hovering aircraft. "Lucy? Is that you?"

"Yes. What's that racket?"

"What?"

"Never mind," she shouted back. "You need to come home right away, Matt."

Matt felt his stomach tighten. "Why? What happened?"

"Dad's been arrested for murder."

Four

The clock on the dash of Grace's Ford Taurus read 8:45 p.m. when she reached the outskirts of New Hope. Getting out of Boston had been a nightmare. After two wrong turns, a flat tire and a three-mile traffic jam on I-95, she had finally spotted the sign for Route 29. Fifteen minutes later, she was crossing the bridge that connected Lambertville, New Jersey to New Hope, Pennsylvania.

She knew little about this quaint little town, except that it was situated in the heart of one of the most beautiful and historic areas of Pennsylvania—rural Bucks County. It was a peaceful, quiet town, although a quick check through the archives of a local paper had confirmed what Sarah had told her. Twenty years ago, a nineteen-year old girl named

Felicia Newman had disappeared, and although it was suspected that she had been murdered, her body was never recovered. Five days later, a mentally disturbed man, also a resident of New Hope, was arrested. Since then, there had been little crime in the town—until Steven's murder.

Grace slowed down and glanced at the directions. "A right turn will take you to the cottage," Sarah had said. "To go to the gallery, you keep straight on Bridge Street."

After driving for more than nine hours, the thought of curling up in a warm bed, even a *strange* bed, was infinitely more appealing than an inspection tour of an art gallery. But she couldn't help it. She was curious. She had to see if Steven's pride and joy was as spectacular as he had claimed.

Bridge Street, she soon found out, was partly commercial and partly residential, which made finding a parking space at this time of night, when everyone was home, more difficult than she had expected. She found a slot in front of a shop called Red Hot Momma's, a boutique of some sort that she would definitely have to check out in the morning.

After shutting off the engine, she got out of the car and made her way down the stone walk that led to the gallery. To her surprise, the door wasn't locked, and no alarm went off when she opened it. Letting go of the knob, she ran her hand along the wall in search of a light switch.

Before she could find it, a dark form sprang out and slammed into her with a force that sent her crashing against the wall.

"Hey!" Instincts rather than wisdom took over. As the figure prepared to strike again, Grace let out a bloodcurdling scream, and, using a technique she had learned in self-defense class, she executed a perfect heel-kick to the groin area. From the *Ahrr* sound that came out of the intruder's mouth, she knew she had hurt him.

Thank you, Frye boots.

"You bitch," the man grunted.

He sounded as enraged as a wounded animal, and would have torn her to shreds if she had given him the chance. She didn't. Instead, she raised her foot, ready to deliver a front kick to the knee, but this time, her opponent saw the blow coming. Staying just out of her reach, he gave her a vicious shove and ran out.

She hit the wall again and the back of her head exploded in pain. She felt herself slide down the wall, her eyelids fluttering, as she tried to catch a glimpse of her attacker.

Her vision started to blur. She struggled to remain conscious, but her mind kept playing tricks on her.

Maybe she should scream again. The problem was, she couldn't find the strength to open her mouth. Or keep her eyes focused, so she closed them, welcoming the darkness.

Grace wasn't sure what she saw first—the pale green walls around her, or the handsome man in a white coat shining something in her eye.

"Miss McKenzie?" He smiled and tucked the penlight in his breast pocket. "Welcome back. I'm Doctor Fenley, and you are in the Solebury Memorial emergency room. How are you feeling?"

She touched the back of her head. Ouch. "Like I was hit with a cast-iron pan."

He laughed. "Luckily you weren't."

It all came back to her then: the drive to New Hope, her stop at the Hatfield Gallery, her attempt to stop a robber. "How did I get here?"

"The paramedics brought you in a few minutes ago. Apparently, a young couple passing by heard screams coming from the art gallery and rushed to help. A man ran out just as they turned the corner, jumped into an SUV and sped away. They found you on the floor, unconscious, and called 9-1-1."

"Am I all in one piece?"

"As far as I can see. You have a mild concussion

and a bump on the back of your head that will remain tender for a couple of days. How's your vision?"

"I don't see two of you, if that's what you mean."

"Excellent. Any fuzziness?"

"No."

He took a clipboard from the foot of the bed and wrote something in what she presumed was her chart. "We'll keep you here overnight and I'll stop by in the morning to see how you're doing."

She sat up, trying to look perky. "Is an overnight stay necessary? I feel fine." *No, you don't. Stop showing off to the handsome doctor.*

"Standard procedures, Miss McKenzie. Concussions can sometime take a bad turn."

She lay back on her pillow, already sorry for trying to be a hero. "You're the doctor."

"That's my girl. Now, do you feel up to having a couple of visitors?"

"Already? I just arrived in town."

"This is not your standard welcome wagon. I'm talking about New Hope's chief of police and his deputy. They'd like to ask you a few questions."

And she had questions of her own. "All right."

The doctor hooked the chart back on the bed railing. "I'll send them right in, but they shouldn't stay more than a few minutes. If you get tired, you just tell them."

He walked out and she heard him talk to someone, then the curtain parted again, and two men walked in. The first one had a definite look of authority. His step was confident, his dark blue uniform crisp, even at this late hour, and his gaze sharp. He was in his early-to-midforties with brown hair cut flat on top, an acne-scarred face and a square jaw. He reminded her of SpongeBob. The man next to him was younger with an easy smile and light blue eyes.

"Good evening, Miss McKenzie," the older man said in a formal tone. "I'm Chief of Police Josh Nader, and this is Deputy Rob Montgomery."

She was too tired, and too worried about the gallery to waste time on small talk. "Did you catch the robber?"

"Not yet. That's why I'm here. I was hoping you could give me a description."

"It was a man."

The deputy took a small notebook from his pocket. "Is that all you can tell me?"

"It was too dark for me to see more than that." She looked at the chief, trying to gauge his humor level. "He might be walking funny."

His interest perked up. "Did he have some sort of physical impairment?"

"You could say that. I kicked him in the balls."

The deputy let out a hearty laugh that the chief silenced with one glacial look. Okay, humor level, zero.

"Fighting with an intruder is never a good idea, Miss McKenzie."

"It is if you know what you're doing."

"You could have been hurt."

Being careful not to move her head, she sat up. "How did he disconnect the alarm?"

The chief held up a small plastic bag. Inside was a thin strip of metal. "With this."

"What is it?"

"A tool that he placed over the magnetic sensor so the door could be opened without triggering the alarm. We found it still taped to the doorjamb. Thanks to the young couple who ran to your rescue, he had no time to remove it. Hopefully, we'll find some fingerprints."

"I had no idea that it could be so easy to get past a burglar alarm."

"This one wasn't particularly sophisticated. One or two motion detectors would have helped. Unfortunately, there weren't any. You'd be amazed how many business owners have antiquated security systems these days."

"Was anything taken?"

"At first glance, it doesn't appear so. The showroom is undisturbed. Only the back room, or part of it, was searched. Several paintings were tossed on the floor, but there's no way of telling if anything is missing."

"The man I ran into was empty-handed," she said, starting to feel sleepy. "Unless he loaded his car before I arrived."

"He may not have had time to take anything. At any rate, we'll start a full investigation and keep you informed."

Wow. Sarah must have made one hell of an impression on him. "When will I be able to reopen the gallery?"

"Our crime scene team is there now. They should be done in an hour or so. But before you reopen, I'd like you to stop by my office in the morning and give us a statement. My deputy will be glad to pick you up and bring you to the police department."

"I appreciate that. Will my car be all right where it is?"

"Is that the black Taurus with the Massachusetts plates?"

"Yes."

"It'll be fine. In spite of what you've just experienced, New Hope is really a peaceful, law-abiding town."

Tell that to Steven, Grace thought as she closed her eyes.

* * *

Following another thorough examination, Grace was released from the hospital the next morning, and escorted to the police station by Deputy Rob Montgomery, who had arrived promptly at 9:00 a.m. Once there, she had given the chief the same statement she had given the night before, signed it and had accepted the deputy's offer to walk her to the gallery, which was only a few blocks away.

She felt well rested, and except for the tenderness in the back of her skull, there were no symptoms from last night's attack.

Standing alone in the gallery's showroom, Grace took her first good look around. The crime scene team had left the place a mess. White dust was everywhere, furniture had been overturned, and a large, L-shaped desk was in complete disarray.

Grace picked up a chair that had been knocked down and put it back in an upright position as she let her gaze sweep from one end of the room to the other. Steven had made the most of the fifty-by-thirty-foot space by hanging paintings of various sizes close together. Larger works were propped up on easels placed throughout the room. She counted forty-five paintings ranging in price from fifteen hundred to fifteen thousand dollars. A small portion of the work displayed was devoted to western art and established artists. The rest of the inventory was comprised of colorful Bucks County landscapes signed by names she didn't recognize.

She walked across the room to the desk where art catalogs, correspondence, newspapers and invoices were scattered across it. Behind the desk was an archway that led to the back room.

There, too, she found evidence of police work, as well as minor damage left by the alleged robber. Several paintings lay on the floor, facedown, as if somebody, presumably her aggressor, had gone through the stack, one by one, before letting each painting fall. Half a dozen were still standing, suggesting that he hadn't had time to examine them.

Regardless of what the intruder had been looking for, one thing was certain. He had no respect for art.

Except for the white dust used to collect fingerprints, the rest of the room was intact. A Formica counter held a microwave and a Braun coffeemaker, as well as an assortment of frame samples and more art catalogs. A small cupboard housed containers of coffee, sugar and creamer.

A quick check of an upper shelf revealed, of all things, a tackle box, also dusted for fingerprints. To her recollection, Steven hadn't been much of a fisherman. In fact, he had hated the sport.

Curious, she opened the box. It was filled with lures. Not just any lures, but some of the best available in today's market. She should know. Her father was an avid fisherman and had introduced Grace to the sport at an early age.

She looked at the selection in front of her. There were squid manglers, glow-in-the-dark spoons, crank baits, litterbugs, walleyes and bomber flats. She even spotted a Wigg-Lure, which die-hard fishermen claimed was the most phenomenal fishing lure ever invented.

What in the world was Steven doing with state-of-the-art lures?

She put the Wigg-Lure back in its compartment and the tackle box back on the shelf. Steven's new hobbies were none of her business. She had more pressing matters to tend to.

She walked over to the paintings and started to pick them up, one by one, inspecting them carefully as she went. Each painting had a Post-it stuck to it with the name of the artist, the title of the work and the price. Only the last painting sparked instant recognition. It was from Eduardo Arroyo, an early twentieth-century artist who had produced more than a hundred paintings in his lifetime. This particular canvas, about twenty-eight by twenty-three inches, was the sixth and last of his Santa Fe series. Showing a typical day in the town square, with merchants displaying their ware on colorful blankets, it was entitled *Market Day*.

What was the work of one of the country's premiere American West artists doing in a back room, instead of being displayed along with the other western paintings in the showroom?

She looked at the Post-it, and blinked. Twenty-five thousand dollars? For a painting that was worth at least four times that?

Steven had been fond of western art, but not particularly knowledgeable, which might explain his underpricing. But what about the dealer, or the collector who owned the painting? Didn't they know what they were selling? And what it was worth?

Fortunately, Sarah had given her carte blanche to do as she saw fit and that's what she would do. She planned to start by taking all sixteen paintings to the front room, including the Arroyo, and check Steven's paperwork for more information on the latter.

She was dusting a frame when someone behind her said, "So *you're* Grace McKenzie."

Five

A woman stood on the threshold of the gallery, leaning against the doorjamb. One hand was on her hip, while the other played with a long, blond curl. She was in her early thirties, no taller than five-three or four, with almond-shaped blue eyes and a small petulant mouth painted a bright red. She wore a celery-green denim jacket with embroidered lapels, snug jeans tucked into ankle boots, and chandelier earrings that shimmered in the October sunlight.

Her expression was curious as she inspected Grace from head to toe. "I'll say this for Steven. He had good taste in women." She gestured toward the door. "I knocked. Guess you didn't hear me."

"Guess I didn't," Grace replied, matching the woman's casual tone.

The visitor moved aside as Grace walked back into the showroom. "I'm Denise Baxter, by the way."

Baxter. That made her the wife of Fred Baxter, the man charged with Steven's murder.

"I figured I'd come and tell you the dirt about me before you heard it from the townspeople. That way you'll know the real scoop."

Grace wiped her hands on a paper towel. "You don't need to tell me anything, Mrs. Baxter—"

"Please, call me Denise. Everybody does."

"All right, Denise. As I was saying, you don't owe me any explanation. And if it makes you feel better, I was never big on gossip, idle or otherwise."

The young woman studied her for a moment more, then bobbed her head. "Yup, you're exactly like Steven described you—straight to the point." Her gaze shifted to a spot on the floor, halfway between the desk and the front door. "It feels strange being here. It's my first time since…" She stopped, as though she couldn't say the words.

Grace followed her gaze. "Is that where they found Steven's body?"

Denise nodded. "Nobody was allowed near the place while the yellow tape was on. All I saw, a couple of days later, was the chalk outline. Then the investigation was over and Mrs. Hatfield had the entire gallery scrubbed clean." She returned her gaze to Grace. "She hated me on sight."

Grace smiled. "Don't take it personally. Sarah is very hard to please. Trust me on that."

"Steven blamed her for the breakup between the two of you."

How like Steven to put the blame on someone else. "Did he really?"

"Oh, don't get me wrong. He told me how he messed up, but he felt that if it hadn't been for his mother being so hard on you, you would have forgiven him and stuck around."

"In that case, he was deluding himself. I broke up with Steven because he cheated on me. Pure and simple. Call me old-fashioned, but trust and loyalty rank high on my list of priorities, especially between a man and a woman about to be married. As for Sarah, she had nothing to do with my decision. I had come to terms with her attitude toward me by simply ignoring it."

Denise looked at her with undisguised admiration. "You have more guts than I have. One look at the woman and my knees turned to jelly." She paused before adding, "I can see why Steven was so fond of you. You don't take any crap from anyone."

Grace smiled. "Is that what he told you?"

"No, that's what I've been hearing all morning. The way you fought back that robber last night is the talk of the town. Where did you learn to kick like that?"

"In kickboxing class. When you live in the city and work until late at night, self-defense becomes a necessity."

"Do you have to defend yourself often?"

"Actually, this was my first time. Hopefully my last."

"Are you all right? Lorraine at the café says that you spent the night in the hospital."

News traveled fast in a small town. "I'm fine. Just some bumps and bruises."

Denise sat on the stool in front of the desk, making herself at home. "You seem like a good person."

"You can tell that after only a few minutes?"

"I'm a good judge of character. How about you? Are you a good judge of character?"

"I like to think so."

"Let's put you to the test. What do you think of me?"

Grace laughed. The woman was relentless, and yet, there was something about her that was endearing. "I think you're very pretty."

"That's not what I mean."

"All right." Grace sat down in the swivel chair behind the desk and put her arms on the armrests. "I think you're honest—a little insecure, perhaps, but that doesn't seem to interfere with your candor. And in spite of what you say, I think you're very gutsy. The fact that you're here proves it."

"Hmm."

"Am I right?"

"Pretty much. You and I could be friends, you know. God knows I could use a friend. As you'll soon find out, I'm not the most popular person in town these days."

"Because of your affair with Steven?"

"That, but mostly because of Fred's arrest. The people in New Hope worship him. He was so much more than their police chief. He was their friend, their champion, their advisor. They could talk to him about anything. Fred was always there, ready to help. I can't even tell you how many marriages he saved, just by making each couple talk to each other. The residents revered him almost as much as they do Father Donnelly, who's pretty much of a saint in these parts. And now, Fred's in jail and it's all my fault."

"Guilt is a heavy burden to carry, Denise. And it doesn't change anything. All it does is make you feel bad."

"I wouldn't feel half as bad if Fred was guilty, but he isn't. He didn't kill Steven!"

There was a conviction in her voice as she spoke

those words that made Grace pay instant attention. "I don't understand. From what I heard—"

"I know what you heard. None of it is true. My husband did not kill Steven Hatfield."

"Wasn't his gun found outside the gallery? With his fingerprints on it?"

"*Pft.*" Denise gave a disdainful toss of her blond curls. "Do you think for one second that anyone with an ounce of intelligence would drop the murder weapon as he fled? Which is what Chief Nader says happened."

"It does sound a little…"

"Sloppy. And Fred is anything but sloppy. That's what I told Josh. The man worked with Fred since the day he got out of the army. He knows him better than anyone."

"But you said there was an investigation."

She rolled her eyes. "If you can call that an investigation. The little Josh did, he did for show."

"What do *you* think happened?"

Looking restless, Denise stood up and started walking around the gallery, stopping to look at a painting every now and then. "It all started at Pat's Pub, where Fred likes to stop for a beer every evening, you know, just to shoot the bull with his friends. That evening, he walked in on a conversation that sent him into orbit. Cal and Lou Badger, two hopeless morons, were talking about me and Steven, apparently in vivid details.

"Fred would have killed them with his bare hands if Eddie—that's the pub's owner—hadn't stopped him. Then he stormed out, and because he was in such a rage, everyone assumed he was on his way here, to the gallery."

"He wasn't?"

"Fred isn't the type to make a scene in a place of business. He's much too decent to do that. He went home to wait for me."

"So you can vouch for him? You can give him an alibi?"

"No." Denise's shoulders slumped. "I was working on a new line. I make jewelry," she explained. "And I didn't leave my shop until about seven. When I got home, the police were there, hand-cuffing Fred."

"If your husband didn't do it, then who did?"

"Take your pick."

That was a strange comment. Steven wasn't the type to have enemies. "What do you mean by that?"

"Steven had his share of enemies in this town, starting with Buzz Brown."

"Who is Buzz Brown?"

"He owns a large farm on Route 232. Six months ago his wife became very ill. Buzz tried to sell his property to a developer so he could move Alma to Arizona, but Steven, who was a member of the township planning board, strongly objected to the developer's plan to build three hundred single-family homes on the site.

"When the township residents heard that the subdivision would destroy the character of the area, increase traffic and raise taxes, they started attending the planning board meetings and voiced their concerns. As a result, the application was denied and a few weeks later, Alma died. Buzz held Steven personally responsible for his wife's death. They never spoke after that."

"Six months is a long time, don't you think?" Grace asked. "Assuming that Buzz Brown was mad enough to kill, why didn't he do it right away?"

"Because if he had, he would have been the number one suspect."

Obviously, Denise had given the case a lot of thought. "You said that Steven had his share of enemies? Who are the others?"

"The dean of the local college, John Amos."

"The same college where Steven taught an art course twice a week?"

Denise nodded. "As you know only too well, Steven was a hopeless womanizer. One of the coeds reported him for sexual harassment. The dean wanted to fire Steven on the spot, but the faculty intervened in his favor and he was allowed to stay. The dean was furious."

"Why was he allowed to stay?"

"Why do you think? Steven's mother stepped in, made a generous donation to the college, and that was that. John Amos is lucky *he* didn't get fired."

The incident must have been humiliating for the dean, but hardly a reason for murder. "Who else?"

"I can't name anyone *specifically*," Denise said. "But the way Steven flirted with the women here in town..." She rolled her eyes again. "They all loved the attention, but the husbands and boyfriends, well, that was another matter."

"Was he sleeping with any of the women?"

For the first time, Denise's gaze faltered. "No." She looked away. "He wasn't."

Grace gave her a long look. The question had made Denise uncomfortable.

Perhaps sensing Grace's doubts, Denise turned around. "If you think that *I* killed Steven," she said, "forget it. I can't shoot to save my life. Ask Carmine, who runs the shooting range. He'll tell you. Fred took me target shooting a few times, before he finally gave up. Besides, like I said, I was at the shop. A lot of people saw me there."

Like art, people were never quite the way they seemed. There were layers to be peeled and angles to study. Denise's seemingly forthright manner had taken a different turn. She was hiding something, perhaps to protect herself, perhaps to protect her husband.

"I'm sure a competent attorney will unravel the mystery," Grace said.

Another *pft*. "Miles sucks. I wanted to hire someone with clout, a seasoned lawyer, experienced in criminal cases, but Fred won't talk to me. I haven't seen him since they took him in." She sounded resigned, and a little defeated.

Grace couldn't think of anything adequate to say except, "I'm sorry."

"That's all right. I can put up with that. All I want is for Fred to go free. And now for the first time in a little over a week there's hope." Her expression brightened. "Matt is on his way."

"Matt?"

"Matt Baxter, Fred's son. Lucy—that's my step-daughter—called him. Fred didn't want to bother him. He kept saying that Josh would come to his senses soon enough. When it was obvious that he wouldn't, Lucy called her brother. He should be arriving today."

"Does he solve murders?"

"He's an FBI agent," she said as if that statement required no other explanation. "One of the best. He and Fred are a lot alike—tough, stubborn, short-tempered, but very smart. Good people."

Grace smiled. "You sound as if you care for your husband very much."

"I *love* my husband," she said, meeting Grace's eyes. "I know that sounds weird, considering what I did, but it's the God's truth."

"May I ask a personal question?"

Denise shrugged. "You've earned it."

"Knowing what you knew about Steven, and feeling as you do about your husband, why did you have an affair in the first place?"

"For the same reason every female in this town went a little dopey whenever Steven was around—his charm. He oozed it, as I'm sure you know. And he truly loved women. He loved being around them, complimenting them, remembering their birthdays, or some other special occasion. When he talked to a woman, he made her feel as if she was the only person in the room. And no matter how bad you looked, Steven Hatfield could make you feel like a beauty queen. I was no exception, even though I was happily married. But Fred was always busy, helping someone through a crisis. As a result, there wasn't a lot of time for the two of us to do anything fun. When Steven started paying attention to me, it went to my head."

"Even though you knew his reputation with the ladies?"

"I wasn't thinking about that at the time."

Once again, the comment seemed to make her uneasy, and this time, Grace chose not to push it. "How old is your stepdaughter?"

"Nineteen."

"Her father's arrest must have been hard on her."

"Terrible, but she's coping. Fortunately, she and I are very close. We comfort each other."

Grace couldn't hide her surprise. "She's forgiven you?"

Denise gave a slow shake of her head. "No, and I'm not sure our relationship will ever be quite the same as it was, especially if her father is convicted, but right now, she realizes that we need each other."

She waved her hand, causing the bangles around her wrist to jingle. "That's enough of me. I want to hear all about you."

"I'm afraid I'll have to get back to work," Grace said. "There's an awful lot to do, much more than I expected. And I still have to go to the cottage to unpack."

"Okay, I'll get out of your hair, but how about lunch?"

"Actually, I was planning on skipping lunch."

"You can't work on an empty stomach. I'll make us a couple of sandwiches and we can eat while I give you a tour of the town. Everyone is dying to meet you, or at least have a glimpse of you."

"How do you know?"

"Lorraine told me. She owns the Everything Goes Café and is the only person in town, except for Father Donnelly, who still speaks to me."

Oh, what the hell, Grace thought. She could work on Steven's books after lunch. And Denise did look like she needed a friend, even if the friendship would only last a week.

Six

Matt always had mixed feelings when he came back to New Hope. Not that he didn't like coming home. On the contrary, after several months' absence, driving down Main Street and waving to his old neighbors never failed to lift his spirits.

The downside was Josh Nader. No matter how hard he tried not to run into him, Josh was always there, his sixth sense as sharp as a hound's nose. They would talk for a while, pissing each other off, the way they used to when they were teenagers, then one of them would walk away, tired of the game.

It would be different this time. With Matt's father in jail and Josh calling the shots, the police chief would take full advantage of the situation and enjoy every minute of it. He was probably sharpening his tongue right now, waiting for Matt to show up at the jail so he could bust his balls.

Matt reminded himself to play it cool. Losing his temper at the first taunt wouldn't help the situation, or his father.

It hadn't always been so tense between him and Josh. In fact, there was a time when they had been close friends. In the first grade, Matt, Josh and George Renchaw had formed a bond that had lasted for years. They had called their little trio the Three Musketeers, not a very original name, but they were little kids and they looked up to anyone with a sword and a plumed hat. Together they had done their share of pranks and mischief. George kept them straight. Studious and level-headed, he was the one who made sure his two buddies never went too far.

Then in eighth grade, everything changed. A new girl moved next door to Josh's house and all three boys fell head over heels in love with her. When Mary Ellen Sanders chose Matt, George gracefully accepted defeat, but Josh declared war on Matt.

Long after Mary Ellen had left their lives, Josh's animosity toward Matt kept on growing. Matt and George graduated from college at the same time Josh got his army discharge. That summer, another in-

cident had pulled Matt and Josh even further apart.
Matt's former girlfriend, nineteen-year-old Felicia
Newman, disappeared. When foul play was suspected
and several young men were interrogated, Josh was
quick to point the finger at Matt, claiming he had
heard the couple argue. Fred Baxter, the chief of
police at the time, had no choice but to bring his son
in for questioning. A few days later, Dusty Colburn,
a mentally retarded man with a crush on Felicia, was
arrested, and Matt was cleared.

The unfortunate incident had left the town bewildered and unsettled, with a handful of people not
completely convinced that the right man had been
arrested. And while no one believed that the chief's
son was the culprit, Josh's unfounded accusations
had taught Matt one important lesson: New Hope
wasn't big enough for the two of them. When Josh
announced that he was planning to join the New
Hope police force, Matt decided he should be the
one to leave. Two months later, he was entering the
FBI Academy in Quantico, Virginia.

After his graduation from the FBI Academy, the
news that a hometown boy was now a federal agent
kept the town abuzz for weeks. Jealous of the attention Matt was getting, Josh, by then a rookie with the
New Hope PD, applied for a job with Interpol, the

international police force that specialized in global crimes. But although Police Chief Baxter gave the young officer a good report, it wasn't good enough to be accepted into that elite organization.

Angry and bitter, Josh had nonetheless put up a good front, but Matt knew that deep down, he blamed Fred for ruining this unique opportunity. His animosity may have tapered off when Fred recommended him for the position of chief a year ago, but with Josh, it was hard to say.

George Renchaw had done equally well. A corporate attorney with a large New York City firm for many years, he had left his job and returned to New Hope, where he still practiced law while serving a second term as mayor. There were rumors that he was being considered for a higher office, but nothing had been officially announced. As for Matt, after twenty-one years with the bureau, he was now a special agent based in Philadelphia, where he headed the antiterrorism task force.

Flashing lights in Matt's rearview mirror ended his trip down memory lane. He pulled to the side, slowing just enough to let the police cruiser pass, but the car slid behind him, lights still flashing.

Matt brought his Jeep Durango to a stop and glanced in the rearview mirror. Josh, looking fit in his dark-blue pants and shirt, got out of the car and walked toward the Jeep, taking his time.

"Great," Matt muttered under his breath. And immediately reminded himself to be civil.

"Hello, Matt. Welcome home." Josh tilted his hat back and smiled, bracing his big hands on the window's edge. He looked the same as he had a year ago, when he had attended Fred's retirement party—tall, fit and in control.

"Is this a personal welcome, Chief?" Matt said casually. "Or was I going over the speed limit?" Surely that was civil enough.

"Actually I'm tempted to ticket you for going *under* the speed limit. What's the matter? The signs aren't written big enough for you?"

Matt kept his smile pasted on. "I was just taking in the scenery. A year is a long time to be away."

"Well, like I said, you're always welcome here."

Matt refrained from telling him that welcome or not, he didn't need his permission to visit. "I'd like to stay and chat," he said instead. "But I'm anxious to see my father. So if you don't mind—"

"What makes you think that I'm going to let you see him?"

Matt took a breath and counted to five. "It's his right to have visitors. Or haven't you read that part of the manual yet?" He probably shouldn't have said that, but dammit, the bastard had it coming.

"He's been charged with murder one," Josh said. "Which significantly alters his rights, but since I'm a good guy, I'm going to let you come and go as you please. For old time's sake. And while you're visiting your dad, tell him to do himself a favor and take a guilty plea. It'll save the taxpayers money and get him a lighter sentence."

"You can't ask an innocent man to plead guilty."

"He did it, Matt. You've got to accept that."

Matt's fists tightened around the wheel. "Are we done here?"

Josh moved away from the SUV. "For now. Just don't abuse my kindness."

"Wouldn't dream of it, Chief."

Seven

Although Matt had prepared himself, seeing his father behind bars hit him harder than he had expected. The only comfort was Fred himself. At sixty-three, the police veteran had never looked better. He was leaner and more muscular, probably because now that he was retired, he had time to work out. And in spite of the confinement, he seemed totally relaxed as he sat on his bunk, his back against the dingy wall, one ankle propped on his knee and reading the *Bucks County Courier Times*.

"What's the matter, Pop? You couldn't stay away from your old stomping grounds, so you got yourself arrested?"

Fred looked up, his blue eyes lighting up instantly. He tossed the paper aside and stood up. "Hello, son."

He took in Matt's tall, lean shape. "You're looking good. And tanned. Been skiing?"

"You could say that." Matt never discussed his assignments and his father knew better than to ask for more details.

The two men reached through the bars and clasped hands. "How come they haven't transferred you to the county jail where you wouldn't have to put up with Josh?" Matt asked.

"Haven't you heard? Last month's floods badly damaged the building. It looks like I'm going to be here for quite a while."

"Not if I can help it, Pop."

"Josh isn't going to make it easy for you."

"Josh is an ass. Why you recommended him for the job of chief, I'll never know."

"Nobody's better qualified. He's dedicated, fair—"

"You want to rethink the fair part, Pop?"

Fred shrugged. "He's just doing his job, Matty. And he's got to do it under extreme pressure—from the town, who wants me out of jail, and from the D.A. who wants to make sure I stay in."

"Not if your new attorney has anything to say about it."

"What new attorney?"

"Lucy wasn't happy with Miles Stewart, so I contacted a friend of mine who used to be with the bureau and now practices in New York City. He's one of the best criminal lawyers in the country. Unfortunately, he's wrapping up a case and can't be here until November twentieth."

"I don't need a fancy attorney, son." He grinned. "I have a lot of faith in *your* abilities, even if I don't approve of Lucy calling you."

"I'm glad she did."

As an afterthought, Fred asked, "You're staying at the house, aren't you?"

"Not this time, Pop. I checked into the Centre Bridge Inn."

"Lucy will be disappointed."

"I'll talk to her."

"Okay, but remember, my house is your house. Nothing will ever change that."

"I appreciate that." He leaned against the wall. "Now, how about you give me your version of what happened?"

Fred was silent for a long time. Matt folded his arms and just waited.

"You were right, you know," Fred said at last.

"About what?"

"Denise. I shouldn't have married her. She was too young, too energetic, too unpredictable." He paused.

"Neither one of us had any luck with the Newman sisters, did we? You were the smart one, though. You had enough sense to break up with Felicia before things got too far. I, on the other hand, allowed my infatuation with Denise to turn into something so powerful, I couldn't have walked away if I had wanted to."

"We don't have to talk about that now."

"Yes, we do. Your disapproval of Denise changed our relationship, and I hated that. The truth is, I was too blind to see her for what she was."

"She made you happy."

"That she did. Until I heard about her affair with Steven Hatfield. It's true what they say, the husband is always the last to know."

"Lucy said that you didn't find out about Hatfield until last week. Is that right?"

Fred ran a hand through his gray hair. "Yeah. I had been visiting some friends in Doylestown, and on the way back I decided to stop at Pat's for a beer. The Badger brothers were already there, drinking and telling dirty jokes. That's when I heard Denise's name being mentioned."

"What did they say?"

"Something about knowing all along that she'd be a good lay, and maybe they'd have to ask Steven Hatfield just how good she was."

"They happened to say that just as you walked in?"

"Yeah. I was too steamed at the time to think much about the timing. Later, I wondered the same thing."

"What happened after you heard that remark?"

"I should have ignored them, but I didn't. I was pissed off."

"You picked a fight with them." It wasn't a question. Lucy had already told him about their sweet old dad trying to take on two men the size of Texas.

"Wouldn't you have?" Fred asked. "If they talked about your wife that way?"

Matt made a mental note to talk to the notorious Badger brothers, two former little punks who had grown into bigger punks. "Probably, but go on."

"Fortunately, Eddie split us up before we could do any real damage to his place. I stormed out and went home to confront Denise. She wasn't back from the shop yet. Before you ask, no one saw me come home."

"And everyone at Pat's assumed you were going to the Hatfield Gallery."

"What was I supposed to do? Carry a sign?"

"Why didn't you just walk over to the jewelry shop?"

"Because I didn't want to make a scene. I was never much for airing my dirty laundry in public. And while I was home, Steven was being murdered."

"With your gun." When Fred remained silent, Matt added, "Mind telling me how it ended up in the flower bed of the Hatfield Gallery?"

"If you mean, do I have an idea who could have planted it there, no, I don't. And make no mistake, it *is* a plant, made to look as if I dropped it in my haste to get away. As if I would do a dumb thing like that."

"Who knows where you keep your gun?"

"It's no secret to those who know me well that I keep my guns locked up in the bedroom armoire."

"So whoever framed you not only had the key to your house, but the key to the armoire as well? Is that what you're telling me?"

"When I come home, I'm in the habit of dropping my keys on the kitchen hutch. The kitchen is where I read my paper and have coffee with my friends, or whoever feels like dropping in. It wouldn't be hard for someone to make an impression of both keys at the first opportune moment."

"Any idea who that someone might be?"

Fred shook his head. "Nope. Some weeks I can't even tell you how many people stop by, especially now that I'm retired."

He wasn't exaggerating. Fred Baxter had been just as popular when Matt was growing up. The house was always filled with friends and neighbors who came to chat, to tell the chief their troubles, or to just play a few rounds of poker.

"So the question is, who hated Hatfield enough to kill him?"

"He wasn't very well-liked, especially by the men. Did they hate him enough to kill him?" Fred shrugged. "I don't know. Maybe. I wanted to kill him myself when I heard about him and Denise."

"Who would you put at the top of that list?"

Fred was thoughtful for a moment. "Once I would have said Buzz Brown, but too much time has gone by. He was pissed off, though, blamed Steven for his wife's death."

"Why was Steven so set on not having that land developed?" Matt asked.

"Oh, the usual reasons—traffic, taxes, overpopulated schools. Buzz didn't buy it, though. He thought it was personal."

"Personal how?"

"Don't know. You can ask Buzz when he comes back from his trip to Kansas in a few days. Or you could talk to Duke Ridgeway. He sits on the planning board and played golf with Steven. He might know something."

"I'll give him a call, and talk to Buzz as well when he gets back. Who else is on your list?"

"Hatfield was the town's heartthrob. He got in trouble at the local college where he taught a weekly art appreciation course. A sexual harassment complaint from a young coed almost got him fired. And then there was this artist from Milford. Steven had promised to feature her in a one-woman show but never did. Witnesses saw them at the gallery, shouting at each other."

"Do you have her name?"

"Elizabeth Runyon. She works part-time at her aunt's antique shop on Church Street."

Matt wrote the information down. "It won't hurt to check her out, but I wouldn't hold too much hope with those two," Matt warned. "There isn't much of a motive for murder with either one."

"And that's why I'm the only viable suspect. With me, they've got it all, Matty—motive, opportunity and the kind of evidence not even Clarence Darrow could dismiss."

Matt tried to stay optimistic. The last thing his father needed right now was for his own son to tell him that his case was hopeless. But the truth was, the killer had engineered and executed what looked, at least on the surface, like the perfect crime.

"Something odd happened last night, though," Fred said as an afterthought.

Matt's antennae went up. "I'm listening."

"You may not know this yet, but in his will, Steven left the gallery to his ex-fiancée, a curator at some Boston museum. She arrived in town last night, presumably to take over, and surprised an intruder inside the gallery. Foolishly, she tried to stop him and got pretty banged up in the process. She spent the night in the hospital and was released this morning. Her name is Grace McKenzie. She was engaged to Steven about ten years ago and apparently, they had remained friends."

"Was anything taken from the gallery?"

"The police don't know yet. A few paintings were thrown to the floor, but the rest of the place was undisturbed, so Josh ruled out vandalism."

"It sounds to me like the robber was looking for a particular painting."

"Maybe. Miss McKenzie will be able to tell what's missing after she does an inventory."

"That break-in could be important, Pop. Is Josh investigating it?"

"He has to. The news is out and a few people in town want the investigation into Steven's murder reopened."

"What is she like, this Grace McKenzie? Do you know?"

"According to Rob, she is pretty, sassy, smart and gutsy. Not too many women would try to stop an intruder in the middle of the night." He chuckled. "I heard that she packs a nasty kick."

"She hurt the guy?"

"I'll say. She hit him in the balls with the heel of her boot."

"Ouch."

"My sentiments exactly. Josh was impressed, and as you know, he doesn't impress easily."

Matt smiled. "You're pretty well informed for a guy who spends all his time behind bars."

Fred looked smug. "My former deputy keeps me au courant."

"Is that okay with Josh?"

"Hell no, but who cares?"

Eight

"Sarah, please." Grace switched her cell phone to her left ear as she stopped at a traffic light. "There is no need for you to come to New Hope. The gallery is fine. I'd like to tell you that nothing was taken, but the truth is, I haven't had a chance to check the inventory yet. As soon as I do—"

"For heaven's sake, Grace, I'm not worried about the inventory. Chief Nader told me you had a concussion. That's why I called. I'm concerned about *you*."

Was she? Really? "The doctor gave me a clean bill of health before I left the hospital." The light turned green. "I've got to go, Sarah. I hate to talk on the phone while I drive. Is it okay if we talk later?"

"Call me anytime."

After saying goodbye, Grace snapped her phone

shut and dropped it on the seat next to her. Sarah had mellowed over the years, or maybe it was Steven's death that had changed her. Grief had a way of doing that to people. Grace made a mental note to call her tonight, not because she had a sudden yearning to talk to the woman, but because she felt sorry for her. For all her money, her busy social life and a houseful of servants, Sarah was a very lonely woman.

Grace left the town behind and followed North River Road, a narrow, winding thoroughfare that led deeper into the heart of Bucks County. As the morning mist lifted, making way for bright sunshine, she understood why Steven, who had an eye for beauty, had chosen this part of Pennsylvania as his new home. And why local artists never tired of painting those magnificent landscapes.

Grace raised her visor so she could feast on the scenery. Ancient oaks and red maples bordered the road, forming a brilliant canopy of yellow, orange and russet. Tucked behind those majestic trees, centuries-old homes overlooked the Delaware River, one of the most historic waterways in the nation. It was difficult to look at this setting and not recall how history was made, right here in Bucks County.

Steven's cottage, although small, took her breath away. Half-timbered and Northern European in style, it was barely fifteen feet wide, with wood beams on the exterior walls and cedar shingles on the roof. The windows, all leaded glass, were small, but in perfect balance with the rest of the house.

Grace pulled her car onto the graveled driveway, half of which was covered with dry leaves, and went to unlock the door. She found herself in an attractive living room with comfortable sofas and chairs in a plain navy fabric, and plush wall-to-wall carpeting in a neutral shade. A corner of the room had been made into a dining area, with a round maple table and four chairs. The high ceilings and natural flow from one room to the next made the cottage seem bigger than it was. A flight of stairs in the middle of the living room led to a second floor.

She put her suitcase down and took time to look at the mementos Steven had accumulated over the years—an antique peg hook where he had hung art work, a whimsical white gourd lamp and a garden urn that served as a side table. Family photographs were everywhere; some she had seen before, others she didn't know. On the mantel, above the stone fireplace, was one photograph she knew very well. It had been taken in Santa Barbara, where she and Steven had attended an art festival a few months before their breakup.

The snapshot brought back vivid memories of their two years as a couple, the plans they had made to someday own an art gallery together and the young artists they hoped to discover, all in spite of Sarah's strong objections.

As the wedding date drew near, however, Grace began to fear that as much as she tried to ignore her future mother-in-law's criticism, the strain of that relationship would eventually affect her and Steven's marriage.

"That's what we call getting cold feet," her father had cautioned. "If you're not ready to get married, don't do it."

Maybe that's why Steven's betrayal hadn't hurt her as deeply as she had expected. Although wounded at first, after a few days, she was able to look at the breakup as a blessing rather than a tragedy. A few months later, when Steven had called to ask if she could take a look at a sculpture he was thinking of buying, she had surprised herself by saying yes.

She was glad that he had fulfilled his dreams, Grace thought as she kept gazing at the photograph, and saddened that he had enjoyed his success for such a short time. She wasn't sure why he had kept this snapshot, though. Sentimentality? A memento of what could have been?

After putting the snapshot back, she picked up her suitcase and carried it upstairs. The single bedroom was large and mostly white, with a four-poster brass bed and an adjoining bathroom in the same color scheme. The look was clean and uncluttered without being harsh.

Steven's clothes hung neatly on the rack in the walk-in closet. There were shirts from Savile Row, cashmere jackets, custom-made suits and designer ties. Shoes and boots in various styles and colors were on an upper shelf.

Glad that she hadn't packed much, she hung her clothes in the facing rack. Then, remembering that she had a date with Denise Baxter, she stripped and went into the bathroom to shower.

"Believe it or not," Denise said, taking her role of tour guide seriously. "New Hope started as an industrial town, with mills that were busy manufacturing paper, quarrying stone and grinding grain."

She unwrapped a sandwich and gave half to Grace. "But even in those early days," she continued, "the beauty of Bucks County did not go unnoticed. Soon artists began settling along the Delaware River and New Hope became an artists' colony."

"I can see why," Grace said. "The scenery from North River Road is nothing short of spectacular."

"And it only gets better."

As she ate her tuna salad on rye, Grace took in the many shops along Main Street, all filled with an assortment of merchandise—candy, antiques, rare books, gourmet food, garden decorations. Business owners had welcomed fall with planters of colorful mums outside their doors and huge corn stalks wrapped around the telephone poles.

"Some of the architecture is beautiful," she remarked. "Do any of those buildings come with a pedigree?"

"Lots of them. For example, the Logan Inn we passed a moment ago is on the National Register of Historic Places. In fact, New Hope itself is registered as a National Historic Site. That big stone house over there—" she pointed "—is the Parry Mansion, and was once the home of Benjamin Parry, a wealthy mill owner."

"I've already counted five art galleries. Wasn't Steven worried about the competition?"

"All the time. The one that concerned him most, though, was the Haas-Muth Gallery, just up the street from the Hatfield Gallery. The owner is an artist, but he doesn't just display paintings. He also sells Oriental rugs, which brings a lot of traffic. Steven was thinking of doing something similar, not with rugs, but maybe with antique clocks." Her voice turned a little somber. "He never had the chance."

"Who is that?" Grace asked, nodding in the direction of a twin-spiraled church.

"Father Donnelly. He's our pastor. He first came here as a young priest many years ago, but the church likes to move their people around and he was sent to another parish. Now he's back."

She smiled at the handsome, fortysomething man watching them approach. He wore black pants and a black jacket with a white collar peeking through. "Hello, Father. Were your ears ringing? I was talking about you."

"I'm flattered." He rested his gaze on Grace. "You must be Miss McKenzie."

She extended her hand. "I'm glad to meet you, Father."

"Welcome to New Hope. I hope you're recovered from that unfortunate incident last night."

"Completely, thank you."

"In that case, you might find time to attend Sunday mass?" His eyes shone with youthful mischief as he talked.

Grace wasn't much of a churchgoer, but how could she refuse such a gracious request? "I'll make a point to do that," she promised.

"You're incorrigible, Father," Denise said. "Always trying to garner more parishioners."

"That's my job, Denise, as well as my pleasure. Now if you'll excuse me, ladies, I have to make my hospital rounds. You both have a good day."

"There goes a good man," Denise said as the pastor walked away. "He's been a huge comfort to me. He never preaches, never criticizes and he never pushes you to say anything you don't want to say. He sits with me and we just talk. He gives me the strength I need to face the day." She took a bite of her sandwich. "This morning I asked him to look at some earrings I made and give me his opinion."

"Did he try them on, too?"

Denise laughed. "No, silly, but he would have if I had asked him to. That's how he is. And speaking of earrings, here's my shop."

They had stopped in front of a store named, appropriately, Baubles. Denise unlocked the front door and Grace found herself in a bright, colorful store that was a perfect reflection of its owner. Two glass cases held an assortment of beaded necklaces, rings, bracelets and earrings of every shape and color. On the counters, yards of silver and gold chains hung on small racks, competing for space.

Grace walked around, admiring Denise's work.

"You're very talented," she said as she picked up a necklace with a small citrine pear hanging from it. "And very versatile. There's something for every taste."

"Thank you. I love my work. It keeps me busy, especially now that Fred is...away."

Grace kept moving along the cases, studying the delicate workmanship. "How did you learn to do all this?"

"A friend of mine used to own this store. She gave me a job as a salesgirl the day I graduated from high school. I learned a lot from her over the years, not to mention that we got along like two sisters. That's why I continued to work after I married Fred, for the love of it. Then one day, Alice announced that she was selling the store and moving to upstate New York. She was hoping I'd make her an offer, but I wasn't about to ask Fred for that kind of money. A week later, Fred handed me the keys and told me the store was mine. I thought I would faint."

"Seems to me like he made a sound investment."

"Go ahead." Denise came to stand behind her. "Pick something. As my welcome gift to you."

"That's very kind of you, Denise, but I can't accept."

"I insist." She took the citrine necklace out of the case and held it against Grace's neck. "This would go well with your hazel eyes. Unless you'd prefer something else. The coral bracelet maybe? I saw you looking at it."

It was impossible to say no to this woman once she had made up her mind. "Are you in the habit of giving away merchandise, instead of selling it?"

"No, just you, because I like you. So?" She held the necklace in one hand and the bracelet in the other, moving them up and down. "What will it be?"

"The necklace. And thank you very much."

"You're welcome." Denise walked back behind the case and started wrapping the necklace in white tissue. "You can wear it tonight."

"I'm not going anywhere special, but I'll still wear it."

"You have somewhere to go now. Lucy is dying to meet you, so I thought I'd make us a nice home-cooked dinner. Do you like Italian food?"

Grace laughed. "Are you kidding? That's my favorite kind."

"Then you're in luck, because I make the best lasagna this side of Napoli." She fitted the narrow box with a lid and handed it to Grace with a flourish. "Seven o'clock. Our house is on Bridge Street, a couple of blocks from the gallery. You can't miss it. It's the blue Colonial with the American flag out on the front yard. Come hungry."

Nine

Duke Ridgeway had to be close to eighty by now, but the years didn't seem to have slowed him one bit. After Pat's Pub, New Hope Hardware was the busiest place in town, and Duke, who had owned the store for the last forty years, ran it like a finely tuned machine. Born and raised in Bucks County, he was a respected businessman and a fair and incorruptible member of the planning board.

"Well, if it isn't little Matty," he said, adopting the nickname only Matt's father and his sister used from time to time. He made change for a customer, thanked him and closed the cash register. "How are you, my boy?"

"Not too bad. What about you, Duke?"

"Ah." He made a disgusted gesture. "The old leg

is starting to let me down." He scratched his head, pretending to be puzzled. "You don't suppose I'm getting old, do you?"

"You? Never. Besides, age is only a piece of paper."

Duke laughed. "I'll remember that. How's your pop holding up?"

"Pretty good, considering."

"You've got to get **him** out of that cage, Matty. It ain't fair him being there."

"I'm trying, Duke. In fact, that's why I'm here. I was hoping you could help me with something."

"I'll do what I can, you know that, but if there was a way for me to clear your daddy, I'd have done so by now."

"I know that, but something came up during a conversation with my father that still puzzles me. I'd have asked Buzz, but I understand that he won't be back until the end of the week."

Duke nodded. "He's thinking of moving to the midwest." He slid a cardboard ad for latex paint to the end of the counter. "So what brings you by, son?"

"You remember that application for the development of Buzz's farm?"

"You bet I do. Kept us in session for months."

"Do you have any idea why Steven opposed it so much?"

"Mostly because of the increase in taxes New Hope would have to shoulder. Now mind you, the developer presented a good case. He explained how self-sufficient that community was going to be, the economic growth for local businesses, a regulated traffic pattern and a homeowner association that would pay for many of the services the residents would need."

"That didn't satisfy Steven?"

"It wasn't just Steven. A couple of other members agreed with him. When the developer failed to explain how he could keep the children from playing in the detention basins, Steven started getting a lot of support. Soon the entire town was determined to keep the developers away. From the way everyone was talking, you'd have thought there was gold buried in those woods."

"Was the vote unanimous?"

"Not quite. I voted yes and so did Mel Frisk."

"Was there any bad blood between Steven and Buzz? Or Steven and the developer?"

"Nobody knew the developer until he came to town, and as far as I know there was no bad blood between Steven and Buzz before then, but you can bet your last dollar that there was after that. Buzz hated his guts."

He removed his glasses and started to wipe them with a corner of his flannel shirt. "You don't think Buzz shot him, do you? Because I'll tell you right now, Buzz could no more kill another human being than your pop could."

"I know. I'm just trying to fit the pieces of the puzzle together." He watched Duke put his glasses back on. "How did Steven get along with the other planning board members?"

"Good. I was the only one he socialized with, but they liked him okay. He was smart. Came to the meetings on time, didn't talk down to people and expressed himself well. I know what some of the townspeople are saying about him, and maybe some of it is true, but as far as I'm concerned, he was just a good guy trying to fit in."

"He didn't flirt with some of the wives?"

Duke let out a hearty laugh. "Now, I don't mean to be disrespectful of my fellow board members, but I can tell you that they had nothing to worry about. Steven wouldn't have given any of those ladies a second look if they had been the last females on earth—and if you repeat that to anybody, I'll call you a liar."

Matt laughed. "It will be our secret." A customer walked in and Matt stuck out his hand. "Thanks a lot, Duke. I'll give your regards to my father."

"You do that. And be sure to have a little chat with Buzz. He might not feel like talking, because the pain of losing Alma is still so damn raw, but it's worth a shot."

Founded in 1893 by Everett J. Anderson, a wealthy mill owner, Anderson College was a private institution that offered a diverse range of degree programs, including a strong art department, which was the reason Lucy had chosen the local college. Located on Route 202, the sprawling campus now boasted more than a thousand students from all walks of life.

Finding a parking space was a challenge, but Matt lucked out when two male students jumped into a Nissan parked two spaces from the front entrance and drove away. Matt was leaning against the Durango, arms folded when a human wave of laughing, jean-clad young women poured out of the main building. With individuality practically nonexistent, picking out his sister among the crowd wasn't easy. Not only did all the girls wear similar attire, they also wore their blond or brown hair long and straight.

At last he spotted Lucy, her blond locks bouncing with every step. But although she made an effort to keep up with her friends' ebullient chatter, she seemed quieter, more subdued. Matt's heart went out to her.

Born when Matt was already in college, she had taken a special place in their parents' heart, especially Fred, who adored his little girl. They had grown even closer after the death of their mother ten years ago.

"Luce!"

At the familiar nickname, she looked up and a huge grin split her pretty face. Her worries temporarily forgotten, she ran toward Matt and threw herself in his arms. "Oh, Matty, I'm so glad to see you."

He caught her, trapping her books between the two of them, and held her tight for a moment before he put her down. "I'm glad to see you, too, Goldilocks. Let me take a good look at you."

He held her at arm's length and took a quick inventory. She had their late mother's good looks—silky hair so pale it almost looked white, a fair complexion, large blue eyes and a small mouth that was made for smiling.

"You look good, kiddo."

"You, too."

As if to confirm her last statement, Lucy's two friends came to stand beside her. Ginny Peruso, who had been Lucy's soul mate since they were toddlers, smoothed down her brown hair while Barb, a stunning blonde, struck a pose. "Hi, Matt," they said in unison.

Feeling suddenly very old at forty-one, Matt wrapped an arm around his sister. "Ladies."

"Are you going to be in town long?" Barb had always been on the precocious side, but the coy looks and sexy tone were new. Matt reminded himself that they weren't little girls anymore, or awkward teenagers. Almost overnight, they had become women. As had Lucy.

"I'm not sure yet."

As though sensing that her big brother needed rescuing, Lucy took his arm. "Okay, guys, enough with the flirting already. Ginny, I'll see you after dinner." Then, not waiting for an answer and ignoring the two girls' look of disappointment, she pointed at the Jeep. "Is this yours?"

"Yup."

She jumped in and waited until he was behind the wheel before saying teasingly, "You took a huge chance coming here. You could have had all your clothes ripped off."

Matt pulled out of the parking space. "By two nineteen-year-olds?"

"By a swarm of red-blooded females," she corrected. "It isn't every day that those hallowed halls are graced by the presence of a hunk like you."

"I'm more than twice their age."

"And therein lies the attraction, big brother."

Matt threw his head back and let out a hearty

laugh. "Okay, what's with all the compliments? You need money? A new car?"

"I don't need or want anything. I'm speaking the truth. Didn't you notice the hungry looks you drew? Even Professor Adler couldn't take her eyes off you."

"Professor Adler can't see farther than her nose."

"She had laser surgery. *And* a boob job. Could you tell?"

It felt good to hear her giggle. "Now that you mention it," he replied playfully. "She did seem... fuller."

Lucy laughed and wrapped an arm around his shoulder as he drove. "Where are you staying?"

"The Centre Bridge Inn."

"You know that you're welcome to stay at the house, don't you? Denise said to tell you that your old room is always ready."

"Thanks, Luce, but I like it better this way. It's easier to come and go without having to give anyone a lot of explanations."

"That's not why you're staying away."

He took the coward's way out and ignored the comment. "How about some lunch?" he asked as he slid into a parking space in front of the Everything Goes Café. "I'm famished."

"How about an answer to my question?"

He held her gaze for a moment and recognized in them their mother's determination. "Okay, if you must know, my relationship with Denise wasn't all that great before, and what she did to Dad didn't do anything to improve it. Any way you look at it, he's in this mess because of her."

"I'm mad at her, too, Matt, and it may take me a long time to forgive her, but she's truly sorry. I hear her cry sometimes at night, and I have to admit that it breaks my heart."

That was Lucy, tenderhearted and always ready to go to bat for the underdog. "I can understand that. She's been like a mother to you over the years. Just don't expect me to be as kindhearted, that's all."

But Lucy wasn't ready to give up just yet. As they stepped onto the sidewalk, she said, "Did Dad tell you that she attacked Josh when he came to arrest him?"

"Attacked him? Physically?"

"When Josh tried to put the cuffs on Dad, Denise pushed him against the wall and told him to 'put his handcuffs where the sun don't shine'—her words, not mine. Josh was so intimidated, he tucked the handcuffs back in his pockets and told Dad to get in the car."

Matt chuckled at the image. "I'll say this for her, the woman has guts." He opened the door to the café. "Now, about that lunch?"

Although the lunch hour was over, the brightly lit café was packed with college students nibbling on cheese fries and thick slices of Lorraine's mile-high apple pie. Delighted to see Matt, Lorraine quickly cleared a table for them and handed them a menu. "I put aside a little care package for your dad," she told Matt. "I was going to deliver it in person, but since you're here, you might as well take it to him. Is that all right?"

"You're a doll, Lorraine. Thank you. I'm sure my father will be thrilled." He waited until she had moved away before asking, "Does she do that often?"

"Send Dad his favorite food?" Lucy opened her menu. "Every day. She worships him." She leaned over the table. "I think she had designs on him," she whispered. "But then Denise came along."

"Really?" He watched Lorraine lift a tray over her shoulder and carry it across the room. "I never knew that."

"You were in some other part of the world, chasing bad guys."

"How did she take it? Denise coming into the picture, I mean."

"She was a good sport about it. She didn't hold a grudge against Denise or anything. In fact, she's one of the few people in town who still speaks to Denise."

"Did she know Steven well?"

Lucy looked surprised at the question. "Lorraine? I don't think so. Why?"

"Just curious. How about the rest of the town? How did everyone react when they heard that Steven Hatfield had died?"

Lucy put her fist on her hip and pretended to be upset. "Matthew Frederick Baxter. Are you pumping me for information?"

"How else are you going to earn your lunch?"

She hit him with her menu. "You rat."

"The more I know, the better I can help Dad."

"True." She looked around her and lowered her voice a little. "There were mixed reactions. I guess Dad told you that Steven wasn't very well-liked."

Matt nodded. "Did anyone go to his funeral?"

A busboy placed two tall glasses of water in front of them and disappeared. "A few members of the planning board went," Lucy replied. "One professor from the college, a few students. The rest of us attended a mass conducted by Father Donnelly here in town. Several people showed up, other business owners, suppliers, town officials."

"What about Denise?"

"She didn't go." Lucy looked suddenly uncomfortable as she started reading her menu, but Matt had perfected the art of observing people over the years, and he could read Lucy like a book. She was hiding something.

He took a sip of his water. "Why do you think that is?" he pressed.

"I don't know." She kept her eyes downcast.

"That's odd, don't you think? Considering her relationship with Steven?"

"The people in this town haven't been very nice to **her these** past couple of weeks. That's why she thought it best to stay away."

A waitress stopped by their table and greeted Lucy by name. Although Matt had never seen her before, she seemed to know him quite well. "You're Matt, aren't you? I'd recognize you anywhere." She gave him an enticing smile. "Did anyone ever tell you that you look like George Clooney?"

"Who?"

"George Clooney. The actor?"

Matt unfolded his paper napkin. "Never heard of him."

"You're kidding, right?"

Lucy was laughing softly. "You must forgive my brother, Renée. He doesn't get around much, but she's right," she told Matt. "You do look like George Clooney. Especially when you smile."

Matt cut short the conversation by handing Renée his menu. "We'll have two BLTs on wheat toast and two Cokes. Is that okay with you, Luce?"

"Sure." As soon as the waitress was gone, Lucy's face turned serious again. "How are you going to help Dad?"

"By talking to people, poking around, that kind of stuff."

"What do you hope to find out?"

"If Steven was expecting someone the night he was killed, and if he or she showed up. The problem is, at this time of year, the downtown businesses start to wind down at about four. I've talked to a few people so far, and everyone closes at six sharp, if not sooner, which means they didn't see or hear anything."

"Did you talk to Elizabeth Runyon? She was steaming mad when Steven welched on his promise to feature her in a one-woman show."

"I did talk to her. She didn't do it."

"What makes you so sure?"

"She has an airtight alibi. She and her aunt were out to dinner that night. At least fifty people eating at the same restaurant can vouch for that, including the waiters."

"People sneak out of public places all the time with no one noticing."

"How would you know that?"

"I watch *Desperate Housewives*."

He gave her a blank look.

"Oh, my God, where have you been? *Desperate Housewives* is the hottest show on television. It's filled with intrigue, sex and hanky-panky."

He smiled. "It's a little different in real life, honey."

The frown between her blond eyebrows reappeared. "Are you saying that Dad's case is hopeless?"

He took her hands in his. They were cold. "Absolutely not," he said with more optimism than he felt. "I don't expect it'll be easy, but I doubt our killer committed the perfect crime. Few murderers do. It's just a matter of finding out where he screwed up." He gave her hand a quick squeeze. "Would you like to help?"

Her face brightened, just as he knew it would. "To clear Dad? Are you kidding? What do you want me to do?"

"Tell me what you know about that Boston curator. I understand that she inherited Steven Hatfield's gallery."

"That's what I heard."

"Have you met her?"

"No, but Denise has. She says she's nice and very pretty."

"How did they meet?"

"Denise went to the gallery and introduced herself. They sort of hit it off."

Matt wasn't surprised. Denise had always been outgoing. That's how she had charmed his father.

The waitress returned with their orders and smiled invitingly at Matt before leaving. Lucy picked up her pickle and bit into it. The gleam in her eyes had returned. "Would you like an introduction?"

He raised a brow. "To Renée?"

"No, silly. To Grace McKenzie. I'm sure Denise could arrange it."

"I don't need anyone to *arrange* an introduction to a woman for me, thank you very much."

"Aren't you planning to talk to her?"

"When I do, I'll handle my own introduction." He chewed in silence for a moment before speaking again. "What about Steven Hatfield? I didn't know him very well. What was he like?"

Lucy picked up her sandwich. "Nice. Friendly. A good teacher." She took the tomato slice out of her sandwich and laid it on the side of her plate. "He loved art, and anything that had beauty in it—flowers, antiques, the sunset."

"Women?"

"Well…yes, that was a known fact."

"Do you have names? Anyone I could check out besides Denise?"

"Why would you check out Denise?"

"Because spouses and lovers are always the first suspects."

Lucy shook her head. "Denise would never kill anyone. Besides, she was at Baubles until seven that night."

"Did you see her there?"

She hesitated. "No, but—"

"No one else did, either. I asked. The stores on each side of the jewelry shop are closed on Mondays, and both Jay Dunn and Gloria Saunders across the street closed at five-thirty that night. They both *think* that the lights in Baubles were still on when they left, but they can't swear to it. Nor do they know if Denise stayed at her shop until seven as she claims."

"As she *claims*?" Lucy gave another shake of her blond head. "Denise may have cheated on Dad, but she would never let him go to jail for something she did."

"That *something* is first-degree murder. Punishable

by death. That would put a snag on even the best of intentions."

"When did you turn into such a cynic?"

Matt picked up a piece of crisp bacon that had fallen from his sandwich, and ate it. "I'm just being thorough, Luce."

Ten

Well-fed and equally well-informed on the habits and eccentricities of a small town after her walking tour with Denise, Grace returned to the Hatfield Gallery, ready to work. She sat behind Steven's large desk, palms on the leather blotter and waited a few seconds before opening the file cabinet, where, hopefully, she'd find the names and phone numbers of the people she needed to contact.

Steven's system of record-keeping was nothing short of pathetic. Lacking proper space, he had bulked his client files in a single cabinet without bothering to label them. Also in the cabinet were dozens of bills for a variety of services—framing, dry cleaning, wood refinishing and landscaping, all clipped together in a system only Steven could understand. Some of the bills had been paid promptly, others had needed a second and third notice. Paying bills on time had never been one of Steven's priorities.

Amid this mumble-jumble, Grace found a list of the paintings currently on display in the gallery, along with copies of letters to clients, proof of authenticity on the work he took on consignment, and provenance papers. Sorting everything out and identifying the paintings proved to be time-consuming and often frustrating, but she managed to put everything into some sort of order.

At the same time, she kept searching for information on the Eduardo Arroyo painting. Eventually, she found an agreement between the Hatfield Gallery and a Philadelphia art dealer by the name of Victor Lorry. The document stated that the painting was to be displayed for a period of fifteen days, starting on October 5th. If, after that period, the painting remained unsold, the dealer would take it back.

Puzzled, Grace reread the contract, signed by Steven and Lorry. The short consignment period bothered her. Why only fifteen days, when all the other paintings were on consignment for thirty, sixty and even ninety days?

The folder still open in front of her, she took out her cell phone and dialed Angie's home. After four rings, her friend's cheerful message clicked on. "Hi, folks. Sorry I can't pick up right now, but you know what to do." Grace left a detailed message and hung up. Then, with the name and phone number of the various artists whose work was on consignment, she started making her calls.

Many of the people she talked to already knew about Steven's death, while others had no idea that he had been killed. All expressed concern about their respective art work, but seemed relieved when they found out that Grace was a curator at the Griff Museum and that the conditions spelled out in their agreements with the Hatfield Gallery would stand.

She wasn't as lucky with Victor Lorry. After calling him twice and getting nothing but an answering machine, she left a message, asking him to call her back at his convenience. While she waited for his call, and Angie's, she went through the invoices, bank statements and income tax returns the police had returned.

It didn't take her long to realize that business wasn't exactly booming. That surprised her. She had talked to Steven three or four times a year in the four years he'd had the gallery, and each time he had boasted about its huge success. Yet, his overhead expenses took a big chunk of his profits, leaving him with enough to live comfortably but not as grandly as he had claimed.

By nightfall, neither Victor Lorry or Angie had returned her calls. Remembering her date with the Baxters, she looked up and glanced at the clock above the backroom doorway, and let out a gasp.

Framed in the small side window and illuminated by the streetlight was a man's face.

He had bright red hair, shaved high on the sides and ending up in thick curls at the top. He appeared to be in his early thirties, but could have been younger. His eyes, big and round, turned fearful when she wrapped her hand around the first weapon she could find—a letter opener shaped like a dagger.

The face disappeared.

Weapon in hand, Grace ran to the door, hoping to catch a glimpse of the peeping Tom or his car, but he had vanished.

Shaken, she hurried back into the gallery, locked the door and flipped the closed sign over. Then, searching through her bag, she found the number Chief Nader had left with her that morning, and dialed it.

A deputy she didn't know answered and took the information down. "We'll come and take a look, Miss McKenzie," he told her. "Are you at the gallery now?"

"I'll be leaving in a few minutes. The chief can

reach me on my cell phone or at Denise Baxter's house. I'll be there for the next couple of hours."

"Maybe you should stay where you are until we get there."

"The Baxters' house is just two blocks away." She looked at the letter opener, which she intended to take with her. "I'll be all right."

After hanging up, she slipped into her red leather jacket, set the alarm and turned off the lights, leaving only the desk lamp turned on. Then, after making sure that no one was lurking in the shadows, she left.

The Baxters' house was a lovely Colonial with several carved pumpkins and corn stalks decorating the front porch. In a corner, an antique wheelbarrow held a brilliant assortment of golden mums. Grace looked down at the yellow mums in her hands. She hadn't been very imaginative, but at least they wouldn't clash.

Denise opened the door, wearing a welcome smile and an apron that invited guests to kiss the cook. She made a big fuss over the mums. "Thank you, Grace. How did you know yellow was my favorite color?"

"You have a lot of yellow in your shop. I made a wild guess."

"Aren't you observant."

She led Grace into a large, eat-in kitchen where a bright fire crackled. The smell of tomatoes, garlic and olive oil was enough to make Grace's stomach growl with anticipation.

A young woman, no older than twenty, was at the sink, shredding romaine lettuce into a salad bowl.

"You must be Lucy," Grace said, not waiting for Denise to introduce her.

The girl, a pretty blonde with shimmering blue eyes, took the offered hand and shook it. "And you're Grace." She took Grace's jacket and hung it on a peg near the window. "You don't look like a museum curator. None that I know, anyway."

Grace laughed. "If that's a compliment, thank you."

"It is and you're welcome."

Denise poured red wine into waiting long-stemmed glasses. She handed one to Grace and one to Lucy before picking up her own. "Welcome to our home, Grace." Lucy echoed the salute and the three women clinked glasses.

"You wore the necklace," Denise said, looking pleased. "I was right. It looks perfect on you."

Grace touched the stone. "I love it. Thank you again, Denise."

The wine was good, an Italian Ruffino that slid

down Grace's throat easily, erasing the tension of the last several hours.

Denise was observing her above the rim of her glass. "What's the matter, Grace? You seem out of sorts."

Grace let out a nervous laugh. "Does it show?"

"You keep looking out the window."

Seeing no reason to hide what had just happened, Grace told the two women about the incident at the gallery.

"It's probably the same man who attacked you last night," Denise said, outraged. "The nerve of him to—"

"It wasn't," Grace interrupted. "This man was much smaller. And I would have noticed the red hair last night, even in the dark."

"Red hair?" Lucy and Denise said in unison. They looked at each other.

"Big blue eyes?" Denise asked.

"I couldn't see the color, but he did have big, round eyes."

Denise nodded. "That's Bernie Buckman. He is— was—a friend of Steven's. Don't ask me why. We were all baffled when we found out they were spending so much time together. Those two had as much in common as knitting and pole dancing."

Grace smiled at the metaphor.

"And not to mention," Denise continued, "that Bernie is a loner. He has no friends and no relatives except his sister. That's why Steven's death hit him so hard."

"What would he want with me?"

"He's probably curious about the gallery's new owner, like the rest of the town."

"Why didn't he come in if he wanted to talk to me?"

"He's much too shy to do anything so bold," Lucy said. "That letter opener probably scared the daylights out of him."

"I feel terrible," Grace said, shaking her head to a wine refill. "Is he going to get in trouble with the chief?"

"Why should he?" Denise said. "He didn't do any harm. Just play it down when the chief questions you. Say that you've been a little jittery since last night and made too much out of nothing."

"I'll do that." She put her glass down. "You said that Bernie and Steven had nothing in common?"

Denise swirled her wine. "Unless you count fishing."

"Fishing?"

"You know." Denise made a casting gesture.

Grace thought of the tackle box she had found in the gallery. "That's odd, because Steven didn't fish."

"That's what I thought, too. He was too finicky to gut fish or hook live bait." Denise took a lasagna out of the oven and set it on a trivet. Golden-brown cheese, mixed with tomato sauce, bubbled invitingly. "Yet he walked over to the river every morning to talk to Bernie. That's how they became friends." She shrugged. "Maybe he did learn how to fish for all I know, but if he did, he never said anything to me. I certainly never saw any fishing gear at the gallery, or at the cottage."

"I did."

Both women looked at Grace.

"I found a tackle box filled with lures in the gallery's back room earlier today," Grace explained. "Everything looked new."

Denise nodded. "Steven told me he was going to buy a tackle box for Bernie's birthday. He loves fancy lures, but with the salary he makes working as a caretaker at the cemetery, live bait is about all he can afford."

"In that case, I'll make sure that he gets it."

They were interrupted by a loud knock on the door. Denise rolled her eyes. "That would be Chief Nader. God forbid he should use the bell like everyone else."

She walked away and came back a few seconds later, Chief Nader in tow.

"Good evening, Lucy. Miss McKenzie." He removed

his hat. "You reported another intruder?" Was it her imagination or did he sound a little skeptical?

"No. I mean yes," Grace amended when he raised a brow. "Actually, it was all a mistake."

"A mistake?" He frowned. "You didn't see a man outside your window?"

"I did, but it turned out to be nothing." She laughed nervously. "Last night left me a little jittery," she said, borrowing Denise's words. "I jumped to conclusions. There's nothing to worry about."

"Why don't you let me be the judge of that?" He took out his little notebook again. "Can you describe him this time? Or was it too dark again?"

This time she hadn't imagined it—his tone was clearly sarcastic. "It wasn't the same man. Please don't do anything to him, Chief. I'm not pressing charges."

"Do you know his identity?"

She glanced at Denise, who jumped right in.

"It was Bernie."

Josh turned back to Grace. "Carrot hair, short on the sides, thick on top? Big blue eyes?"

Grace nodded. The chief sighed and tucked his notebook back in his pocket. "That's Bernie all right."

"We figured he was curious about Grace," Denise offered as an explanation. "So let him be, you hear. The kid's been through enough."

"Give me a little credit, will you, Denise?"

Denise raised a defiant chin. "I will when you let Fred go."

Chief Nader put his hat on. "Good evening, ladies. Stay out of trouble."

Grace waited until he had left before asking, "Bernie's not going to get in trouble, is he?"

"No. Josh's a big pain in the behind, but he's a man of his word." She picked up the dish of lasagna and carried it to the table. "Anyone hungry?"

"Starving," Grace said, her mouth watering.

"In that case, take a seat and, as they say in Rome, *mangiamo!*"

A cold wind blew in from the river when Grace left the Baxters' house a little after ten that night. Dinner had been wonderful, and Lucy was a delight—a little quiet, but that was understandable, considering that her father was facing a murder charge.

An art student, and encouraged by Steven, she had had aspirations of moving to Provence for an entire summer to do nothing but paint. But with the events of the past few days, those plans had come to a screeching halt.

In spite of Denise's infidelity, the two women seemed to have a good relationship, understandably, since Lucy had been only ten when her father had remarried. Snippets of conversation, however, had told Grace that the relationship between Denise and Lucy's older brother, Matt, wasn't as pleasant.

She had just taken her car keys out of her bag when she heard a faint rustling coming from the path that paralleled the canal behind the building. At the same time, she caught a thin beam of light, arcing from side to side.

"Not again," Grace mumbled under her breath.

She started to take the letter opener out of her bag when her gaze fell on a shovel propped against the side of the building. Trying not to make a sound, she gripped it hard and held her breath as she approached the path. Enough light came from the lamppost to allow her to see the intruder.

Standing with his back to her, he held a penlight in his right hand, and moved it back and forth across the leafy ground. He seemed totally absorbed in his task. He was tall, broad-shouldered and, except for that faint noise she'd heard a moment ago, quiet as a mouse.

He was definitely not Bernie Buckman, but he *could* be the man who had given her that nasty bump on the head.

Grace raised the shovel above her shoulder and

held it as she would a baseball bat. "Don't move," she warned, trying to sound tough, "or this time, *I'll* be the one to give you a concussion."

Eleven

The man turned around, but instead of scurrying away as he had the previous night, he just stood there and gave her a long, appraising look.

"That's a pretty good stance you have," he said, not sounding the least bit concerned. "Ever thought of trying out for the majors?"

A comedian. And a bad one at that. "Move under that streetlight where I can see you." She gave the shovel a shake. "And put your hands up in the air."

"Yes, ma'am."

Cool as a cucumber, the stranger did as he was told. Grace estimated that he was between thirty-five and forty, with dark hair, eyes that watched her with undisguised amusement and a little lopsided smile that, at any other time, would have made her want to smile back. Not this time.

"Maybe you should put your weapon down before it misfires—"

"And maybe you should stop cracking jokes and take this situation a little more seriously."

"Sorry."

"Are you aware that breaking and entering is a crime?" Resting the shovel on her shoulders and holding it with one hand, she used the other to take her cell phone out of her bag. She hoped she hadn't lost all credibility with the New Hope police department.

"I wasn't breaking and entering."

"You did last night. I have the bump to prove it."

"I'm sorry about the bump, and the concussion, but the man who inflicted those injuries wasn't me."

Her finger above the nine key, she stopped. "How do you know about the concussion?"

"My father told me." When she frowned, he added, "I'm Matt Baxter."

The phone almost dropped out of her hand. Matt Baxter. The FBI agent.

"Is it safe for me to put my hands down?" he asked.

She let the shovel fall into the flower bed. "Yes. And you shouldn't be sneaking around like that. It gives people the wrong idea."

"I'm sorry if I frightened you. Can we start over?" He gave her a disarming grin. "Hi, I'm Matt Baxter."

This time she did smile, and shook his hand. "Grace McKenzie."

"I know. You're the new owner of the Hatfield Gallery."

"And you're here to investigate Steven's murder."

"I would have told you that, if you had given me the chance."

"What were you looking for?"

He leaned against the lamppost. "Any kind of evidence Steven's killer may have left behind."

"The police already did that. They found nothing."

"With all due respect to our police department, the authorities are not always as thorough as someone who has a vested interest in breaking the case. Like me."

"Does that mean that you found something?"

"Not out here." Another charming smile. Denise hadn't mentioned that smile when she had described him. "I was hoping you'd let me take a look inside."

Charming *and* direct. A good combination. "Inside the gallery?"

"Is that a problem?"

She didn't answer the question. "Sarah Hatfield had the entire place scrubbed clean."

"I'm aware of that."

"But you still want to take a look?"

"If you don't mind."

How could she mind? She would have done the same thing for her own father. And he seemed quite nice actually, not overbearing as she had expected him to be, but instead rather…humble. He was also very handsome—not that she was a pushover for good looks, but she wasn't made of stone. She noticed those things, in spite of what Angie thought.

Without a word, she walked around the building and went to unlock the front door, moving aside to let him in. She got a whiff of his aftershave as he walked past her, a woodsy scent spiced with a hint of nutmeg. Nice.

He was a younger version of his father, whose photographs she had seen at the Baxters' house, only better looking. His eyes were a deep blue, almost navy, and the light stubble of beard made him look rugged and sexy. He wore black cords, and a black leather bomber jacket over a cream shirt that was open at the neck.

"I understand that the man who broke in ransacked the back room," he said.

"He didn't exactly ransack it. He knocked a few paintings down. Everything else was undisturbed."

"So it's safe to say that he was looking for a particular painting?"

"That's my guess. I haven't had time to do a complete inventory yet, but as soon as I do, I should know which painting, if any, is missing."

He pointed at the doorway behind the desk. "Is that the back room?"

"Yes."

"May I?"

"Sure." She went ahead of him and flipped the light switch.

He stood in the doorway, taking in the room's contents in one swift glance before approaching the paintings, now neatly stacked against the wall. He studied each one for a few seconds. "Steven seemed to specialize in landscapes by local artists."

"Mostly."

"Did the police take all his files? Contracts, phone records, bills?"

"They took some, returned others."

"His laptop?"

"Still at the police station. His cell phone, too."

Her own phone rang. She selected a key from her key chain and held it out to him.

"What's that?"

"The key to that file cabinet in the bottom of the desk." She checked the caller ID. It was Angie. "I have to take this," she said.

She moved to the far side of the showroom. "Hi, Ange."

"Sorry it took me so long to get back to you. My computer crashed and I had to go to the museum to retrieve the information you needed."

"Any luck?"

"The Arroyo exhibition you mentioned was held at the Griff in the spring of 2000. The painting in question, *Market Day*, was one of the forty-two paintings exhibited. It was owned at the time by a Ronald Sutherland, who loaned it to us along with two other Arroyos. Sutherland passed away about a year ago, so it's possible that the painting was sold, either privately or at auction. I've been trying to contact his widow to find out more information for you, but Mrs. Sutherland is in Japan and won't be back until after Thanksgiving."

"Do you have any idea how much the painting is worth now?"

"At the time of the exhibition, it was listed at eighty-five thousand dollars. I checked with a friend in California, who specializes in western art. He told me that because *Market Day* is the last of a series, you could not buy it today for less than a hundred thousand dollars.

"Considering Arroyo's popularity," Angie continued. "I can't imagine why anyone would sell it for less. Unless, of course, Steven or the dealer, or both, were interested in a quick sale."

Grace saw Matt open a folder. "Thanks, Ange. You're a doll."

"Hey, hey, not so fast, girlfriend. How's New Hope?"

Matt took his gaze off the file in time to meet Grace's gaze. They smiled at each other. "Full of surprises," she replied.

"Do tell."

"Later. Good night, Angie. I owe you a dinner."

"Just as long as you're not planning on cooking it."

"Smart-ass."

She hung up and walked back to the desk. "Found anything yet?"

"Nothing of interest." His eyes swept over an invoice. "How do you like running the Hatfield Gallery?"

"I haven't had time to form an opinion. I'm not even open for business yet."

"But you've been here before? When Steven was alive."

She walked across the room and sat on the edge of the desk. "No."

He closed a folder and opened another. "Tell me about the Griff. How long have you been there?"

"Four years."

"And before that?"

"I spent three years with the Poltiss Foundation, where I worked as an archivist. And before that I worked at the Beacon Hill Gallery."

He looked up, smiling. "Is that where you met Steven?"

"No. I met Steven in Philadelphia. We were both attending an auction. He was going to art school at the time, and after meeting me and spending a few weekends in Boston, he decided to transfer there."

"Where you became engaged."

She was impressed by how easily he could talk and work at the same time, especially as the work demanded focus. Grace suddenly realized that the friendly, seemingly harmless chitchat revolved entirely around her. Was he being polite or was it something more than that? Duplicating his innocent smile, she asked, "Why are you so interested?"

He shrugged. "The way you handled that intruder last night has made you somewhat of a celebrity, so naturally, I was curious."

"Hmm, I don't think so. You're asking very specific questions." She leaned over the desk. "Are you suspecting *me* of having killed Steven, Agent Baxter?"

"Not exactly."

Well, he certainly didn't mince his words. "What does that mean?"

"It means that I work backwards, eliminating people as I go until I'm left with the obvious. Don't be offended. Put yourself in my place. Here you are, the dead man's former fiancée and the unexpected heir to a valuable business. I don't need to tell you that people have killed for less."

"And I don't need to tell you that federal agents aren't always right."

"That's true. We make mistakes, like everyone else. I'd like to apologize for mine."

She was much less offended than he seemed to think. The truth was, she had rather enjoyed this little banter. "Does that mean that I've been eliminated as a suspect?"

"Until you give me a reason to reinstate you."

"In that case, apologies accepted."

"Thank you. Will you let me make it up to you?"

"That's not necessary."

"Please, I insist. How about lunch tomorrow?"

He was a little too charming, a little too smooth, a little too quick on his feet, but he pulled it off very effectively. She said yes.

Twelve

"Thank you, Mrs. Vernon," Grace said, walking her very first customer to the door. "Enjoy the painting."

"Oh, I will." The white-haired woman cast one last glance at the Arroyo Grace had placed on an easel, with the new price—one hundred thousand dollars—beside it. "And as I said, my husband is going to want to take a look at that painting. Eduardo Arroyo is one of his favorite artists, you know."

"I'm looking forward to meeting Mr. Vernon. Do you need help with this?" Grace pointed at the package under the woman's arm. "It's raining pretty hard."

"I'm fine. You've done an excellent job of wrapping it."

Grace waited until her customer had secured the painting in the back of her station wagon before shutting the door. Her first client. She was proud of herself, not only because the gallery's bank account would be a few thousand dollars richer, but because the Arroyo was already generating the interest it deserved.

She was sliding Mrs. Vernon's check into the cash box when the gallery's phone rang. She walked over to the desk to answer it. "Hatfield Gallery."

She didn't recognize the soft, almost timid voice of her caller, but recognized the name.

"This is Bernie Buckman," the man said. "Denise Baxter told me I scared you last night. I'm sorry. I didn't mean to do that."

"That's very nice of you to say that, Bernie. It's a shame that you didn't come in last night. I would have loved to meet you. In fact, I have something here that belongs to you."

"You do?" He sounded surprised.

"It's a tackle box and a great selection of lures that Steven bought for you."

He let a couple of seconds pass before asking, "Are you sure?"

"Very sure. Denise Baxter told me that Steven had planned to give it to you for your birthday. I'll be glad to drop it off to you, if you'd like. You work at the cemetery, right?"

"You don't have to come all the way here. I can stop by the gallery."

"What about today? I close at six. Is that all right?"

"I clean offices at night and I don't finish until about nine."

"That's not a problem. I'll take the tackle box home with me and you can stop at the cottage. Do you know where it is?"

"Yes, ma'am."

"Then I'll be expecting you tonight, after nine."

"I'll be there. Thank you, Miss McKenzie."

"You're welcome, Bernie."

As soon as she hung up, the phone rang again.

"This is Victor Lorry," the caller said rather bluntly.

Grace let out a sigh of relief. "Mr. Lorry. I'm so glad you called. I don't know if you're aware of this, but Steven Hatfield passed away and—"

"I *am* aware of it." Barely pausing, he added, "Did you sell the painting? Is that why you called?"

A man who didn't waste words. She could appreciate that—to a certain extent. "Actually, I wanted to discuss the Arroyo with you."

"What is there to discuss?"

"For one thing, it's grossly underpriced."

"How do you know? Are you an expert?"

His rudeness was beginning to grate on her nerves.

"I'm a museum curator, Mr. Lorry, and while I'm not an expert in western art, I know people who are. That's how I found out that Market Day is worth considerably more than what Steven Hatfield thought. I've already repriced it at one hundred thousand dollars."

"You had no right to do that!" he barked.

Grace was taken aback. "I beg your pardon?"

"I said, you had no right to do that. Steven already had a prospective buyer, for the agreed-to price. His name and phone number are in my files. All you have to do is contact the man and make the deal."

"I've already called Mr. Lombardi. When I explained the situation to him, he said that he needed to think about it a little while longer."

"Don't hold your breath. He's not going to buy it, not at that price." He made an impatient sound with his tongue. "Look, I'll stop by today and take the painting back."

Grace was trying hard to remain calm and businesslike. "You can't take it back, Mr. Lorry. Not yet anyway. The contract specifies that Market Day is on consignment until—"

"The contract was between Mr. Hatfield and me."

"No. The contract is between you and the Hatfield Gallery. As the new owner, I—"

She never had a chance to finish her sentence. He had hung up.

Perplexed, she stared at the receiver for a few seconds before lowering it back into its cradle. In all the years she had worked with collectors and dealers, she had never come across one as rude as Victor Lorry. What was his problem? Why was he getting all worked up at the thought of making more money?

Grace's stomach tightened as she recalled Angie's comment. *"Unless of course, Steven or the dealer, or both, were interested in a quick sale."*

She could think of two reasons why a dealer would want to sell a painting quickly. The art work was either stolen or forged.

Trying not to jump to conclusions, she sat down and opened her laptop. The museum Web site had a code-restricted page that enabled authorized personnel to access a list of stolen art work. After entering the password, Grace scrolled down the list. The names of stolen art, their value and the date they were stolen slowly unrolled in front of her eyes.

Market Day was not listed.

Troubled, she logged off and went to stand in front of the painting, considering the second possibility. Even under close scrutiny, she couldn't tell if *Market Day* was the real thing or not. But although western art was not her specialty, she knew certain things about Eduardo Arroyo. He had been a meticulous artist, paying extraordinary attention to details until the people in his paintings looked so real, they could have walked off the canvas.

She saw that quality now. She saw it in the finely crafted Aztec jewelry spread out on the colorful blankets, in the merchants' faces as they sat in the shade of the arcades and in the sun-baked roughness of the unpaved village square.

Conflicted and uncertain, she let her fingertips trail over the painting. How could such exquisite work be the product of a forger?

Thirteen

From as far as Matt could remember, Pat's Pub, on the corner of Main and East Mechanic Streets, had always enjoyed a busy clientele, especially after five, when local contractors and factory workers stopped by to unwind.

Eddie O'Hara, now forty-one, had taken over for his father more than a decade ago. Like Pat, he knew how to keep his customers happy while making sure that friendly discussions didn't get out of hand. He and Matt had played ball together as kids. Both had shown great promise, but Eddie was the one whose pitching arm had caught the attention of the pros.

Six months before graduating from college, he was recruited by the Reading Phillies to be their starting pitcher. He'd had ten great years with the minor league team before an injury had ended his career.

He was behind the bar, serving cold drafts to half a dozen hard hats when Matt walked in. He was almost as tall as Matt and although he no longer ran bases the way he used to, he could still throw a curveball faster than anyone in the county.

"Matt!" He waved him over. "Come over here and let me take a closer look at that ugly mug of yours."

The two men reached over the bar for a quick hug and a pat on the back. "How's everything, Eddie?" Matt asked. "How's your old man?"

"Cranky as ever. He drives my mother crazy, so every now and then she sends him here so he can drive *me* crazy." Suddenly serious, he squeezed Matt's shoulder. "I'm sorry about Fred. For the record, I think those charges are completely bogus."

"Thanks, Eddie. That's good to hear."

"Hell, the entire town feels that way." He placed a bottle of ice-cold Heineken in front of Matt. "I hear you're investigating the case."

"That's why I'm here."

"Got any leads yet?"

Roaring laughter broke out behind him. Matt turned around to see the Badger brothers, sitting at a table, stealing glances in his direction and having a grand time. "A couple," he said, moving toward the two men.

Although they were a year apart, Cal and Lou Badger resembled each other enough to pass for twins. Both had shaved heads the shape of bowling balls, bellies that hung over their belts, and arms covered with tattoos. Cal favored topless mermaids while Lou was into snakes and motorcycles. Born and raised in Hunterdon County, their nasty pranks had spread across the county line and kept the authorities on both sides busy. Both now worked for Hawkins Construction, and routinely stopped at Pat's Pub before going home.

"Hello, boys. Having fun?" Matt asked.

Lou snickered. "Hello, bureau man. Caught any spies lately?"

"Hey, Matt." Cal's shoulders shook with laughter. "Let me see you talk to your watch."

Matt rested his hands on the table and brought his face inches away from Cal's. "I'm not in the mood to listen to your half-witted jokes, Calvin." He kept his voice low and flat. "So if you know what's good for you, you'll shut that dumb trap of yours and just listen. You got that?"

"I'm shakin' in my boots, bureau man." The words

were tough, but Cal sounded a lot less confident than he had a moment ago.

Across the table, Lou shifted uncomfortably in his chair. "What do you want with us?"

"I have a few questions about the night Steven Hatfield was killed."

Cal and Lou exchanged glances. Those two jerks weren't even smart enough to control their reactions. "We don't know nothing," Lou said.

"You were here when my father came in."

"Oh, that." Lou took a mouthful of beer and wiped his mouth with the back of his hand. "Like I told the police, Fred came in and ordered a St. Pauli Girl like he always does."

"And you two were just having a conversation."

"What's wrong with that?"

"A conversation about Denise."

"So?"

"So I find the timing a little odd."

Lou's expression went blank. "Huh?"

"I find it odd," Matt said, speaking slowly and enunciating clearly, "that since you had been at Pat's for a whole hour, you picked the exact moment when my father came in to start talking about Denise's affair with Steven Hatfield."

"Maybe we were finished with our other conversation," Cal said, and let out a laugh.

"Or maybe somebody put you up to it, told you what to say and when to say it."

"Like who?"

"I don't know. Why don't you tell me?"

"Can't." He spread out his hands. "I don't know what the hell you're talking about."

"How did you find out about Denise and Steven?"

Lou licked his lips. "Don't remember."

Matt turned to the other man. "What about you, Cal? How's *your* memory?"

Cal shrugged. "Hanging 'round here, you hear lots of stuff."

Matt grabbed him by the collar. The man weighed at least two hundred and fifty pounds, but Matt lifted him out of his chair as if he were a rag doll. "You don't want to piss me off, Cal. You don't know what I can do when I'm pissed off."

"Get your fucking hands off me!" Cal yelled.

Matt was about to drag him out when a firm hand stopped him.

"Easy, Matt," Eddie said. When Matt's grip didn't lessen, he squeezed harder. "Let him go."

Matt expelled a long breath and let Badger go.

The expression in the man's eyes was one of regret. The bastard had been spoiling for a fight.

"Come on." Eddie dragged Matt away. "Your beer is getting warm."

Calmer now, Matt returned to the bar.

"Don't get me wrong," Eddie said when he was back behind the counter. "I'd love nothing more than to see somebody give that jackass a good workover. I just don't want that someone to be you." He filled a bowl with cashews and put it in front of Matt.

Matt popped a handful of nuts in his mouth. "Because you think I couldn't take them on?"

Eddie laughed. "You forget that I've seen you make bigger men than Cal beg for mercy. No, I stopped you because right now, Josh is looking for any excuse to throw you in the slammer. Don't make it easy for him."

Eddie was right. A public brawl with those two morons wasn't the answer. There were other ways to find the information he wanted. For now, Matt would have to be satisfied knowing that his visit here had rattled them up.

Fourteen

An unexpected flow of visitors had kept Grace busy for most of the afternoon, and while she had not sold any more paintings, the Arroyo continued to attract interest. She was saying goodbye to a dozen senior citizens on an art tour when a dark-haired, wide-shouldered man with a scowl on his face walked in.

"I'm Victor Lorry," he said, his attitude as unpleasant in person as it had been on the phone a few hours earlier. "We spoke—"

He came to an abrupt stop when he saw the Arroyo, his expression a mixture of dismay and anger. He turned to face Grace. "What did you do?"

"What do you mean?" she asked, knowing damn well what he meant.

"The price!" He pointed an accusing finger at

the discreet tag beside the painting. "I precisely told you not to change it, but you went ahead and did it anyway."

"And I tried to tell you before you hung up on me, that we had a binding agreement, one that clearly states that the gallery reserves the right to change the price of any work it takes on consignment."

She started to ask him why he was in such a hurry to sell *Market Day* but stopped herself in time. The last thing she wanted right now was to arouse his suspicions.

"I'm too busy for this," Lorry said impatiently. "It's clear that you and I cannot do business together." Without warning, he took the painting off the easel.

"What do you think you're doing?" Grace asked, alarm rising in her voice.

"Taking back what's mine."

"I don't think so." She gripped the painting on both sides and held it firmly. "You signed a legal contract, and unless you let go of this painting right now, I'll be forced to call the police."

"Is everything all right here?" a calm voice said from the doorway.

Grace and Lorry turned at the same time. Matt Baxter stood in the doorway, blocking any possible exit. Grace held back a sigh of relief. She no longer had any doubt that the Arroyo had to be authenticated.

The problem was, she didn't think she alone could have kept Lorry from walking out with the painting.

Taking advantage of the dealer's surprise, she gave one last tug to free the Arroyo from his grip. "It is now," she replied. She put the Arroyo back on the easel. "I'll let you know when I sell the painting, Mr. Lorry."

Lorry didn't answer. Instead, he assessed Matt for a few seconds as if he was considering taking him on. Matt just stood there, looking relaxed.

"I'll be back," Lorry said to Grace. Then, after one last dark look at Matt, he walked out.

"Charming fellow," Matt commented after he'd left. "Friend of yours?"

"He's an art dealer with whom Steven did business."

"He looks more like a two-bit hood than an art dealer."

Grace walked over to the desk, took a dust cloth and came back to wipe the frame where Lorry's fingers had left a few smudges. "He was just angry."

"Any particular reason?"

"He claims that his agreement was with Steven and now that Steven is dead, he refuses to work with me. He came to take his painting back and I wouldn't let him."

"What was he trying to do? Wrestle you for it?"

"Apparently."

Matt walked over to the painting. "What's wrong with the painting?"

Grace wasn't ready to share her suspicion with a federal agent, especially one she had known less than twenty-four hours. "There's nothing wrong with it," she said. "Why?"

"Oh, I don't know. Its owner was hell-bent on taking it back. You were hell-bent on not letting him. It made me curious."

"Victor Lorry and I had what you call a personality clash. Now that the matter has been settled, I feel a little silly."

"Nothing that a good lunch won't fix."

"You're right. Just let me go freshen up."

Once in the back room, however, Grace didn't touch up her lipstick, but unclipped her cell phone from her waistband and dialed a number in Boston.

At the fourth ring, Professor Fishburn's answering machine picked up and the familiar voice instructed her to leave a brief message and a phone number. Trying to be both thorough and brief, Grace told her old friend what she suspected and asked if he would be willing to come to New Hope to put her mind at ease. She gave him her cell phone number and hung up, praying the professor wasn't on a trip somewhere, hunting for rare art.

* * *

"So, what exactly does a curator do?"

Matt watched Grace wrap her hands around one of Lorraine's hefty sandwiches and take a healthy bite.

"Well…" She chewed, swallowed and took a sip of her iced tea. "Do you want the short version or the long version?"

He laughed. "Give me one I'll understand."

"Okay." She took another bite of her pastrami and melted cheese on rye. "As a general rule, curators plan and oversee the arrangement, cataloging and exhibition of various art collections. We also schedule lectures, workshops and fund-raisers. In a smaller museum, like the Griff, a curator might be called to perform a number of additional tasks. I run the American Impressionists department."

Assigned to the art and antiquities fraud unit in the late nineties, Matt knew all there was to know about curators, archivists and conservators, but he pretended ignorance for the sole pleasure of watching Grace while she talked.

The rumors hadn't done her justice. She wasn't just pretty, she was fascinating. And what made her even more appealing was that she didn't seem to have a clue about the impact she was having on people. She didn't notice the open stare of the few men in the café, or the women's more covert glances. Her attention was totally focused on him and their conversation.

Her eyes were mesmerizing, although he couldn't quite make up his mind if they were green or gray. The rest of her features were perfectly proportioned—high cheekbones, a strong, determined chin and a wide, sensual mouth she covered only with a thin layer of pink gloss. She would have looked terrific in any hairstyle, but the short layers of her ash-blond hair worn in that sexy, tousled do suited her particularly well. Her clothes were classic—well-tailored gray slacks and a black wool jacket over a crisp white shirt.

He found himself wondering what she wore in the privacy of her own home. Cozy flannel, maybe. Thick socks on her feet. No bra.

Something she said brought him back to earth. She moved her hands a lot, sandwich and all, as she talked about the museum director and his rigid ways.

"He passed on exhibiting an important collection once because he could only get it for January and February and he thought the museum would lose tons of money. Granted, winter in Boston is brutal, but would the foul weather keep art aficionados away from a major exhibition? Hardly. So what happened?

Another museum did the show and broke attendance records. Are you going to finish your chips?"

"No." He pushed his plate toward her. "Be my guest."

"Thanks."

"May I ask you something?"

She helped herself to a potato chip. "Sure."

"What are you? Five-four? A hundred pounds?"

The question didn't seem to faze her. She kept on eating. "A hundred and ten. Why?"

"How can you eat so much? Where do you put it?"

She laughed. "Oh." She took another chip. "A lot of people ask me that. The answer is simple. I can't cook, so whenever I go out, I stock up, you know, like a camel with water."

"You don't cook at all?"

She shook her head. "Pathetic, isn't it? That's what happens when you grow up without a mother."

"You were raised by your father?"

"Yup. Just the two of us. He did all the cooking, plus a million other things. He's wonderful. You'd like him."

He smiled at the way her voice had softened. If he hadn't already taken her off his suspect list, he would have done it at that exact moment. Killers didn't talk about their dad this way. "Does he live in Boston?" he asked.

"Not anymore. He moved to Napa Valley a few

years ago to become a winemaker. He sold everything he owned, packed his clothes and a few mementos into his Bronco and moved to California."

"How's the business going?"

"Great. Winemaking is hard work, but he's happy."

"How often do you see him?"

"A couple of times a year." She finished the rest of her iced tea. "What about you? How often do you come home?"

"Not often enough. Traveling is tough on family relations."

"Lucy said that your job was dangerous."

"Lucy worries too much."

She smiled. "I get it. You don't like to talk about what you do."

"Actually, I'd much rather talk about you."

"Didn't I just finish telling you my life story?"

"Not quite. What's the deal with Victor Lorry?"

She shrugged. "I told you. He's not keen on doing business with me, that's all."

"Any particular reason?"

"He felt uncomfortable leaving such a valuable painting in the hands of someone he didn't know. He's fine with that now."

She was a lousy liar. Three years in profiling had taught Matt a lot about people's behavior. From the way she kept avoiding his gaze and trying to find things to do with her hands, now that she no longer had any food, he guessed that there was a lot more to the situation he had witnessed than she admitted. And that Mr. Lorry was anything but fine. Whether or not he had anything to do with Hatfield's death was something Matt intended to find out, but not behind Grace's back.

"I have a confession to make," he said, looking directly at her.

"I knew it. I'm boring you to tears and you've just remembered an errand you have to run."

He laughed. "Hardly. The reason I seem so interested in your Mr. Lorry is because he doesn't quite ring true to me. You see, I used to be attached to the art and antiquities fraud unit some years ago, and I've seen my share of art traffickers and art thieves. Lorry fits the profile to a T."

No longer amused, she folded her hands on the table and gave him a stern look. "So you were just pretending to be interested in my work?"

"I was not pretending."

"Then why didn't you interrupt me? Why let me go on and on about the details of daily life in a museum if you already knew all about it?"

"Because I loved listening to you. It's not every day

that I get to meet someone so passionate about her job."

She seemed to mellow a little. "Are you planning on investigating Lorry?" she asked after a while.

"Would you mind if I did?"

"No—"

"Well, son of a gun," someone said behind him. "If it isn't my old friend Matt."

Matt glanced over his shoulder and grinned as George Renchaw, now New Hope's popular mayor, approached their table, his jacket open and his ample stomach protruding. Although he had tried every diet in the book, he was quickly losing the battle of the bulge, thanks to his wife's superb cooking.

"George, you old rascal. It's good to see you." Matt stood up and shook his friend's hand before moving aside. "Have you met Grace McKenzie?"

The practiced politician smile snapped on as he took Grace's hand. "I haven't had the pleasure yet, but I've heard a lot about you, young lady. I'm Mayor Renchaw."

"Glad to meet you, Mr. Mayor."

"I heard what happened on your first night in our town," he went on. "And I want you to know that our police department is doing everything in its power to find the perpetrator."

"Thank you, Mr. Mayor. I appreciate that."

"I hope you don't think that what happened is indicative of what New Hope is all about. It's not. Matt can vouch for that. We are a peaceful, law-abiding community with one common goal—the well-being of our citizens and the good people who visit us."

"All right, George, enough with the political speech," Matt said. "Your re-election campaign doesn't start until next year, so chill out."

"I see that the two of you have some catching up to do," Grace said, rising. "And I have a gallery to run. Mr. Mayor, it was a pleasure to meet you. Matt, thanks for the lunch."

"You're welcome. Let's do it again."

George watched her leave before taking the vacated seat. "She's one hell of a looker." His eyes shone as he looked at Matt. "Is there something going on between the two of you?"

"Not that it's any of your business, but the answer is no. I've known her less than twenty-four hours."

George smoothed down his tie. "I knew I wanted to marry Louise the first moment I met her." He was interrupted by the ring of his cell phone, which he had placed on the table. He glanced at the name on the display and sighed. "It's Thelma at city hall. I have to take this."

"Go ahead."

As he talked his way out of some citizen group meeting, Matt picked up his coffee cup and leaned back. George had done well for himself. A straight-A student through high school, he had earned a full scholarship to Harvard before being accepted into Harvard Law. Two weeks after graduating, he had been hired by a large New York firm where he had eventually made partner.

But after seventeen years and two heart attacks, George had left the rat race and returned to his roots. He still practiced law in the town where he was born and raised, but kept a much lighter schedule. Two years ago, he was approached by the soon-to-retire mayor and was asked if he would consider running.

After being reassured by his doctor that he could handle the added responsibilities, George had said yes. He had done a good job. Shortly after taking office, he had hiked the salaries of both the police and fire departments, put an end to no-bid contracts and made sure that the roads were properly plowed during the winter months. His plan to expand the existing high school by adding a new building on Route 202 had met with some resistance at first, but after the skeptics had had a chance to see the plans *and* the numbers, the proposition had passed without a hitch.

"Are you always this busy?" Matt asked when George finally hung up. "Or is this only for my benefit?"

"It depends. Are you impressed?"

"Totally."

George laughed and slipped his phone back in his pocket. "I'm really sorry about your dad, Matt," he said, now serious.

"Thanks, but he didn't kill Steven Hatfield."

"Don't you think I know that? Josh does, too, although he won't admit it. He didn't want to arrest your father, but dammit, man, the way your father stormed out of Pat's with murder in his eyes—"

"He went home to confront Denise."

"But he can't prove it. He has no alibi between the time he left Pat's and the time the police came to arrest him."

Matt leaned forward, his voice barely above a whisper. "He was framed, George. Whoever set him up was very clever about it. He knew my father's habits, knew where he kept his gun and knew that he would go into orbit when he heard about Denise." He straightened up. "And the Badger brothers have something to do with it."

"*What?*"

"Why else would they choose that precise moment when my father entered the pub to start talking about Denise?"

"To rile him. They never liked him, you know that. When your father was police chief, those two spent more time in jail than on the job site."

"I'm not buying it."

George looked around him, as if to make sure no one was eavesdropping. "Look, Matt, Josh is giving you a lot of leeway here, and I'm glad. In fact, I encouraged him to do just that, but going after the Badger brothers?" He shook his head. "That scares the shit out of me."

"Don't worry about me. I can handle the Badger brothers."

"Who said you're the one I'm worried about?"

Fifteen

"I'm glad you called." Sitting on Steven's sofa with her hands cupped around a coffee mug, Denise kicked off her shoes and made herself comfortable.

"I didn't mean for you to come over in this downpour," Grace replied. The intermittent rain had intensified at rush hour, saturating the roads and causing traffic jams throughout the county.

"I didn't want you to be alone when Bernie got here."

"I thought you said he was harmless."

"He is, but…" She shrugged. "I just thought you'd be more comfortable if I was here."

Grace held back a smile. Like it or not, Denise had appointed herself Grace's friend and protector, with everything the title entailed.

"He won't mind my being here," she continued. "I'm one of the few people in this town he likes. Maybe because he knew about Steven and me."

"I wasn't aware of that."

Denise took another sip of her coffee. "He saw us kissing one day in the gallery's back room. I was mortified, and worried, but Steven was cool about it. He just made Bernie promise not to tell a soul, and that was it."

"Who would he tell, if he doesn't talk to anyone?"

"Unfortunately, he must have told someone, unintentionally of course. You can imagine what happened next. That someone told another person, and before you knew it, we were the gossip du jour at Pat's Pub."

"Did you ask Bernie if he had let it slip?"

"He swears he didn't, but I'm not sure I believe him—not that he's a liar or anything," she hastened to add. "It's more like…he was scared or something."

"Scared of—" Loud banging on the front door made Grace jump.

"Help!" a female voice shouted. "Please help! A car went off the road and into the river!"

Denise and Grace scrambled to their feet and ran to the door. A woman in an ankle-length navy raincoat stood on the front porch.

"Maureen," Denise said. "What are you doing here? What's wrong?"

The woman pointed frantically toward the river. "A car just went over the bank," she shouted. "And I don't have a phone!"

"Denise, call 9-1-1," Grace said. Then, turning back to the woman, she added, "Where exactly did it happen?"

"Follow me." The rain had stopped. They started running, crossing the slick, winding road. "That's my car," the woman said, pointing at a van with its headlights turned toward the river. "Can you see it? Can you see the car in the water?"

Grace ran down the embankment. "Oh, God."

It was already half-submerged. Grace could see the driver, frantically trying to open the door. His eyes were filled with panic as he looked back at them.

Denise had caught up with them. "A rescue team is on the way." She bent at the waist, peering through the bright headlights. "Dear God, is that Bernie? Maureen, is that Bernie?"

Maureen came to stand beside her. "It *is* Bernie!"

Grace, too, recognized him. "Do you have a tire iron in the van?" she asked Maureen.

"Yes."

"Get it, please. Hurry."

Maureen was back within seconds and handed Grace the tire iron.

Focusing on only one thing—saving that poor man—Grace walked into the icy water.

"Grace!" Denise cried. "Are you insane? The current! You'll drown!"

"I'll be fine. Go get some blankets."

The water quickly reached Grace's waist as she got closer to the car. She took slow, careful steps, her arms extended over the water for better balance. The current was strong, but fortunately, the car hadn't begun to drift yet. She thanked her father for making her take those lifesaving classes years ago. The training would come in handy, although she never had to do a river rescue before.

The water level inside the car was rising, and only Bernie's head was visible now. The look on his face was one of sheer terror. He was screaming something at her and although she couldn't hear the words, she could read them on his lips. *"I can't open the door!"*

She pointed at her chest, signaling she was going to try.

But just as she reached the handle, there was a loud sucking sound and the entire car disappeared under water.

Sixteen

"I'm going to need help," Grace shouted over her shoulder. "Denise, get in here."

"In the water?"

"Yes, in the water. I'll try one door, you try the other." She held on tightly to the tire iron, ready to use it if she had to.

"I can't swim!"

She couldn't swim? Who couldn't swim? "It's not that deep. All you need to do is hold your breath and follow my lead."

Denise shook her head and took a few steps back. "I can't! I'm terrified of water."

Grace took a deep breath and went down.

The car had settled on the bottom of the river, which, at this particular spot, wasn't very deep.

Grabbing hold of the handle, she tried to open the door, but it wouldn't budge.

Her lungs felt as if they were about to explode. With one kick, she went back up, took a big gulp of air and went back down, aware that Denise was screaming something at her. This time, she swam around the car to the passenger's door, but it, too, was stuck.

She swam back to the driver's side, trying to stay calm, and not look at Bernie's terrified expression. Treading water now, she motioned for him to get away from the window. Then, holding the tire iron with both hands, she broke the glass.

The force of the water rushing in thrust Bernie back, but now that the pressure inside the car was off, Grace was able to open the door and pull Bernie out.

One hand around his waist, she gave a strong kick, then another, and at last, they broke through the surface.

She only had to swim a few strokes until she could stand. Still holding on to Bernie, she pulled herself onto the wet grass and fell to her knees, exhausted.

Denise quickly wrapped a blanket around her shoulders while Maureen did the same with Bernie. "You crazy girl," she said. "You could have drowned." She knelt beside Grace. "Are you all right?"

"Yes." Between deep breaths, Grace looked up. "You really can't swim?"

"Not a stroke. I'm surprised I managed to get this close to water without having a panic attack."

"I don't know anyone who can't swim."

"I almost drowned when I was eight. It took me a year to find the courage to step into a bathtub. I'm sorry. I wasn't much help, was I?"

"Don't worry about it. Bernie is fine, that's all that matters." Grace turned to look at the man she had pulled out of the water. Except for a few cuts on his hands from the glass, he seemed fine.

"Here they come!" Maureen said when the wail of a siren broke through the night. She ran up to the road and started to gesture wildly.

Within moments, the riverbank was flooded with lights. Two men in green scrubs jumped out of a rescue vehicle while a cruiser let out two uniformed officers. A third car pulled up behind them and Chief Nader stepped out, wearing a yellow slicker and a matching hat.

"What the hell happened out here?" he demanded.

While the paramedics examined Bernie's hands, Maureen and Denise gave a rather incoherent account of what had just taken place. Somehow, the chief made sense of it all. He looked toward the river, where

Denise was pointing, before looking back at Grace. "You rescued Bernie from the bottom of the river?"

"It was either that or let him drown."

"You could both have drowned," he said in his chief's voice. "This river can be treacherous at times, especially in bad weather."

"I'll remember that next time," she said dryly.

As though aware that he had been insensitive, the chief tried to make amends. "What you did was very brave, Miss McKenzie. Are you sure you're all right?"

"The paramedics say I am." She just wanted to go home, slip into a hot bath and go to bed, but the chief wasn't finished yet. He was barking orders, telling his deputy to call a crane or whatever was needed to pull the car out of the river.

When he was done, he turned to Bernie. "Now, Bernie, tell me what happened. Were you driving too fast? Or did you fall asleep at the wheel?"

Wrapped in Maureen's blanket and no longer shivering, Bernie gave an emphatic shake of his head. "Neither. Someone in a pickup truck pushed me into the river. *Intentionally.*"

The chief and his deputy exchanged glances. "Pushed you? Maureen didn't say anything about someone pushing you into the water."

"That's because I didn't see it happen," Maureen

interjected. "I was driving up the road when I heard a loud plop and saw the car in the water."

"I was hit from the back twice," Bernie continued. "But I managed to keep the car on the road. That's when the pickup started hitting me on the driver's side. He kept doing it until I went rolling down the embankment."

"Did you recognize the pickup? Or the driver?"

Bernie shook his head.

"What color was the truck?"

"I don't know—dark, maybe dark green."

"Did you read the license plates? Or part of it?"

Bernie shook his head again. "I was too concerned about staying on the road."

Although he looked skeptical, the chief turned to his deputy. "I want a county-wide search for a dark-colored pickup truck, possibly green, with heavy front end and side damage."

He turned back to Bernie. "What were you doing on this road at this time of night? Don't you live clear across town?"

Bernie glanced at Grace, who answered for him. "He was coming to see me, Chief. I found a tackle box that Steven had bought for Bernie's birthday and I wanted to give it to him.

"In fact," she added, "if it's all right with Bernie,

he can come and dry off at the cottage. Steven has a closet full of clothes that I'm sure will fit him."

"I don't know." The chief scratched the back of his head. "The paramedics tell me they want to take you both to the hospital for a checkup."

"I don't need a checkup. I'm fine."

"I don't need a checkup, either." Bernie's tone was firm. "But I'd like to call my sister at the hospital so she won't worry when she hears what happened."

The chief handed him his cell phone. Bernie talked for a little more than a minute before handing it back. "She said it's okay for me to go to the cottage with Ms. McKenzie. She'll pick me up after her shift."

"All right," the chief said. "But I'll need you to stop at the police department first thing tomorrow morning and give me a signed statement. You, too, Maureen."

"I'll be there, Chief. May I go now?"

"Yes."

"What's going to happen to my car?" Bernie asked the chief.

"We're not going to be able to pull it out until morning, but once we do, it'll be evidence in an accident of a suspicious nature. That means that I'll have to impound it. As far as driving it again—" he shook his head "—I'm afraid that after the bath it took, it'll probably be totaled."

Bernie gave a resigned nod, then, at Grace's invitation, he started walking up the slope, followed by Denise.

Seventeen

"You like him, don't you?" Denise asked after Grace had sent Bernie into Steven's room for a shower and some fresh clothes. She had changed first, and was just starting to warm up, thanks to the crackling fire Denise had lit.

"I do, although I'm not sure why. Maybe it's because he was so honest with me earlier, or because I sense genuine grief for Steven's death."

"He lost his best and only friend."

"And now he's lost his car. How will he go to work?"

"I might be able to help him with that," Denise said. "Fred has an old Firebird that he drives from time to time. I'm sure he wouldn't mind letting Bernie use it until the poor guy figures something out." She looked down at her crimson fingernails. "I can't ask him *personally,* but I'll talk to Rob."

"Your husband still refuses to see you?"

Denise shook her head. "I go to the jail every day, hoping he'll change his mind, but I'm just kidding myself."

"I'm sorry, Denise."

She heard footsteps behind her and turned around. Bernie was back. He had chosen gray Dockers and a gray sweatshirt that fit him remarkably well.

"You look great," Denise said.

"Thank you. And thank you, Ms. McKenzie, for letting me wear these."

"You can keep them if you'd like. Are you warm enough?" She patted the chair across from the sofa. "Come and sit here, near the fire."

He laughed, but did as she asked. "You mustn't fuss over me."

"I'm sorry. I don't mean to be so overbearing. It's just that I feel responsible. I shouldn't have asked you to come over in this weather."

"I wanted to come." His gaze shifted to the tackle box on the coffee table. "Is that it?"

"Yes. Go ahead," she said. "Open it. It's yours."

As Bernie flipped the latch, Denise stood up. "I'd like to stay, but I've had enough excitement for one night. And those lures might just put me over the top," she added with a teasing smile. "I'll see you tomorrow, Grace?"

"Definitely." Grace walked her to the door and watched her back out of the driveway before walking back into the living room.

Bernie was admiring one of the lures, holding it to the light. "A Wigg-Lure," he said, sounding like a little boy on Christmas morning. "He remembered."

Grace sat back on the sofa. "I had no idea that Steven was such a fishing enthusiast."

"He wasn't really, but he was interested, so I taught him a few things. In return, he taught me about art."

"He did?"

He seemed more at ease now, and the words came out willingly, without any prompting on Grace's part. "I used to spend a lot of time at the gallery, learning about the various artists Steven represented and their respective techniques. He also taught me about important nineteenth-century artists. My favorites are Johann Berthelsen and Guy A. Wiggins."

Grace smiled. "You like New York City landscapes."

"Yes, I do." He looked up. "What about you? What do you like?"

"My specialty is American Impressionism of the late 1800s and early 1900s."

"Like William Merritt Chase, Childe Hassam and William Leroy Metcalf?"

She looked at him with renewed interest. "Why, Bernie. I feel as though *you* should be running the Hatfield Gallery instead of me. I'm amazed at how much you know."

"Steven was a good teacher."

"Have you ever thought of finding a job in the art field?"

"I don't like to be around people much, although I was starting to get better, thanks to Steven." Gently, he laid the lure in a compartment of its own, and picked up another. "Sometimes, on my days off, he'd let me fill in for him at the gallery if he had errands to run, or a class to teach. Once, I sold a painting." His face glowed with pride. "A Doug Emmerson still life. Steven insisted on giving me a percentage of the sale, as a commission."

"You earned it." A thought suddenly occurred to her. "Did you ever hear the name Victor Lorry?" she asked.

Bernie was thoughtful for a moment. "No. Is he an artist?"

"A dealer with whom Steven was doing business. I thought perhaps he had mentioned him to you."

"Why are you interested in him?"

"Oh, no particular reason," she said lightly. "Steven took one of his paintings on consignment and Mr. Lorry wanted to know if it had been sold."

"Which painting?"

She liked his curiosity. "*Market Day* by Eduardo Arroyo. He's a nineteenth-century western artist. He had it in the back room, with several others."

"I don't know the painting, but Steven liked western art. He often said that if there had been more interest from the public, he would take more in consignment, but in this area, western doesn't sell well."

"I put the Arroyo on display, so anytime you want to stop by and look at it, you're more than welcome. In fact," she added on impulse, "I rearranged the showroom in order to put more paintings on the walls. I'd love to know what you think."

His cheeks colored with pleasure. "You mean it?"

"Absolutely. Come any time."

"I will. Thank you." He glanced at the clock on the mantel. "Are you sure you don't mind my waiting here for my sister? She's a nurse at Doylestown General and sometimes she gets delayed."

"I don't mind at all, Bernie. I enjoy talking to you." Then, realizing the late hour, she asked, "Have you eaten?"

He shook his head. "I usually eat when I get home."

"Then you must be starving." She stood up. "Why don't I see if I can find something in the kitchen?"

"No, no, you've done too much already. I don't want to be a bother."

"It's no bother. I'm a little hungry myself."

She went into the kitchen and checked the freezer, hoping to find a couple of Swanson frozen dinners she could pop into the microwave. No such luck. The freezer was full of packaged meats and frozen vegetables.

The cupboards were equally disappointing. All she found was an assortment of cereals, coffee, jam, herbs and spices. Behind those few staples were two large boxes of Velveeta macaroni and cheese.

She picked up one of the boxes which, according to the manufacturer, contained everything needed for a quick, hearty meal, and read the instructions. *Boil one quart of water.* She could handle that. *Stir one packet of shell pasta into boiling water.* So far, so good. *Cook for ten minutes, drain and stir in cheese sauce.*

How hard could that be?

Leaving the box on the counter, she walked back into the living room. "How does mac and cheese sound?"

Bernie was still admiring his new lures. "Great."

Even though they were about the same age, she

felt like a mother looking after her child. He was a shy but gentle man, and she could see why Steven had liked him.

Back in the kitchen, she found a large pot and filled it with water before setting it on the stove. While she waited for the water to boil, she took a paring knife, cut the strip of Scotch tape that held the box closed and pulled up the lid.

At the look of what was inside, she let out a quiet "oh."

Bundles of hundred-dollar bills, each held with a rubber band, were tightly packed into the box.

After glancing over her shoulder to make sure that Bernie had not followed her, she took out one of the bundles and fanned it out, counting the bills. Fifty bills in each of the twenty-two bundles. A total of one hundred and ten thousand dollars, plus a few loose hundred-dollar bills, suggesting that there may have been more.

Her heart racing, she took out the other box of Velveeta and opened it up the same way she had the first. There was money in there as well, the bundles packed as tight as a sardine can.

And there was one other item. Sitting on top of all that cash was a gun.

Eighteen

Stunned, Grace stared at the gun. To her knowledge, Steven had never owned any kind of weapon. He wasn't a hunter or a target shooter, and he had never given a single thought to personal safety. Nor was he in the habit of keeping large sums of cash hidden in a kitchen cabinet. Only drug dealers did that. And if there was one thing of which she was certain, it was Steven's contempt for drug trafficking and all it represented.

But something was clearly wrong here. With the discovery of what she could only assume was unreported income, she now understood Steven's trips to Europe, the expensive suits, the Rolex and the Porsche.

If the money hadn't come from drugs, where had it come from?

As if on cue, Matt's comment about Victor Lorry came back to her. *"He looks more like a two-bit hood than an art dealer."*

What if Lorry *was* an art trafficker? And Steven had found out about it and threatened to expose him, unless he gave him a cut? Not the thirty-five percent commission specified in the contract, but cash that Steven wouldn't have to report?

Oh, Steven, Grace thought with a sinking feeling in her stomach. What have you gotten yourself into? And what have you gotten *me* into?

Suddenly aware that the water had come to a brisk boil, she quickly turned off the burner and went to peek around the doorway. Bernie wasn't paying attention to anything but his new lures.

She found a roll of Scotch tape in a drawer, resealed the two boxes, and returned them to their original places. She would have to decide what to do with their contents, but not now, with Bernie only a few feet away.

After some more rummaging, she found a can of Hormel chili, a pack of Saltine crackers and a can opener. Not exactly what she had promised Bernie, but he was hungry and hopefully wouldn't mind the substitution.

A few minutes later, she walked back into the

living room, carrying a tray. After assuring her that he loved chili, Bernie wolfed it down while they talked like two old friends. Grace learned that he had lived in New Hope all his life. He had met Steven one early morning about six months ago while he was fishing at his favorite spot, a couple of hundred feet from the cottage. Steven, who had been jogging, had stopped to introduce himself. They had quickly become friends, which Bernie agreed was unusual since he didn't make friends easily.

"I guess you could say that he brought me out of my shell," he said as he finished the last cracker.

"But if he knew nothing about fishing, and you didn't know anything about art, what did the two of you talk about those first few days?"

For the first time since they had met, Bernie seemed uncomfortable. "Oh, this and that." He stood up and picked up the tray. "I'll take care of the dishes."

"You don't need…"

"Please. I'd like to."

Grace watched the kitchen doorway for a while, listening to the sounds he made as he filled the sink with water. The fact that he seemed to have no problem finding what he needed, suggested that he had been here before, and while he wasn't trying to hide his familiarity with Steven's home, he seemed uncomfortable discussing certain aspects of their relationship. Why? He had been open enough about everything else. So what was it about that last question that had made him so uneasy?

A knock on the door cut her speculations short. An attractive woman in her fifties stood outside. She had Bernie's fiery red hair, which she wore in a neat ponytail, a small oval face and inquisitive dark eyes. Under the tan raincoat, Grace caught a glimpse of a colorful top over white pants.

"You must be Judy," she said, opening the door wide to let the woman in. "I'm Grace. Please come in. Here, let me take your coat."

"Thank you." She glanced toward the living room. "I feel so guilty," she said. "I should have come right away, but he swore that he was all right, and the pediatric floor was particularly busy tonight."

"He's fine." Grace hung the raincoat on a hook. "Go see for yourself."

Bernie walked back into the living room at the same time Judy did. He grinned and came to give her a hug. "Hi, sis."

"I'm sorry I'm late, honey." She immediately saw the Band-Aids on his hands. "What happened here? You told me you hadn't been hurt."

"I wasn't. Those are just scratches. Ms. McKenzie had to break the car window to get me out."

Judy turned around. "Where are my manners? I haven't thanked you for what you did." Emotion filled her voice. "You were amazing. It's true," she added, when Grace shook her head. "Chief Nader filled me in. I don't know how Bernie and I can ever repay you."

"If I fall into the river sometime, you can come and rescue me. How's that?"

Judy's serious face broke into a lovely smile. "You've got yourself a deal." Her gaze fell on the coffee table. "Are those the famous lures Bernie told me about?"

"Aren't they something?" Bernie's eyes lit up again. "Look at this one, sis. It's the Wigg-Lure."

"I'm sure you'll put it to good use. Right now, we'd better go. We don't want to abuse Ms. McKenzie's hospitality. I also want to stop at the police station and talk to Deputy Montgomery."

"Why?" Bernie asked.

"I want to make sure they're doing everything they can to find the driver of that pickup truck."

"I'm not sure they believe my story, sis."

"We'll see about that." She watched her brother close the tackle box before turning to Grace. "Who would want to do something so awful to him?" she asked, low enough so Bernie wouldn't hear. "And why? Bernie has never hurt anyone."

Later that night, as Grace went to bed, she wondered the same thing.

Nineteen

Ari Fishburn had provided more entertainment for Grace over the years than any man she knew. Born in Greece and adopted by American parents when he was ten, his passion for art had manifested itself at an early age. During a career that had spanned five decades, he had worked as a lab technician, an archivist, a conservationist and a curator. He had also spent ten years as director of the Lakeside Museum in Chicago before finally retiring. He now worked part-time as a consultant, specializing in western art and American Impressionism.

Experts claimed that he was one of the best authenticators in the country. Many agreed, including the FBI, who called on him occasionally.

He was a tall, slender man, with clear blue eyes

and a head of hair almost as white as the trademark suits he wore, summer and winter. As punctual as ever, he arrived in a chauffeur-driven car at noon sharp the following day, looking very dapper in a white Armani suit and a matching fedora.

Grace met him at the curb as he stepped out of the car, dragging the thick black briefcase he called his "lab on wheels" behind him. "Hello, Ari." At his request, she had stopped calling him professor long ago, while they were still working together in Boston.

"How are you, my dear?" He removed his hat and embraced her warmly. "Still as fetching as ever, I see."

"And you're still an incorrigible flatterer."

"I speak nothing but the truth."

They walked along the stone walk together, arm in arm. "I still feel guilty about taking you away from your golf game," she said as they went down the stairs. "Had I known—"

"You should not feel guilty. I would have been very upset if you had called on anyone else. Besides, you saved me from making a complete fool of myself on that course. I'm a terrible golfer, you know. The only reason my friend Ray called is because they were short a player and they needed a quick replacement for their foursome."

He stopped abruptly. They had just entered the

gallery and the Arroyo stood on the easel in the center of the showroom, a stream of sunlight bathing it in a soft, golden glow.

"Here it is, Ari. *Market Day*. The sixth of Eduardo Arroyo's market series."

"He was always one of my favorite artists."

"That's why I called. I knew you would enjoy seeing an authentic Arroyo—provided, of course, that it *is* authentic."

"Well, then, let's get to work, shall we?" He opened his briefcase. Inside was everything he needed to authenticate a painting outside his lab. Occasionally, the forgery was so masterful that it required taking the canvas back to his Boston lab for more extensive tests. Most of the time he was able to authenticate the work with nothing more than his portable X-ray machine and his magnifying glass.

After studying the painting carefully through the glass, he asked Grace to close the blinds. Then, he took the painting down from the easel and laid it flat on the desk where he had set the X-ray instrument.

Grace stood to the side, watching his expression, hoping she'd get an early clue about the verdict.

At last, he turned the machine off and straightened up. "This is very good," he said, still looking at the painting. "The paint is properly layered. Arroyo's thumb strokes, here and here," he pointed at a couple of archways around the village square, "are where they should be, and the shadow and light effect that you see here, falling on the blanket, is as good as any I have seen."

He turned to face Grace. "Unfortunately, none of that makes it real."

Although she had suspected as much, her heart gave a quick thump. She was already thinking of the scandal this would cause, the bad press for the gallery, and for Sarah. "You are absolutely sure?" she asked, still hoping.

"Come here." He waved her over and handed her the magnifying glass. "Look at this. In order to be authentic in depicting unpaved village roads, Arroyo liked to mix desert dirt with his paint. This technique, which very few people are aware of, by the way, gave the road a grainy, almost pebbly quality that is discernible to the naked eye."

"I see it," she said, focusing on a section of the road.

"Yes, but the effect you see, although well reproduced, is not due to the mixing of dirt with paint. It was achieved by using a textured brush. The X-ray fluorescence, which, as you know, can determine the purity of paints and other substances, did not reveal any desert dirt."

She lowered the magnifying glass.

"I'm sorry, Grace. I know that in spite of your suspicions, you were hoping for a different diagnosis."

She didn't know what she had feared more—dealing with a forgery or a stolen original. Either one was bad. "I would have found out the truth eventually."

"What are you going to do?"

"Report the forgery. I'm just not sure how it will affect the future of the Hatfield Gallery."

"I suspect it will survive, just as others have. Even famous museums experience their share of forgeries. When I was curator at the O'Keefe Auction House in Seattle, forty percent of all works proposed to me were forgeries. Once, when I was attending an auction, one of the Old Masters featured that day looked as authentic as any Raphael I had ever seen. Yet a week later, when the new owner had it appraised, he found out that it was a fake. Many thought that the scandal would bankrupt us, but it did not. The O'Keefe is as thriving as ever. It's quite possible that Steven was unaware that he was dealing with a forger, in which case he can't be held accountable."

Then explain to me why he had a quarter of a million dollars and a gun hidden inside a kitchen cabinet?

As he started to pack up his equipment, she said,

"Please don't leave yet, Ari. Let me buy you lunch. We'll catch up."

"My dear Grace, I'd like nothing better than to have lunch with a beautiful woman, but tonight is my daughter's thirtieth birthday and I promised I'd be back in time for a family dinner."

"Rain check, then? When I get back to Boston?" She didn't hear his answer. Through the window, she saw Matt's Jeep pull up at the curb. She groaned.

Ari looked up. "What is it?"

"Matt Baxter. He's the son of the man accused of Steven's murder. He's also an FBI agent—a very smart one."

"Are there any other kind?"

"What I mean is that he was on the art and antiquities fraud unit for a while and knows quite a bit about forgeries."

"Does he know about the Arroyo?"

"He suspects something."

"Then perhaps you should tell him the truth. It's a rather heavy burden to carry all by yourself, don't you think?" He looked at Matt coming down the path leading to the gallery. "Do you trust him?"

"I haven't known him very long."

"When in doubt, trust your instincts," he said.

Matt walked in and quickly assessed the scene—

Ari packing his equipment, and the Arroyo still on the desk. "Am I interrupting something?" he asked.

"No." Not nearly as nervous as she had expected, Grace made the introductions. "Matt, this is an old friend of mine, Ari Fishburn. Ari, say hello to FBI Special Agent Matt Baxter."

"How do you do?" Ari said, shaking the offered hand.

"*Professor* Ari Fishburn?" Matt asked. "The same Ari Fishburn who helped the bureau catch Joseph Reid, one of the most skilled forgers of our time?"

Ari looked pleased. "That would be me, young man."

"It's an honor to meet you, sir. I signed up for one of your classes once. Unfortunately, I was called away on a case and had to cancel."

"You have an interest in art, Special Agent?"

"I worked with the fraud division for two and a half years."

"I still consult with your boss every now and then…Carlton Brown?"

"I know him well."

Ari snapped his case shut. "I'd love to stay and chat, but as I told this beautiful young lady here, I have an important dinner to attend." He kissed Grace on the cheek, whispering in her ear. "I'm a fairly good judge of character, by the way, and I like this man." Out loud, he added, "It was a pleasure seeing you again, my dear. Keep in touch."

"I will. Thanks, Ari."

She watched him leave before turning around. "So," she said, "what brings you by?"

"I heard about your little midnight swim and wanted to find out how you were."

"Fully recovered, thank you."

"You took a big chance, Grace."

"That never entered my mind. Besides, Denise was there. She wouldn't have let anything happen to me."

"Denise can't swim."

"A minor detail."

"I'm glad that you've kept your sense of humor. How's Bernie?"

"He was scared at first, but he's fine now. He says that he was pushed."

"So I've heard. I stopped by the police station. They pulled the car out of the river this morning."

"Did they find green paint on it?"

"Forensics is inspecting the car right now. They shouldn't have any problem finding traces of paint from another vehicle, provided Bernie is telling the truth."

"Why should he lie?" she asked defensively.

"Don't get upset. I'm only repeating what I was

told. You can understand why the chief would rather have Bernie roll into the river because of possible inattention than because someone intentionally pushed him in. Josh's peaceful little town is starting to get bad press and it's reflecting on him."

"I didn't mean to snap at you. I'm sorry. This whole thing has me on edge and until it's resolved, I'm going to remain on edge."

"I have just the remedy for that."

She smiled, feeling some of the tension drain away. "I bet you do."

He pretended to be offended. "I don't know what you're thinking, young lady, but what I had in mind was a drink at Left Bank Libations in Lambertville. My friend Glenn makes the best metropolitan in town, guaranteed to relax those knots in the back of your neck after the first sip."

Yes, what exactly *had* she been thinking? "How do you know I have knots in the back of my neck?"

"I'd like to dazzle you with my psychic powers, but the truth is much more simple. You keep rubbing that area. Now, how does that drink sound?"

She brought her hand down. "Better and better."

"Afterward we could have a relaxing dinner."

"Any more relaxing and I'll fold like a rag doll."

"Does six o'clock sound good?"

He was persistent. She liked that in a man, and she liked it a little more coming from *this* man. "Yes." She picked up the painting, but instead of putting it back on the easel, she took it to the back room and closed the door.

"Was your Arroyo a bad boy?" Matt asked in a teasing tone.

"I'm not ready to show it just yet."

"Why not?"

She gave him a long look. "I think you know."

"Is it a forgery? Is that why Professor Fishburn was here?"

"I've been suspecting something ever since that argument with Victor Lorry yesterday. Ari confirmed those suspicions. The Arroyo is as phony as a three-dollar bill."

"Tough way to start a new business."

"What do you mean?"

He made a broad gesture. "All this is yours now, isn't it?"

She didn't want to lie to him anymore. "Only if I accept it. Which, for your information, I have no intention of doing."

He studied her for a long second, as though he was making a complete reassessment of her. "You're turning down the gallery?"

"That's right."

"In that case, what are you doing here, open for business and selling art work?"

"Because Steven had already anticipated that I would turn down the inheritance and asked that before I made my final decision, I spend one week here."

"For what purpose?"

"He hoped I'd change my mind."

"And you haven't?"

"No, Matt, I haven't. I happen to love my job. And in case you haven't noticed, this town doesn't seem to agree with me. I've had nothing but mishaps since I've arrived."

"Do you realize what you're turning down?"

"I do." A sigh escaped her lips. "Which reminds me, I need to report a felony." She rearranged a stack of art catalogs on the desk. "I hate to think what this will do to Sarah. She always knew that her son was no saint, but a trafficker of forged art? How will she explain that to her bridge group?"

"Is it possible that Steven was unaware of the forgery?" Matt asked, echoing the professor's words.

"I was inclined to think that, too, until…" She bit her lips. Did she want to tell him *everything*?

Matt's eyes narrowed. "Until what?"

She took a deep breath. "I found a quarter of a

million dollars and a gun hidden in Steven's kitchen cabinet."

Matt let out a long whistle. "I take it he didn't make that kind of money selling landscapes, original or otherwise."

"No."

"So this money that you found must have come from a different source."

Grace nodded.

"I'm guessing blackmail, unless you tell me that Steven was above that sort of thing."

"All I can tell you is that he loved money and all that it could provide. He never had to worry about it until his mother cut off all financial support. Even after they made up, she was far less generous than she used to be."

"When did she cut the purse strings?"

"A long time ago, when Steven decided to pursue a career in art instead of becoming a politician, like all the men in his family. Steven hated doing without the luxuries he was accustomed to, so it's not inconceivable that he would turn to fraud for extra cash."

"And it's equally possible that Lorry, who would go to any lengths to get his forgery back, is the man who assaulted you the other night."

"One more reason to report the professor's findings," she said, picking up the gallery's phone.

Matt touched her arm. "Before you make that call, would you do me one favor?"

"*Another* favor?" She allowed herself to relax a little. Ari was right. Matt was a very likable person. "I'm going to have to start a list."

"I'll make it worth your while."

"I'm counting on that. What do you need?"

"I'd like to talk to Lorry."

"Before the chief does?"

"I don't trust Josh to ask the right questions."

Grace put the phone down. "Do you really think that Lorry will agree to talk to you? The two of you were in the same room for only minutes and his mistrust of you was almost palpable."

"I'm well aware of that. However, I have an idea."

Twenty

Matt had kept it simple. The last thing he wanted was for Grace to be in any kind of danger, or in trouble with the law. He wouldn't put it past Josh to throw the book at her for helping his archenemy.

Earlier, Grace had called Lorry and told him that she had sold the painting to Steven's prospective buyer after all, not for the price she had hoped for, but for considerably more than the twenty-five thousand dollars Lorry and Steven had previously agreed to. His check, minus her commission, was ready and he could pick it up anytime. To ensure that he came today, she had added that the gallery would be closed for inventory all day Friday.

"He's here," Grace said suddenly. "He just pulled up."

"The black Suburban?"

"Yes."

Slipping deeper into the back room, Matt watched Lorry step out of his SUV. There was a little spring in his step, and he looked much happier than he had the previous day. Money did that to some people.

Matt threw a quick glance at Grace. She had been on pins and needles while they waited, but now that the show was about to begin, she sat calmly behind her desk. She knew what to do, which required very little risk on her part. She would greet the "art dealer," and while she pretended to go get his check, Matt would come out of hiding and start grilling him.

As Grace straightened up a stack of files, Matt looked for signs of nervousness. There didn't seem to be any. Just looking at her, you'd think that trapping criminals was an everyday occurrence.

Her head came up just as the dealer entered the gallery. "Hello again, Mr. Lorry." She flashed him a dazzling smile, as though yesterday's quarrel had never happened.

Lorry, on the other hand, didn't waste any time on civilities. He looked around him, then, satisfied that they were alone, he came straight to the point. "You have the check?"

"I'll get it for you," she said, rising.

Just as she disappeared from his line of vision,

Matt came out, smiling affably. "Ah, Mr. Lorry." Moving quickly, he walked around the desk. "Just the person I want to see."

"What the hell is this? Who are you?"

Matt flipped out his credentials. "Special Agent Matt Baxter, FBI."

Matt caught Lorry's panicked look, but as he started to close the distance that separated them, the art dealer surprised him. Moving with incredible speed, he bolted and was out the door before Matt could blink.

"Shit!"

Grace ran out. "What's wrong?" She looked around her. "Where's Lorry?"

"Gone. Call the police."

As Matt stepped out on the sidewalk, he saw Lorry make a run for his car, but a Coca-Cola delivery truck had double-parked beside it, blocking the black SUV.

Lorry let out a curse, then realizing that Matt was closing in on him, he started running.

Matt took off after him, launching himself into the midday crowd of tourists, store clerks on their lunch break and young mothers pushing baby strollers. The dealer, several feet ahead of him, ran fast, zigzagging between bewildered pedestrians and knocking down a sidewalk display of scarecrows and broom-flying witches.

At the intersection of Bridge and Main, he crossed the street just as the light turned red. A van heading straight for him came to a screeching halt. The driver blasted his horn and stuck his head out the window, shouting obscenities.

Matt let him go. Ignoring other irate drivers, he sprinted across the street, dodging cars coming at him from both directions. Lorry was now a whole block away, and heading for the bridge that connected New Hope to Lambertville.

Matt sailed through the crowd, shoving people aside. A few onlookers had realized that something was going on and moved out of the way. He heard someone ask, "Are they shooting a movie?"

Abruptly, instead of taking the bridge, Lorry ran down the small embankment. As a twenty-foot motorboat started to pull into a private dock, Matt realized what the fleeing man was up to.

He was going to escape by boat.

"Oh, no, you don't," Matt muttered under his breath. Sliding down on his behind, he sprang back to his feet inches from the water, and lunged, grabbing Lorry's jacket.

Under the startled eyes of onlookers, the two men

rolled down the bank and into the river. Lorry put up a good fight, swinging wildly while trying to land a few punches, but he was no match for Matt. After two shots to the jaw, the art dealer looked as if he was about to pass out.

"Give me a hand, will you?" Matt asked the boatman.

"Sure."

The kid, barely out of his teens, jumped off his Donzi and grabbed Lorry's other arm. Together, they dragged him to the grassy edge.

"Let me through!" someone shouted. "New Hope PD. *I said, let me through.*"

Josh stopped in front of Matt, fists on his hips, eyes spitting venom. "You'd better have a damn good explanation for this."

"He does, Chief." Grace pushed her way through. "And I can corroborate every word."

Josh looked disgusted. "Miss McKenzie. Why am I not surprised?"

"She has nothing to do with this," Matt said. He looked at Grace. "Shouldn't you be at the gallery?"

"Denise is watching it for me."

"Stop your babbling," Josh ordered, looking from one to the other. "I'm sick and tired of the two of you turning my town into a circus. First, *she* jumps into

An Important Message from the Editors

Dear Reader,

Because you've chosen to read one of our fine novels, we'd like to say "thank you!" And, as a **special** way to thank you, we're offering you a choice of <u>two more</u> of the books you love so well **plus** an exciting Mystery Gift to send you — absolutely <u>FREE</u>!

Please enjoy them with our compliments...

Pam Powers

Lift here

Peel off seal and place inside...

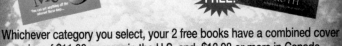

The Reader Service — Here's How It Works:

Accepting your 2 free books and gift places you under no obligation to buy anything. You may keep the books and gift and return the shipping statement marked "cancel." If you do not cancel, about a month later we'll send you 3 additional books and bill you just $5.24 each in the U.S., or $5.74 each in Canada, plus 25¢ shipping & handling per book and applicable taxes if any.* That's the complete price and — compared to cover prices starting from $5.99 each in the U.S. and $6.99 each in Canada — it's quite a bargain! You may cancel at any time, but if you choose to continue, every month we'll send you 3 more books, which you may either purchase at the discount price or return to us and cancel your subscription.

*Terms and prices subject to change without notice. Sales tax applicable in N.Y. Canadian residents will be charged applicable provincial taxes and GST.

If offer card is missing write to: The Reader Service, P.O. Box 1867, Buffalo, NY 14240-1867

BUSINESS REPLY MAIL
FIRST-CLASS MAIL   PERMIT NO. 717-003   BUFFALO, NY

POSTAGE WILL BE PAID BY ADDRESSEE

THE READER SERVICE
3010 WALDEN AVE
PO BOX 1341
BUFFALO NY 14240-8571

NO POSTAGE
NECESSARY
IF MAILED
IN THE
UNITED STATES

the river to save a drowning man, then *you* jump into the river. What is this? A contest?"

He looked down at the drenched man. "And who the hell is this?"

"This bozo," Matt said, yanking Lorry to his feet, "is the purveyor of forged art. He's been swindling the public for years. I strongly suspect that he's the man who broke into the Hatfield Gallery the other night and assaulted Grace McKenzie. He may also have killed, or contracted to kill Steven Hatfield."

At those words, Lorry almost choked. "*What?* Are you out of your mind? I didn't kill anybody. I wasn't even in the country when Hatfield died."

"Can you prove that?" Josh asked.

"Hell, yes. Look at my passport. Ask my neighbors. Gary Wickers, next door, picked up my mail while I was gone."

Josh returned his gaze to Matt. "I thought you guys usually got your facts straight before you made accusations."

"I said he *may* have. If he hadn't taken off from the gallery like a lousy thief, the way he did, I would have had a chance to question him."

"It's not for you to question a possible suspect who may or may not have committed a crime in my town."

"Art fraud is a federal offense." Matt wasn't about

to let that stuffy jerk browbeat him. He took out his cell phone.

"Who are you calling?"

"The Bureau. They need to know about this."

Josh knew the law too well to argue with an FBI agent. "Fine," he conceded. "But until your compadres get here, I'll need to question all three of you." He waved his finger around, including Grace.

"You'll have to wait until I go to the inn for a change of clothes," Matt said, looking down at his dripping jacket.

"What about me?" Lorry asked, his teeth chattering. "Don't I get a change of clothes?"

"You bring any with you?" Matt asked.

"Of course not."

Matt shrugged. "Then I guess you get to keep what you have on."

While Matt was getting connected to his superior at the Philadelphia office, Deputy Rob Montgomery handed him a blanket and tossed another to the freezing man still sitting on the grass, holding his jaw. "Here. If what Agent Baxter says is true, that's more than you deserve." He took the man's arm. "Come on. On your feet."

While Matt briefed his boss over the phone, his watchful eye surveyed the crowd. Two dozen people now surrounded the boatman as he gave his version of what had happened.

Something in his peripheral vision moved. Still on the phone, Matt turned around.

Up on the bridge, leaning on the railing, were the Badger brothers.

Twenty-One

"Why, Bernie, they're beautiful." Grace took the bouquet of yellow roses Bernie had just handed her and brought them to her face. "They smell heavenly. And I love roses."

"Judy thought you would. I wanted to do something to thank you for last night. It's not much, but—"

"Bernie, stop it. It's a lovely gesture and I appreciate it very much." She gave him a quick up-and-down glance. "And look at you, all dressed up. You look great."

"Thanks." He smoothed down his jacket. "I call it my Hatfield Gallery suit. Steven helped me pick it. I don't get much use for it anymore, though."

The thought that he had worn the suit just for her touched her deeply. Denise was right. Bernie was sincere, sweet and probably trustworthy or Steven would have never entrusted him with the gallery. "How did you get here?"

"Denise didn't tell you? Chief Baxter—I mean, Mr. Baxter said it was okay for me to use his Firebird until I collect my money from the insurance company and can buy myself another car."

"That was nice of him." She smiled. "A Firebird, huh? Pretty snazzy car."

His cheeks colored. "That's what my sister said."

She watched him for a moment as a thought began to form in her head. "Bernie, I'm having one of my brilliant ideas here and I want to know what you think."

"About the gallery?"

"Come with me in the back. I want to put these flowers in water."

In the back room, she found a vase and filled it with tap water. "How would you like to work here from time to time, like you did for Steven?" she asked, arranging the roses. "I know that you work two jobs already, but perhaps you could help out whenever you have time? Or on Saturdays and Sundays? Denise says that the galleries get crowded on weekends."

Bernie's small chest seemed to grow one size larger. "I'd like that."

"How much was Steven paying you?"

He shook his head. "Oh, no. I couldn't take any money from you."

She walked back into the showroom and put the roses on the desk. "I want to pay you, Bernie. I'm afraid that's a deal breaker."

He hesitated for a moment, torn between doing what he felt was right and his desire to once again spend time at the gallery. "Fifteen dollars an hour," he said at last, "but it was probably too much."

"I don't think so. Fifteen dollars it is. Plus, of course, a ten percent commission on everything you sell. Does that sound fair?"

"Very. Thank you, Ms. McKenzie."

"You're welcome. And now that you're on the payroll, tell me what you think of the way I rearranged the paintings."

He looked around him, nodding approvingly. "I like it. You put more easels out."

"I wanted to make room on the walls for the paintings I found in the back."

"It looks great. I don't like galleries that have that bare look you see sometimes. It's too cold. I like crowded walls, and lots of easels, like you have here."

She kept watching him as he walked toward the new paintings she had hung. "Are those the ones you took from the back room?" he asked.

"Yes. I don't know very much about Bucks County artists. What can you tell me about them?"

He talked for nearly fifteen minutes, pointing out the differences in style as well as the similarities in color and texture. He expressed himself in a simple, unaffected way that she found quite charming. She was amazed by how much he had learned in such a short time. Steven had not only acted as his mentor, he had instilled in this simple man a true appreciation for art.

"I don't see the Arroyo," he said when they were finished with the tour.

"It's no longer for sale." Certain that the news was already making the rounds, she told him about the incident with Victor Lorry. "Matt Baxter is with Mr. Lorry now. Two more FBI agents will be arriving from Philadelphia soon."

Bernie looked upset. "They don't think Steven had anything to do with the forgery, do they?"

"No one is speculating until we hear what Mr. Lorry has to say." Then, before he asked her questions she wasn't at liberty to answer, she said, "I'll tell you what. I have to go to Denise's shop to buy a few gifts for my friends back in Boston. Can you stay and watch the gallery for me? I shouldn't be long." She smoothed down his tie, like a big sister would have.

"You might as well put your Hatfield Gallery suit to good use, if you're free."

The little crease of worry between his eyebrows relaxed. "My shift at the cemetery is over and I don't have to start my night job until six."

"In that case, you're in charge." She wrote her cell phone number on one of Steven's business cards and handed it to him. "Call me if you need me."

Later that night, Grace sat at a window table, looking at the crowd of diners around her. Number 9 was tucked in a charming square in Lambertville, and was one of the area's most popular restaurants, as well as Matt's favorite. Small and cozy, it served unpretentious, homey food everyone seemed to enjoy. The smell alone made her mouth water. An attentive waiter had already brought her a basket of crusty French bread to keep her busy while she waited.

With Bernie watching the gallery earlier, she had been able to run her errands and stop at the police station to give her statement to Deputy Montgomery. She was getting good at it. She could anticipate questions and answer them with clarity and assurance. As a result of her involuntary notoriety, she and Deputy Montgomery were now on a first-name basis.

While Rob was printing her statement, Matt had

come out of the interrogation room long enough to ask her to meet him at Number 9 restaurant in Lambertville at seven. The cocktails would have to wait until another time.

When she arrived at the gallery, more than two dozen people were waiting to hear the latest news. Bernie had done his best to keep everyone calm, but it was obvious by the panicked look on his face that he wished he was miles away.

The moment Grace stepped into the showroom, the excited crowd surrounded her, demanding to know about "the chase." While Bernie had retreated into the back room, Grace had politely escorted the unwelcome visitors out the door and flipped the Open sign over.

She was on her second slice of bread when Matt walked into the restaurant, carrying two bottles of wine. "I wasn't sure what you felt like, so I brought both," he said, setting the bottles on the table. "One red, one white."

She tried to read his face for a sign of what may have transpired at the police station, but as always, his features remained inscrutable.

The efficient waiter was already uncorking the white wine. "Well," she said after he had filled their glasses and left them to study the menu, "don't keep me in suspense. What did Lorry have to say? I know you were hoping he'd turn out to be Steven's murderer."

"That was wishful thinking on my part." Matt picked up his glass but didn't drink from it. "Unfortunately, his alibi couldn't be more airtight. He really was out of the country that week and didn't get back until October third. When he heard about Steven's murder, he decided to play it safe and take the painting back."

"By breaking in?"

"Exactly. Our self-proclaimed art dealer is nothing more than a two-bit crook who was once arrested for misdemeanor and later for breaking and entering. He served his time, changed his identity and embarked on a whole new career, not as a forger, but as the middleman. Lorry has been running his illegal operation for years. He is careful not to do business with large galleries, or auction houses that might have an expert on the premises. Instead he does his homework and finds dealers like Steven, who are knowledgeable enough to run a gallery, but not so knowledgeable that they would spot a good fake with the naked eye."

Grace couldn't help feeling relieved. "So Steven didn't know he was dealing with forgeries?"

"He didn't have a clue. Lorry is also an expert in

forging documents. He provided Steven with the provenance papers and Steven never looked any further."

"Who's the forger?"

"He has several, all of whom are about to be arrested. The one who specializes in western art is a talented artist Lorry met in New Mexico a few years ago. His name is Eric Rossmann. At the time they met, Eric was earning a fairly decent living painting reproductions of artists he admired. Eduardo Arroyo was one of them. Lorry saw the man's potential and talked him into moving to Pennsylvania, a move that benefited both of them."

"He was never caught?"

"Like I said, Lorry knows how to pick his marks. You were the curveball he wasn't expecting. Once he heard that you, a respected museum curator with access to art experts, was taking over, he couldn't afford to leave the painting with you."

Matt took a sip of his wine. "He hadn't expected to find such a feisty, combative opponent." He smiled. "He still winces when he sits down."

"I have very little sympathy for him." Grace toyed with her bread. "There's just one little problem that remains unsolved."

"What's that?"

"According to Steven's records, he and Lorry

have been doing business for a little over two years. Steven sold several paintings for Lorry so far, all by different artists."

"Right."

"All the sales were properly recorded, and the commissions Steven made don't amount to the quarter of a million dollars I found in the cottage. Far from it."

"I asked Lorry about the cash. He categorically denies being blackmailed. Whomever Steven was blackmailing is still out there. If my guess is right and he is the murderer, he must be feeling pretty twitchy by now."

"He's not the only one. I have a kitchen cupboard full of money that no one wants—" A sudden thought occurred to her. "Unless Sarah can use it to repay those disgruntled, defrauded clients."

Matt shook his head. "Afraid not. If the money came from blackmail, which is a crime, the entire amount must be handed over to the police, who will return it to the person who was being blackmailed. It can't go into the blackmailer's estate because it wasn't his to begin with. Did you mention the money to Deputy Montgomery?"

She nodded. "He said that the presence of cash in someone's home doesn't necessarily mean that it's illegal money. He can't confiscate it until he knows where it came from. Neither can he take the gun. It was properly registered in Steven's name."

"You might want to put the money in a safe-deposit box," Matt suggested. "You'll sleep better. And if it turns out that it is legitimate money after all, you can turn it over to Sarah."

"But until then, she has to use her own money to reimburse Steven's clients."

"Not unless she wants to." He lowered his menu. "Contrary to what a lot of people believe, an inheritance is a gift, free and clear of all claims and obligations. Collectors can file a claim against the estate, provided there are other assets, such as properties, bank accounts, stocks and bonds, etc. The person who ultimately inherits the gallery may choose to repay the injured parties, but he or she has no legal obligation to do so. The gesture would be purely voluntary, perhaps to protect the gallery's good name."

"So it would be up to Sarah to decide how she wants to handle the situation?"

"Entirely."

One phase of the mystery had come to a close, but its conclusion had done nothing to advance the search for Steven's killer. She looked at Matt, who had put his life on hold to help his father, and tried to imagine his frustration. "I wish it had turned out differently," she said. "For your sake, and your father's."

"Thank you, Grace, but I'm not ready to give up just yet, especially now."

"Something came up?"

"You could say that. Dark-green paint was found on Bernie's car. Almost every dent on the driver's side has a sample of it."

"Then someone did try to kill him!" she whispered.

"Seems like it."

"But why?"

"You want my theory?"

She smiled. "Another one?"

Instead of addressing her quip, he reached across the table and took her hands. "You're not going to like it."

She glanced at his strong hands, gently holding hers. "I guessed that much. Tell me anyway."

"The decision to kill Bernie may have been made when you invited him to come to the cottage. Someone, maybe Steven's killer, found out about the impending visit and tried to stop him."

"I find that hard to believe. How can an innocent visit from a totally harmless man be a threat to anyone?"

"Because it's possible that Bernie knows something about Steven's murder. I don't know what or how, but the fact is, Steven and Bernie were an odd match—"

"Are you saying you don't think Steven's friendship with Bernie was genuine?"

Matt finally let go of her hand. "At the risk of having my sister call me cynical again, no, I don't. Maybe it developed into a genuine friendship after a while, but initially, I think Steven sought Bernie out for a specific purpose."

"And what would that be?"

"I don't know. Yet."

"Assuming you're right, how would the killer know that Bernie was coming over that night? I didn't tell anyone, except Denise. As for Bernie, I can't imagine who he would tell."

"He could have been watched. Or his phone could have been bugged."

"Now you're talking like an agent."

He shrugged. "As I said, it's just a theory."

"I don't want to think that Steven used Bernie. He and I had a chance to talk last night while he was waiting for his sister to pick him up. Steven was his hero. I don't know what it will do to him if he finds out that his friend was nothing but a con man."

Matt smiled. "You're fond of Bernie, aren't you?"

"Very much so."

The waiter came back for their orders. Realizing that she was starved, Grace glanced at the menu. "I think I'll start with the goat cheese tart," she said. "And the asparagus vinaigrette."

"Certainly. Will the second appetizer take the place of an entrée?"

"No. For my entrée, I'd like the braised short ribs. And could I have a helping of mashed potatoes to go with that?"

"In place of the haricots verts?"

"In addition."

The waiter wrote it all down. "Very well."

"With gravy on the mashed potatoes?"

She heard Matt chuckle. "I didn't have lunch," she explained. "Or breakfast."

Matt looked thoroughly entertained. "And you're stocking up. I understand." He gave the waiter his order—a sedate Caesar salad and the pan-seared salmon.

"Are you trying to shame me?" Grace asked when the waiter was gone.

"Not at all. I love a woman with a hearty appetite."

"A former boyfriend told me once that I was an expensive date."

"Is that why he's now a *former* boyfriend?"

"No, I dumped him because he failed to tell me that he was married."

"Oh."

"You must think that I'm very stupid."

"Everyone is entitled to one mistake."

"How about four?"

Matt put his glass down. "Four?"

"Uh-huh. Before Preston there was Michael. He broke up with me when he found out that I was a Republican. My second boyfriend was a controlling freak, a flaw I first mistook for strength."

"And the one after that?"

"A hypochondriac. Name an illness and he had it."

Matt covered his mouth with his fist to conceal a chuckle.

Grace leaned back and folded her arms. "Are you rethinking the stupid part?"

"No. I think you're just unlucky."

"And you're being polite."

"Maybe number five will be the charm?"

"I don't intend to find out."

"Now *that* could be regarded as stupid."

Grace quietly studied him for a moment. She had never revealed so much of herself in such a short time to any man before, and while she would have loved to keep this light, easy chatter going, she couldn't allow herself to forget Bernie, especially now that *she* may have been the one to jeopardize his safety.

"Now that you know all my secrets," she said, "could we change the subject?"

"You want to discuss *my* love life?"

She laughed and found herself flirting back. "How long would that take?"

"At least the rest of the night."

"Then we'll save that conversation for another time."

"You don't know what you're missing, but if you insist, sure, we can change the subject. What did you have in mind?"

"Bernie. If the killer felt threatened by him, why didn't he kill him at the same time he killed Steven?"

"It would have looked too suspicious. Or, he may not have grasped the extent of the threat until now."

Grace felt the heavy pressure of guilt bearing down on her. "I feel terrible. This is all my fault."

"You couldn't have known."

"It doesn't matter. I put Bernie in deadly danger and I don't know what to do to fix it."

"Would you feel better if I got him out of the way? Put him in a safe house until this investigation is over?"

"Yes, I would," Grace said eagerly. "The problem is, I'm not sure Bernie will agree."

"He will if he's scared enough."

Twenty-Two

Matt stood on the front porch of the home where he was raised, remembering the good times—Halloween, Christmas, birthday celebrations, Lucy's much anticipated arrival and the bad—his mother's illness, and death.

That time of their lives had been tough on all three of them, but particularly on his sister, who was only ten at the time. Giving Lucy the mother she needed may have been one of the reasons Fred had remarried only one year after his wife's death. But when Matt pointed out the twenty-eight-year age difference, Fred had replied with a few sharp words.

"That's *your* hang-up, son, not mine. I love Denise, but not for the reasons you stated. She is fun, she is kind and she has restored my zest in life. Now is that so wrong?"

But although Matt hadn't been convinced, he'd had to admit that the former babysitter's fondness for the Baxter family could not be disputed. At a time when Lucy and Fred had desperately tried to resume a seminormal life, Denise had been there for them. She had brought food to the house, had provided Fred with a list of housekeepers, and made sure that Lucy got to her ballet lessons on time. And when the ten-year-old had come home in tears because she no longer had a den mother, once again, Denise had come to the rescue.

Matt had no doubt that she had done it all from the goodness of her heart. That's how the Newmans were—trusting, kind, selfless and generous.

Felicia had been the exception—the black sheep, as some liked to refer to her. Beautiful and popular with the boys, she enjoyed being the center of attention and seldom worried about others' feelings. She was particularly spiteful to Dusty Colburn, the man who was eventually arrested for her kidnapping. Her lack of sensitivity, which most of the time she concealed very well, was the reason Matt had ended their relationship. Nonetheless, her disappearance had shaken him as much as it had the rest of the town.

But while most of New Hope had accepted the police theory, Denise, only fifteen when her sister disappeared, hadn't agreed with that scenario. "The police arrested the wrong man," she told anyone who would listen. "We all know that Dusty doesn't have a nasty bone in his body, and the fact that he can't defend himself is no reason to lock him up."

Because of her open criticism of the New Hope PD, many had expected the Baxters to fire her as their babysitter. They hadn't, primarily because Lucy adored her, but also because she was one of the most caring, dependable babysitters in town.

Matt hadn't felt the same way. In his opinion, Denise was much too young for a serious, settled man like Fred Baxter. How long would it be until his pretty young wife went looking for someone else?

Matt would have done anything not to be right. Unfortunately, his predictions had come true, and the consequences had been disastrous.

He rang the bell and within a few moments, Denise opened the door. Not shy when it came to colors, she wore a bright orange sweater with a sequined pumpkin on the front and tight black pants. Her blond hair was pulled back in a ponytail, revealing black-and-white "ghost" earrings dangling from her ears.

There was a brief moment of surprise before the

quick, friendly smile appeared. Denise had never been one to hold grudges. "Matt! What a pleasant surprise. Have you changed your mind?"

"About?"

"Staying with us."

"No. I just stopped by to talk to you. You have a minute?"

"I do. Come in. What can I get you?" she asked as she walked ahead of him and into the familiar kitchen. "Beer? Soda? Coffee?"

"Nothing." He cleared his throat. Her cheerfulness made his task a little more difficult. "Denise, this isn't a social call."

Far from stupid, she got the message instantly. "That's right. You've been making the rounds, haven't you? Talking to people, building a list of suspects. I was wondering when you'd get to me."

"It's nothing personal."

"Of course not. You want to sit down? Or is that too…social?"

He sat down at the old table where his family had shared so many meals. Filled with nostalgia, he looked around him, noticing a pumpkin pie on the island—Lucy's favorite.

"So." Denise crossed her legs and wrapped her hands around her knees. "What do you want to know?"

"You could start by telling me where you were the night Steven was killed."

If the blunt question offended her, she didn't show it. "Didn't you read the police report?"

He had read every page—the coroner's and ballistic findings, statements from various witnesses at Pat's Pub, as well as Denise's. "I'd like to hear it directly from you. If you don't mind."

"Not at all." Under the nonchalance, however, he sensed a certain level of anxiety. "I was at the shop, working on a new design. I didn't pay attention to the time until I looked up and saw that it was past seven. I'm sure that if you ask around, some of the other business owners will confirm that."

"That's where I'm having a little bit of a problem, Denise. Jay Dunn and Gloria Saunders don't recall seeing you in your shop when they left. They're not even certain the lights were on."

"Can I help it if they're not observant?" she asked defensively. "Does that make me a murderer?"

"No."

"But that's why you're here, isn't it? To pin this murder on me."

"I'm not trying to *pin* a murder on anybody, Denise. I'm trying to get to the truth. And the only way I'm going to do that is if I get straight answers."

"I didn't kill Steven. Is that straight enough for you?"

Matt waited a beat before asking his next question. "Were you and Steven getting along?"

She laughed. "Lovers usually do."

"Every relationship has its ups and downs, and we both know that Steven had a roving eye."

"We were getting along just fine." Her tone had sharpened slightly.

"You never had a spat? You didn't resent his little escapades?"

"He didn't have 'little escapades.'"

"That's not what I hear."

"He was a flirt, Matt, that's all. An incorrigible flirt. I knew that going in."

"And it didn't bother you?"

"Not as long as he didn't act on it. Men are the way they are. No woman is going to change that."

A door banged shut. "Matt, is that you?"

Seconds later, Lucy walked in, saw him and ran to give him a warm hug. "I didn't know you were coming. Did you change your mind? Are you going to stay with us?"

"No, Luce." He was suddenly uncomfortable. "I thought you had a morning class," he said, hoping to change the conversation.

"It was cancelled." That keen sixth sense he had

always found so spooky suddenly kicked in. "What's going on?" she asked, looking from him to Denise.

"Your brother just stopped by to say hello," Denise said, bailing him out. "Isn't that nice?" She laughed. "There's hope for us after all."

"Uh-uh." Lucy shook her head. "I don't believe it." She dropped her books on the table. "Why are you really here, Matt?"

"Doing my job, Lucy."

"By *interrogating* Denise?"

Again, Denise tried to intervene. "Lucy, please—"

Lucy cut her short. "No, I won't let him do that to you. You leave her alone, do you hear me, Matt?"

Denise wrapped her arms around Lucy's shoulders. "I really don't mind, honey. I have nothing to hide."

Matt would have been tempted to believe her if it hadn't been for Lucy. Not nearly as practiced in the art of deception as an older person might be, she shot her stepmother a quick, fearful look that was a dead giveaway.

Something was going on between those two.

Denise gave Lucy's shoulder a gentle shake. "I'm afraid you've got your little sister upset, Matt. Could we do this at some other time?"

What choice did he have? "Sure." He stood up, his

gaze on Lucy. Her eyes were heavy with resentment. "Are we still on for lunch?" he asked, rising.

She wouldn't meet his eyes. "I'll let you know."

"Good enough." He walked over and kissed her cheek. For a moment, he expected her to pull away but she didn't. Nor did she return the kiss. "'Bye, Luce." Above the blond head, his eyes met Denise's. Her eyes had filled with tears.

"I'll see myself out," he said.

Twenty-Three

Concerned that Chief Nader, who tended to dramatize, would call Steven's mother and tell her about the events of the last twenty-four hours, Grace had called Sarah the next morning to give her a simpler version.

She didn't get far. At the word *forgery*, Sarah became indignant.

"Dear Lord, Grace," she said, her tone filled with reproach. "How can you remain so calm and matter-of-fact? This isn't some trivial offense one can simply brush away. It's a serious felony."

Grace bit her lip before replying. "The crime and consequences have been thoroughly spelled out to me, Sarah. And if I gave you the impression that I'm treating this matter lightly, I apologize. I'm quite aware of the gravity of the situation. However, as I explained earlier, reimbursing Steven's clients should minimize the problem. That's entirely up to you. So, the question is, what do you want to do?"

There was a long silence. When Sarah spoke again, her querulous tone had mellowed considerably. "What would *you* do?"

Amazing. The woman could be reasoned with after all. "If I were in your shoes," Grace replied, "I'd call each client personally, explain what happened and offer to reimburse them."

"That's all?"

Wealth *did* have its rewards. "It'll be expensive, but yes, that should do it."

"What will happen to the gallery?"

"To quote a friend of mine, it will survive. Thefts and forgeries are fairly common in the art world."

"It's so humiliating. How will I explain to my—"

"I've tracked down all seven clients," Grace continued, determined to stay on track. "I'll be glad to call them for you. Unless, of course, you'd rather do it."

"Heavens no. I wouldn't know what to say to them." She paused. "Are you absolutely sure that Steven was not involved in this scam?"

"Steven was as much of a victim as the collectors who were swindled." She didn't have the heart to tell her about the money she had found, and where it may have come from. Sarah didn't need to deal with hypotheses right now.

She heard a soft sigh at the end of the line. "All right, then, do what you have to do and let me know how much I owe."

"It will take a couple of days, but I'll get back to you."

Grace hung up and returned to the list of names Victor Lorry had provided. In the next two hours, she was able to contact four of the seven clients, apologize to each one and assure them they would be fully reimbursed. Two of them had taken the news fairly well, the other two had required a little more diplomacy, a little more coaxing, but after dealing with temperamental museum directors for years, Grace knew exactly how to pacify an irate customer.

As she continued to make her calls, a few people, mostly fellow business owners, stopped by to say a few kind words, for which Grace was grateful. Being an outsider was bad enough, but finding yourself in the middle of a scandal seventy-two hours after arriving in town was depressing at best.

A little after noon, Denise called, inviting her to share another brown-bagged lunch. Looking forward to a well-deserved break, Grace accepted.

"What's your pleasure?" Denise asked when Grace walked in, carrying two tall cups of Starbucks coffee.

"Mortadella and provolone on pumpernickel? Or turkey and Swiss on a wheat bagel?"

Grace put the coffee on the counter. "You're spoiling me. How will I be able to readjust to Boston and *my* cooking, after gorging myself on this wonderful food for a week?" She pointed at one of the unwrapped sandwiches. "The mortadella and provolone sounds great."

Denise slowly handed it to her. "Readjust to Boston? What are you talking about?"

Oops. She hadn't meant to let the truth slip out, but now that it had, she was glad. Denise had become a good and trusted friend, and deserved the truth. "I'm afraid I haven't been entirely honest with you," she said.

"In what way?"

"I'll be returning to Boston in another few days."

"No, you won't. You've inherited Steven's gallery."

"I'm turning down the inheritance."

There was a short silence, during which Denise seemed to process the news. "Did you just decide that?"

"No. I knew it all along. I told Sarah when she first came to see me in Boston."

"Then what are you doing here, running the gallery as if you were the owner?"

Once again, Grace explained the terms of Steven's

will. "I didn't have to honor that request," she said when she was finished. "But it meant a lot to Sarah, and I had time on my hands, so I thought, why not."

She saw the dispirited look on Denise's face and felt bad. "I'm sorry if I misled you. It seemed easier at the time."

"Isn't that just my luck." Denise put her bagel down. "I make a new friend, someone I can finally trust, someone who understands me, and what happens? I lose her, all in the space of a week."

"You're not losing me. You can come up to Boston and visit me anytime you want."

"You'll forget me."

Grace laughed. "I don't think so, Denise. You're not someone who can be easily forgotten."

Denise picked up her sandwich again. "This town isn't going to be the same without you. *I* won't be the same without you."

"We'll talk on the phone every day. I'll even call you from California."

"You swear?"

"Cross my heart, hope to die." She made a cross sign on her chest.

Denise shivered. "Don't say that, not after everything that's already happened." She started to eat. "Does anyone else know that you won't be staying?"

"Matt."

Denise's sunken spirits seemed to lift a little. "You two seem to have hit it off."

"I like him. He's straightforward, fun to be with and devoted to his family."

"Present company excepted."

"Don't lose hope. Men have been known to be just as unpredictable as women."

"I hope so. Whenever I feel down, I try to think about others with more serious problems, like Bernie. It can't be easy knowing that someone is trying to kill you, having to look over your shoulder all the time, wondering where and when the killer will strike again."

"If this is how you cheer yourself up, you might want to think about something else."

"I thought you were worried about Bernie, too."

"I am, but I won't agonize over it. Matt offered to put him in a safe house, but he won't go. He doesn't want to leave his sister or his job, even for a short time. Matt had no idea Bernie could be so stubborn."

"Does that mean that whoever tried to kill him will try again?"

"Hopefully not. Matt thinks that after the attempt on his life the other night, another one would be too risky."

"What do you suppose he knows that makes him such a threat?"

"Matt is trying to find out, but he's not getting anywhere."

"Maybe Father Donnelly should have a try. He and Bernie used to be close. But that was a long time ago. Then Bernie's mom died and the poor kid was never the same after that. Not even Father Donnelly could help him. Still, it's worth a try."

Grace wiped her fingers on a tissue and Denise immediately jumped off her stool. "I'm sorry. I forgot the napkins. I'll get some in the back. In the meantime, why don't you take a look at my new design?" She pointed at a wall-mounted glass case on the other side of the counter.

Grace approached the display. "I like it," she said. "It's very different from what you've been doing."

"I'm trying to branch in a different direction." Denise disappeared behind a beaded curtain. "I have a couple of other items in progress in that shoe box under the cash register. Check them out."

Grace found the box, put it on the counter and opened it. On top of several layers of pink tissue was a necklace made of freshwater pearls from which hung a lovely pear-shape purple stone. "That necklace is stunning. Is that an amethyst?"

"Alexandrite," Denise said from the other room. "They're cheaper than amethysts but just as pretty."

Grace pushed aside the wad of tissue and gazed at another piece, a gold bracelet, one half of which was studded with small diamonds. Curious because it didn't look like one of Denise's designs, she picked it up.

Attached to the bracelet was a small card with the handwritten words: *Forgive me. And come back to me.* It was signed, *Steven.*

Twenty-Four

Grace glanced at the curtained doorway, then back at the card. *Come back to me*. What did that mean? Denise hadn't mentioned a breakup.

Before Grace had a chance to put the bracelet back in the box, Denise walked in, a pack of napkins in her hands. When she saw the bracelet in Grace's hands, she stopped short. "Where did you find that?"

"Under the tissues. I'm sorry if—"

Denise took the bracelet from Grace's hand and dropped it back into the box. "Never mind." She closed the box and put it back under the cash register.

Grace let the next few awkward seconds pass before she asked gently, "What did he do?"

"I beg your pardon?"

"Steven. What did he do that he had to ask for your forgiveness?"

Denise took two napkins out of the pack and set them on the glass counter. "I can't remember—something stupid, I'm sure."

"For something stupid, the Steven I knew would bring flowers and chocolates. He saved the expensive jewelry for major blunders."

"Grace, please, let it go. It's really none of your business."

The sharp tone stung a little. "That's quite a reversal on your part, don't you think? Only a few days ago, *I* was the one who was telling you that your personal life was none of my business, but you insisted on telling me everything about yourself. You got me involved, Denise. You made me care. You made me your friend. I didn't want to be a part of your life, but like it not, here I am. Live with it."

Denise's eyes remained downcast.

"You broke up with him, didn't you?"

"No."

"Come on, Denise. He asked you to come back to him."

Silence.

"Was he seeing another woman?"

Denise's cheeks flared. "Why must everyone

always think that? Just because he was a hopeless flirt doesn't mean that he chased every skirt in town."

"Wasn't that his reputation?"

"He wasn't seeing anyone else, okay?"

She was interrupted by the sound of the door chimes. Grace looked up to see Chief Nader. His face was as solemn as ever as he removed his hat.

He looked from one to the other. "Ladies."

"What can I do for you, Josh?" Denise asked.

The chief turned to Grace. "Would you excuse us, Miss McKenzie? This is police business."

"Of course." Grace started to walk around the counter, but Denise stopped her.

"Grace stays."

The chief didn't fight her. "As you wish."

She drained the last of her Starbucks and tossed the cup into a wastebasket. "Are you bringing me good news?"

"Maybe. I came to let you know that a dozen or so residents have started a petition, calling for a new investigation in the murder of Steven Hatfield."

"I'd call that good news, and I can't say that I'm surprised. You're the only one who believed that Fred was guilty." She folded her arms. "Are you going to do it? Start a new investigation?"

"I might look into their reason for the request."

"And what's that?"

"They suspect that Steven was having an affair with someone else, someone other than you, Denise."

Grace threw a quick glance in Denise's direction and saw her pale.

"Is that true?" the chief asked.

"No, it's not," she said with the same conviction she had showed earlier. "Believe me, I'd know." She moistened her lips. "Are the petitioners basing their suspicion on anything specific?"

The chief shook his head. "Just Steven's reputation in general. They believe that he may have dumped another woman and in so doing, gave her a motive for murder."

Denise laughed. "The *woman scorned* theory? Isn't that a little melodramatic?"

"The other theory is that you found out about the affair and killed Steven in a fit of jealousy." He watched her closely as he spoke.

"Chief!" Grace moved close to Denise, showing her support. "How can you say something like that? For all you know, that petition could have been started out of pure vindictiveness toward Denise."

"I realize that Denise is not very popular amongst the townsfolk, but nonetheless there are enough names on that sheet of paper to warrant an investigation into the love life of Steven Hatfield."

"Go ahead and investigate all you want," Denise said. "My conscience is clear. And for the record, I stand by my earlier statement. I was here, at Baubles, until seven the night Steven was killed."

"In that case, you have nothing to worry about, do you, Denise?"

"Who's worried?"

They held each other's gaze for a few seconds. Then, when the chief couldn't think of anything more to say, he put his hat back on and walked out.

When he had disappeared, Grace turned to Denise, whose color was slowly returning. "What was that all about?" she asked.

Denise shrugged. "Oh, you know the chief, always grandstanding."

"It was more than that this time. He came to warn you, Denise."

"Don't worry about it. I'm not."

"Yes, you are. I know it and more importantly, the chief knows it." Grace lowered her voice. "What's going on, Denise? Tell me. I might be able to help you."

"Nothing is going on."

"I don't believe you. You're hiding something, and whatever it is, you're not handling it well at all, so why don't you confide in me? Isn't that what friends are for? Helping each other?"

Denise took her time rearranging the small racks on the glass counter. She moved a ring to where a bracelet had been, then picked up a necklace and hung it on the other rack. Grace didn't hurry her. Some secrets were harder to share than others.

"You can't tell anyone," she said at last. "And that includes Matt."

"Does it have anything to do with Steven's murder?"

"I won't say another word until you promise."

"All right, I promise not to tell anyone."

Denise stopped playing with the display. "He *was* seeing someone else."

Grace kept her expression blank, remembering another time, another place. Same man. "How did you find out?"

"I followed him one day after his last class." She looked up, her eyes burning hot and angry. "I hated him for making me do that, for turning me into this jealous shrew I despised."

The outburst took Grace by surprise. She would have never guessed that Denise was capable of such rage. "Where did he go?" she asked.

"The cottage, where she was waiting. The son of a bitch didn't have the decency to take her to a hotel.

He had to screw her right there, in the same bed he shared with me. Can you believe it?"

Yes, she could. "Who was the woman?"

Denise drew a long breath. "Lucy."

There was a moment of stunned silence during which Grace could only stare at Denise, who was looking at the ring on her hand. "Are you sure?" she asked after a while.

"Her car was there, hidden from the road. Like the masochist that I am, I waited, hidden behind the bushes until she came out. I had almost convinced myself that her visit to the cottage was completely aboveboard. Steven often helped his students after school, although he had never had one come to his home before.

"When the door opened, I realized what a fool I had been." Tears ran down Denise's cheeks but she made no attempt to wipe them off. "Lucy looked so happy, so fulfilled, I knew their relationship was a lot more than what I had hoped."

"Judging from that expensive trinket under the counter, you must have confronted Steven."

"That same night. Do you know what he told me?" She took a tissue from the box behind her and blew her nose. "He told me that she didn't mean anything to him. She was just a passing fancy, a kid who made him feel young and vital. He was so callous, and I was so angry at the way he talked about Lucy, I could have…" She stopped and dabbed her eyes.

A cold knot formed in the pit of Grace's stomach. *I could have killed him.* Was that what she had been about to say?

"Did Lucy know about you and Steven?" Grace heard the catch in her own voice as she spoke.

"Not until I told her, a couple of days later. I love that girl as if she were my own flesh and blood, Grace, and the thought of hurting her was killing me, but I couldn't bear to see her waste her innocence on a creep like Steven Hatfield."

"How did she take it?"

"Not well. She called me a liar, and she accused me of trying to break her and Steven up. When she finally realized that I was telling the truth, she went nuts, yelling and calling him names. I couldn't believe it. If I had known what this would do to her, I would have kept my mouth shut. When she left my shop, she was fit to be tied. That's why I stayed behind that night—not to work, like I told the police, but to pull myself together, and to prepare myself for Fred's fury. I was sure that Lucy had run straight home to tell him about me and Steven. As it turned out, she wasn't the one who told him."

"Was Lucy there? At the house?"

Denise looked away. "No."

"Where was she?"

"I don't know."

"You didn't try to find out?"

"No, Grace, I didn't try to find out, okay?" she said sharply. "I had other things on my mind, like the police taking my husband away in handcuffs."

"I'm just trying to help."

"I know." Her shoulders sagged, and a sob rose from her throat. Suddenly unable to hold her anguish any longer, she covered her face with her hands and burst into tears.

Heartbroken, Grace walked around the counter to comfort her. "Don't cry, Denise. Lucy will be all right. She'll rebound. She already has."

Denise's sobbing continued.

"Is there something else? Something you haven't told me?"

Denise raised her head. Her eyes were red and blotchy, her cheeks soaked with tears. When she spoke again, she sounded utterly broken. "I think Lucy killed Steven."

Twenty-Five

Grace stared at Denise in total disbelief. She had a sudden flashback of Lucy at the kitchen sink, washing lettuce, making conversation, laughing. She was too young, too sweet, too innocent to have committed such a vile crime.

"I can't imagine her killing anyone," she said.

"I didn't want to believe it either, but that night, when she finally came home and I had to tell her that Steven had been killed, she had no reaction." She met Grace's gaze. "She was like a statue, very still and very quiet, as if I had just announced the death of a total stranger." She shivered. "It was spooky."

"She could have been in a state of shock."

Denise shook her head. "Earlier, you wondered

why I hadn't asked her where she was? I lied to you. I did ask her. In fact, that was my first question."

"What did she say?"

"That she was driving around, trying to calm down before she went home."

"People do that when they're upset."

"They don't walk in looking white as a ghost, disheveled and trembling."

"She's just a child, Denise. You can't expect her to control her emotions the same way we do."

"She had access to her father's gun. She's a first-rate target shooter, and she was insanely angry."

"So were you." The words came out without warning.

"Except that *I* didn't kill Steven. I wanted to, but I didn't."

"Couldn't that theory apply to Lucy as well? Just because she *could* have killed Steven, and may have wanted to, doesn't mean that she did."

Denise didn't reply.

"Do you want my feelings about all this?" Grace asked.

An encouraging nod.

"Talk to Matt. Have a family powwow—you, Lucy and big brother, and lay your cards on the table."

"I don't know, Grace. If it was anyone but Matt, I

might have considered taking that route, but he and I aren't what you'd call close."

"You told me yourself he was good at solving problems."

"He is."

"Then put your differences aside for a moment, and talk to him. Don't try to handle this burden on your own. You'll drive yourself crazy." She gave Denise's shoulder a little shake. "Do you trust me?"

"You know I do."

"Then listen to me and talk to Matt."

"Talk to Matt about what?"

Grace and Denise looked up as Matt entered the shop.

He looked from one to the other, eyebrow raised. "That *was* my name you mentioned, wasn't it?" he asked Grace. "Or is there another Matt in town I don't know about?"

Grace remained silent. She had promised Denise to keep her secret and she would not betray her.

"Grace has nothing to do with any of this, Matt. I'm the one who was doing all the crazy talking."

"Are you in trouble, Denise?"

"Here you go again," she said irritably. "Assuming the worst about me. Couldn't you, for once, give me the benefit of the doubt?"

A born gentleman, Matt inclined his head. "You're right and I'm sorry." He pointed at a stool against the wall. "May I?"

Denise shrugged. "You might as well make yourself comfortable."

"That bad, huh?" He winked at Grace before focusing his attention on Denise. "Can I help?"

"Maybe." She cleared her throat and began to tell Matt everything she had told Grace a few moments ago. Matt's expression didn't change until he heard about Lucy's affair with Steven. For a moment, he looked as if he was about to spring out of his chair and drag Steven out of his grave, but somehow he managed to keep a tight rein on his emotions and allowed Denise to go on with her story.

"Thank you," he said when she was finished. "Thank you for wanting to protect Lucy. And for being candid about your own feelings as well."

Grace stood up. "I think the two of you should be alone."

"No." Denise laid a hand on her arm. "Please stay." She looked at Matt. "It's okay, isn't it? I wouldn't be talking to you right now if it weren't for Grace."

"She's right," Matt said to Grace. "Please stay." He waited until she had sat down again before continuing. "I don't want to believe that Lucy is a murderer either, but I've seen too many unexpected developments in my career to think that my own family could be any different."

"What are you going to do?" Denise asked.

"I have no other choice but to talk to Lucy. If the outcome turns out the way I hope it will, we'll proceed to phase two."

"We?" Denise glanced at Grace, who still hadn't said a word.

"In order for me to find Steven's killer, I'm going to need your help."

"You want me to help you *investigate* the murder?"

He smiled. "I wouldn't go as far as that. What I need at this point is for you to recall as much as you can about Steven's personal life, his habits, his hobbies, what he did with his free time, that sort of thing."

"He didn't have many hobbies. He liked to travel abroad, eat in fancy restaurants, attend gallery openings and art shows. Occasionally he played a round of golf with his buddies on the planning board, but that's about it."

"Did you ever notice anything out of the ordinary?"

Her earlier excitement seemed to deflate. "I'm not a very good observer, Matt."

"Try, Denise. It's important."

She was silent for a while. Just when Grace thought it was hopeless, she said, "Actually, there was something I found a little odd about Steven, and that was his sudden friendship with Bernie Buckman. When I asked him about it, all he said was that Bernie was a good guy and he enjoyed spending time with him. I had no reason not to believe him." She brushed a few crumbs from the counter. "Now that a cold-blooded murderer is trying to kill Bernie, I'm not so sure."

"The man who runs the spice shop across the street from the gallery says that Bernie worked there a couple of days a week."

"That's true. He had started to show an interest in art, and Steven sometimes let him fill in for him on weekends."

"When exactly did you and Steven start getting involved?"

Grace could see that the question made Denise uncomfortable, but like the trooper she was, she answered it anyway. "Eight, maybe nine months ago."

"He must have told you a lot about himself during that time."

"Not really. Actually, I told him more about myself than the other way around." She threw him a quick, almost guilty glance. "I told him about Felicia."

"You talked to him about your sister's disappear-ance?"

She nodded, but wouldn't look at him. "He seemed interested, so I told him how my family and I were never completely satisfied with the police in-vestigation. I'm sorry, Matt," she said, finally looking up. "I know your father says he did his best to find her, but we felt that he could have done more. And in case you're wondering if I'm speaking behind his back, Fred and I have had this conver-sation before—many times, in fact. He knows exactly how I feel."

Grace glanced at Matt, hoping to see a glimmer of understanding, but he showed no reaction. He was all business. "You said that Steven seemed inter-ested in your sister's disappearance?"

"Maybe *interested* is not the right word. He was supportive, and compassionate. Then, a few weeks later, out of the blue, he started asking me more questions about the case. I was only too happy to oblige, so I told him everything he wanted to know—who Felicia had dated, the circumstances of the breakups, the county-wide search, the question-ing of witnesses, everything I could think of. Talking about Felicia in such detail hurt a little but in a way, it was therapeutic."

"Did you ask him why the sudden concern?"

"I did and he brushed me off, claiming he was just curious."

"Steven did have a curious nature," Grace said. "He was more than curious, actually. He had a habit of meddling into other people's business that occasionally got him into trouble. He was very much like his mother in that respect."

"You think he found out something about my sister's disappearance?" Denise asked Matt.

"It's possible."

"But if he had, he would have told me."

"Not necessarily," Grace interjected. She looked at Matt, who gave a slight nod.

Denise looked from one to the other. "What's going on between you two? Why the looks? What do you know that you're not telling me?"

"I found some money at the cottage," Grace said.

"Money? As in cash?"

"A quarter of a million dollars in hundred-dollar bills was hidden in his kitchen cabinet."

Denise was too smart not to grasp the implications of what she had just heard. She looked at Matt "You don't think that money came from the forgeries, do you?"

"No," he said quietly.

Her hand went to her throat. "Blackmail," she whispered.

Then, as if a spring had just activated her, she jumped from her stool. "Dear Jesus! He knew who kidnapped Felicia!"

Twenty-Six

As Matt had expected, Lucy had cancelled their lunch date, leaving only a brief message on his cell phone. He had debated between giving her time to cool off and showing up at the end of her last class. Feeling optimistic, he had opted for the latter.

A few students had already started to trickle out, and a few minutes later, Lucy appeared. This time she was alone and walked rapidly, with her head down. She didn't look up until Matt called out her name.

Startled, she stopped. "Didn't you get my message?" she asked. "I told you not to come."

"I like to live dangerously."

He failed to make her smile. "I already had lunch," she said curtly.

"Then we'll go for a walk." He took her arm, cutting short her protest.

He led her toward the canal and towpath that bisected the town and ran parallel to the Delaware River.

"What's so urgent?" Lucy asked.

The direct approach had always served him well. "I know about your affair with Steven."

She threw him a panicked look and her cheeks turned red before she tried, rather ineffectively, to appear nonchalant. "What are you talking about?"

"I talked to Denise, and before you accuse her of betraying you, understand that I didn't give her much of a choice."

She waited a while before asking, "Were you shocked?"

"You can relax, I'm not going to give you the dreaded big-brother lecture."

"Thank you."

"Why didn't you tell me?"

"Because you wouldn't have understood."

"About a nineteen-year-old student having an affair with her professor? A man twenty-one years her senior? You're right. I don't understand. And if you had told me, I probably would have tried to knock some sense into you."

"Because you don't approve?"

"Because my first priority was always to protect you."

"I don't need protecting. I'm a big girl now. I can handle anything."

"Maybe so, but it couldn't have been easy finding out that the man you loved was your stepmother's lover."

She sat down on a bench and stared at the canal's murky water, saying nothing.

"Look, honey," he said, sitting beside her. "I can't help Dad if you don't level with me."

She still wouldn't look at him. "What do you want to know?"

"Tell me what happened the night Steven Hatfield was killed."

"I don't know anything, except what I heard or read in the papers."

"Denise said that you stormed out of her shop after she told you about her and Steven."

"I was mad."

"Where did you go?"

"Why do you want to know?" Her tone had turned cynical. "You think *I* killed Steven?" She searched his eyes for an answer. "Oh, my God!" she exclaimed. "You do!"

"Don't get excited—"

"Don't you think I'm justified? When my own

brother thinks that I'm a murderer?" She shrank away from him as if he had suddenly contracted the bubonic plague. "You actually believe that I took Dad's gun, went to the gallery, shot Steven in cold blood and then dropped the gun so Daddy would be blamed? And that after I committed that evil act, I could still look you and Daddy in the face?" Her expression was a mixture of pain and disappointment. "How could you?"

"I didn't want to believe it, but there are holes in the story you told Denise. That's why I had to talk to you."

She got fidgety again. "What kind of holes?"

"Do you remember the condition you were in when you finally went home that night?"

She let out a dry laugh. "Sure. I was a mess."

"What did you do after leaving Denise's store?"

"I drove all the way to Washington Crossing, crying my eyes out and feeling sorry for myself. I don't even remember driving back home."

"Do you remember Denise telling you that Steven had been murdered?"

"Yes."

"It had to be quite a shock, yet you barely reacted."

She looked down at her folded hands. "There's a reason for that."

Something about the way she averted her eyes

told him he wasn't going to like what she had to say. "I'm listening."

"After Denise told me about her affair with Steven, something happened to me. I went a little crazy. I left Baubles and went home to look for Daddy's gun."

Matt tensed but didn't interrupt her.

"Don't ask me if I would have killed Steven or not, because I don't know. Maybe I just wanted to scare him, make him realize how much he had hurt me."

A gust of wind blew her hair in her face. She pushed it away, tucking a long strand behind her ear. "Daddy's gun wasn't where he usually kept it, so I left and went to the gallery, armed only with my anger. I knew that Steven was working late that night."

"What time was that?"

"A few minutes after six. Maybe six-fifteen."

"Go on."

"I was a few feet from the gallery when I saw a man run out the front door."

Matt almost jumped off the bench. "You saw someone and didn't tell the police?"

She looked miserable. "I couldn't."

"Why not? When you knew it could have cleared Dad!"

She suddenly seemed very small, and very vulnerable. "Because," she said under her breath, "the man was Daddy."

"*What?*"

"I recognized his Eagles jacket, the one he always wears to the games. And his Eagles hat."

"Half the men in this town have Eagles jackets and Eagles hats."

She didn't say anything.

"Did you see his face?"

"No. He was running in the opposite direction."

"Then how can you be sure that it was him?"

She turned to look at him. "I just know."

"Describe him."

She looked confused. "You want me to describe Dad?"

"Describe the man you saw."

"Well, he looked just like Dad, same height, same broad shoulders. And he ran fast, like Dad."

"Honey, that description could fit a lot of men."

"What about the gun? I saw it, Matt."

"What do you mean you saw it?"

"After I saw…Dad." She stumbled a little on the word. "I had a premonition that something was wrong, so I went to the gallery." She closed her eyes. "The door was open and I saw Steven, lying on the floor, in a pool of blood. When I backed away, I saw the gun at the edge of the flower bed. Daddy's gun. I didn't know what to do, where to turn. I had all those thoughts going through my head at once. I didn't want to call the police because I would have had to tell them that I saw Daddy run out of the gallery. So, I got back into my car and started driving until I reached Washington Crossing. I stayed there for a while, then I remembered about the gun. I kicked myself for not taking it with me. I started to go back, but by the time I got there, several police cars were surrounding the gallery, so I went home."

"Oh, Lucy." He pulled her to him. "You poor kid."

She rested her head on his shoulder. "You understand why I couldn't say anything? I would have been the noose around Daddy's neck."

He smiled. "It wasn't him you saw, Goldilocks, just someone *meant* to look like him. It was all part of the setup."

She looked up. "What setup? What are you talking about?"

"The killer—the *real* killer—framed Dad. He took his gun, went to the gallery, killed Steven and threw Dad's gun in the flower bed where he knew the police would find it."

Her young face was filled with outrage. "But that's a terrible thing to do!"

"Yes, it is." He smoothed down her hair. "Are we friends again?"

She threw herself into his arms. "Yes." After a while, she looked up. "How are you going to prove that the man I saw wasn't Daddy?"

"I don't know yet, but while I try to find out, I want you to do one thing for me."

"What's that?"

"Go talk to Denise. She's worried sick about you."

Twenty-Seven

"What can you tell me about Ellie Colburn?" Matt asked his father when he stopped by the jail after his meeting with Lucy.

"Dusty's mother?" Fred looked surprised. "What do you want with her?"

"I have reasons to believe that Steven Hatfield may have been digging for information regarding Felicia's disappearance."

"What would he want with a twenty-year-old case? A closed one, at that."

Fred wasn't going to like this part. "He and Denise talked about it. She told him how she and her family were still not convinced that the police had done all they could to find Felicia, or the real kidnapper."

Fred hit the bars with his fist. "Like hell we didn't! My men worked their asses off, looking for that girl and trying to find who had abducted her. I even brought *you* in for questioning. My own son."

"But isn't it true that Dusty was charged based solely on circumstantial evidence?"

"Sometimes that's enough. I explained all this to Denise. She has no business bad-mouthing me to you."

"Wait a minute, Dad. She never said a cross word against you. On the contrary." What was he doing defending Denise?

Fred waved his hand, signaling he had heard enough. "Why don't we get back to Steven? What exactly was he looking for?"

"That's what I want to find out."

"By talking to Ellie?" He chuckled. "Remember that old shotgun of hers? She still has it, and she's not afraid of using it."

"I'll take my chances. If our theory is right—"

"*Our* theory?"

"Denise has been helping."

"Tell me you're kidding."

"I needed her to tell me what she remembered about Steven and his habits."

"Leave her out of the case, son, before she screws it up permanently."

"Pop, come on. She wants you out of here as much as I do."

Fred pretended not to have heard that last comment. "Ellie's all right," he said, addressing Matt's earlier question. "She did the best she could raising Dusty under the circumstances. Her husband was a boozer and walked out on his family when he found out that Dusty was mentally retarded. Ellie didn't have enough money to put him in a specialized facility, so she homeschooled him herself. He was a good kid, never gave anyone any trouble. Then in his midteens, he hit puberty and started noticing girls. I guess he liked what he saw because he became quite a nuisance, but you know all that."

"It doesn't hurt to refresh my memory."

"He was particularly taken with Felicia," Fred continued. "Ellie tried to get him interested in other things. She found him a few odd jobs, and for a while he did okay. He liked having money of his own. Unfortunately, he wasn't very reliable.

"The night of Felicia's disappearance, he was seen talking with her. Well, you couldn't exactly call it *with* her, because most of the time it was just a one-way conversation, with Dusty doing all the talking. Felicia never paid much attention to him. When she did talk to him, it was always to say something nasty. Anyone else would have given up long ago, but not Dusty."

"Who saw them together?"

"Old Cliff Barnard. He's dead now, but he made a sworn statement at the time."

"No one else saw Dusty and Felicia together?"

Fred shook his head. "There weren't too many people out in the streets that night, if you recall. Everybody was too busy celebrating about one thing or another. You had just graduated from Penn State. George had been accepted into Harvard Law and Josh was yahooing about his army discharge. And we can't forget Eddie, who had just signed a five-year contract with the Reading Phillies and was feeling no pain."

Matt chuckled. "I never knew he could drink that much."

"That's what I mean, the bars were full and the streets empty."

"Who reported Felicia missing?"

"Her mother, the following morning, when she realized that her daughter never came home. Everyone, including my department, assumed the girl had skipped town again. She had a habit of doing that. Then a week later, she'd reappear, with a swagger in her hips and a contrite expression on that pretty face of hers.

"Julia Newman accused us of not looking very hard for her daughter because of Felicia's past antics, but she was wrong. We had divers from three counties searching up and down that river for days. More than a hundred volunteers participated in the search, and it pisses me off to no end that Denise has the audacity—"

"What tipped you off that Dusty was your man?" Matt asked, quickly changing the subject.

Fred waited for the anger to pass. "Five days after Felicia's disappearance, we found him sitting on the side of the road, at the same place where he was last seen with her. In his hands was the scarf she had worn that night.

"He wouldn't talk to us, or to anyone. A doctor later explained that Dusty was experiencing a form of post-traumatic shock, not unlike those suffered by some war veterans. No one was ever able to extract one single word out of him since that day."

"Could he have *witnessed* something traumatic rather than caused it?"

"He could have, and don't think we didn't consider that possibility. But Cliff was a very credible witness."

"What exactly did he say?"

"That Dusty seemed rather agitated that night,

even rude to Felicia, to the point that Cliff felt it necessary to get out of his car and intervene."

"How?"

"He told him to leave her alone and go home."

"Did he?"

"As far as Cliff could tell. He saw Dusty start down the road, back toward the center of town. Then Cliff drove off and he couldn't be absolutely sure that Dusty didn't turn around and come back."

"What about Felicia? It was late at night. She was on a deserted road. Why didn't Cliff give her a ride?"

"He offered. She turned him down. You know how she was, snooty and unpredictable."

He walked back to the door and wrapped his hands around the heavy metal bars. "I did everything I could to make that boy talk," he said. "I used any kind of psychology I could think of. It got me nowhere. Dusty remained totally uncommunicative. Two weeks later, he was found incompetent to stand trial and was sent to a mental facility."

"And he's still not talking?"

"I haven't kept up with his progress, but I'm sure Ellie would have said something if he was."

"Does she still live on Lower York Road?"

"Yes, but as I said, don't expect too much from her, son."

"Why?" Matt gave him a grin. "You don't think the old Baxter charm will work on her?"

"Get out of here, you clown."

Twenty-Eight

The lines on Ellie Colburn's face and the perpetual slump of her shoulders attested that life hadn't been easy for her. Barely past her sixtieth birthday, she looked two decades older.

Arthritic fingers gripped her front door as she inspected her visitor. "What do you want, Matt?"

Not the friendliest greeting in the world, but at least she hadn't slammed the door in his face. "Good afternoon, Ellie. I was hoping you'd have a little time to talk to me."

Suspicious eyes studied him. "About what?"

"Steven Hatfield."

"The man is dead. Can't you let him rest in peace?"

"I mean no disrespect, Ellie, but as you may have heard, I'm investigating Steven's murder."

"I heard."

"That's why I'm here—not because I think that you killed Steven," he added quickly when she started to close the door, "but because there is a possibility that his death was linked to Felicia's disappearance."

The door slowly reopened. "Who told you that?"

"May I come in? Please? I don't think we should discuss this on the front porch, do you?"

She opened the door to let him in, but didn't invite him into the living room. She seemed content to stay where they were, in a small foyer with a credenza against the wall and a crystal chandelier hanging from the ceiling. The house smelled good, like freshly cut balsam. She was impeccable herself, in inexpensive but well-pressed chinos, a crisp white shirt and sneakers.

"I understand that Steven was asking questions around town regarding the circumstances of Felicia's disappearance. I was wondering if he came to see you."

"What if he did? What are you going to do about it? Pick up where he left off and get yourself killed, too?"

Now that was an interesting comment. "You think that's why Steven was killed? Because he got too nosy?"

"What difference does it make what I think? Nobody believes me anyway. When I found out that Steven was killed, I told the police about his visit. They took down every word I said and then they did zilch."

"Who did you talk to?"

"Deputy Montgomery. He said he would talk to the chief, but he didn't. Or if he did, Josh didn't care enough to follow through."

"I'll find out if Rob talked to the chief, Ellie. I promise. In the meantime, are you willing to help me?"

She gave him a long, level look. This was not a woman you could easily intimidate. She'd had a tough life and had survived the worst, but he saw the spark of interest in those calm brown eyes, and something else, something he suspected she hadn't experienced in more than twenty years—hope.

"I've been hearing a lot about you," she said after a while. "People say you're smart, and hardheaded."

Matt smiled. "My father will vouch for that."

Her features softened. "Are you going to get my boy out of that cracker house?"

"I'd like to try."

"He's all I have, you know. They took my spirit away when they carted him off."

There was still some of that old spirit left. "Has he ever tried to tell you what happened that night?"

"He doesn't talk anymore. Either he can't, or he doesn't want to. The doctors say that's what happens sometimes after a traumatic shock. That's Dusty's way of not reliving what he saw."

He noticed that she said *what he saw*, not *what he did*. "You seem convinced that your son is innocent."

"I *know* my son is innocent. The boy may have been a little intense at times, especially around girls, we all know that, but he would never harm anyone, least of all Felicia. He worshipped that girl." Her expression turned bitter. "Not that she deserved it. That little witch was rotten through and through."

"How's Dusty doing now?"

Ellie shrugged. "He has occasional nightmares, but all he does is scream. He never says anything. He reads a lot, though, comic books mostly, as many as I can bring him."

"You visit him often?"

"Every day. He's my boy. He needs me."

"Anyone else come to see him?"

"Steven went, just once. I told him it was useless, but he insisted, so I took him there myself."

"What happened?"

"What I told him would happen. Nothing. Dusty didn't say a word. He just sat there during the entire visit, looking through his comic books while Steven tried to make him talk. I never saw Steven again after that."

"Did he tell you why he was so interested in Felicia's disappearance?"

"I asked him. He gave me some cockamamie story about acquainting himself with New Hope's past."

"You didn't buy it?"

"Hell, no, but I wasn't complaining. I figured that maybe, if he poked around long enough, he might find something that could clear my boy. That's why I went to the police after he was killed. I thought something smelled fishy, but I didn't know what."

"Do you know if Steven talked to anyone else about this?"

"He would have liked to talk to Cliff Barnard, but Cliff died about eight years ago."

"That's the man who saw Dusty and Felicia on Route 32 together."

"That's right. She was hitchhiking. At eleven o'clock at night." Ellie shook her head in disapproval. "The things that girl did. She drove her mother crazy. It's a wonder she wasn't killed any sooner."

"You think she was killed?"

"A pretty girl like that doesn't stay gone for twenty years. Somebody would have seen her."

That was the general consensus. "So, at the moment, you are the only one who sees Dusty?" he asked.

"Except for Father Donnelly. He's been so good to

Dusty. Visits him every week, without fail. I don't think he missed a single week in the last twenty years."

"How can that be? Father Donnelly was transferred eighteen or nineteen years ago, wasn't he? And didn't return to New Hope until recently?"

Ellie nodded. "A year after Dusty was moved to the psychiatric hospital, Father Donnelly was sent to Harrisburg. He stayed there for a few years before being transferred to a small parish in Lancaster County. Eventually, he came back to New Hope, as a pastor."

"And while he was away, he still came to visit Dusty? Even when he was in Harrisburg?"

"Yes, sir. He never missed a visit. Can you believe that? A few years ago, he gave Dusty his personal bible, the one he was given when he came out of the seminary. Dusty's never been very religious, but for some reason, that bible helped him find the faith he never had before. He carries it with him everywhere he goes, and reads it every day. I think it's brought him some peace," she said with a knowing nod.

"I'm sure it has." Matt looked at his watch. "I won't take any more of your time. Thanks for talking to me, Ellie. You were very helpful."

"You won't disappear, like Steven did? You'll keep me informed of what you find out?"

"That's a promise, Ellie."

Twenty-Nine

"Why don't you just move into my office?" Josh said sarcastically. "Take over and help yourself to anything you want?"

"Come on, Josh, don't make it sound as if I'm asking for the moon. All I want is to take a look at Felicia Newman's file."

"And you still haven't told me why you want to do that."

Might as well tell him, Matt thought. He would cooperate more willingly if he was kept in the loop. "The case could be connected to Hatfield's murder."

At those words, Josh's sarcastic expression vanished. "Where the hell did you hear a crazy thing like that?"

"I'd rather keep my sources confidential. The point is that a few months ago, Steven Hatfield became interested in the disappearance of Felicia Newman and started poking around for information."

"That's hogwash. If he was poking around, I'd have heard about it. Or one of my deputies would have. In fact, this department is the first place Hatfield would have come to for information."

"But he went to see Ellie Colburn, and Ellie came here right after she heard about Steven's murder. Rob didn't tell you about that?"

Josh nodded. "He mentioned it to me."

"What did you do about it?"

"What was there to do? Ellie Colburn's agenda was always to get her son out of that mental hospital. Anything she says has to be taken with a grain of salt."

"Maybe you should have followed through."

Josh bristled. "What the hell does that mean?"

"It means that if you had investigated her claim, you would have found out that at Steven's request, she took him to see Dusty. There will be a record of that visit."

"And just what does that prove? That Steven Hatfield was nosy? Or maybe he was one of those amateur sleuths who think they're better than police investigators."

"And maybe, as he kept digging, he found something that the police didn't. That could change everything."

"I don't follow."

"Think, Josh. If Dusty Colburn is innocent and Steven was investigating a case everyone thought had been solved, the real killer must have been squirming."

"Assuming that Hatfield had found something to squirm about."

"Now you're with me."

"No, I'm not, because if he was in possession of new evidence, he would have gone to the police and we would have started a new investigation."

"Unless Hatfield chose to keep quiet and cash in on what he knew."

"You mean blackmail?"

"That would explain the quarter of a million dollars Grace found in his kitchen cabinet, don't you think?"

Josh seemed to process that statement for a second or two. "You're reaching."

"We won't know that for sure until I start looking into the original investigation." He leaned back in his chair, feeling as if he had scored a goal. "Now, how about that file?"

Josh let out a long-suffering sigh, as though he was doing Matt a huge favor. Then, turning his head toward a door, he yelled, "Montgomery!"

Rob stuck his head into the opening. "Yes, Chief?"

"Bring me the file on Felicia Newman."

Rob looked from Josh to Matt and back to his boss. "Felicia Newman? What for?"

"Matt wants it."

"That case was closed twenty years ago."

"I know that, Montgomery!" Josh said, exasperated. "Just get it and give it to Matt." As Rob disappeared, the chief pointed a finger at Matt. "I want that file back on my desk in twenty-four hours."

"Thanks, Josh. You're a real prince."

A cold front had moved in during rush hour, bringing temperatures into the forties and sending shoppers scurrying for warmer surroundings.

Wishing she had packed a warmer coat, Grace raised the collar of her leather jacket and kept her head down as she walked toward the church, where she hoped to find Father Donnelly preparing for the eight-o'clock evening mass. Matt hadn't believed that the priest would be able to convince Bernie to go into protective custody, but knowing what she knew about Father Donnelly, she felt differently. And if he couldn't help, at least she had tried.

As she neared the parking lot, the back door to the church flew open and a man ran out. It was Bernie, heading toward Ferris Street.

"Bernie!"

He didn't stop, or acknowledge her presence in any way. How could he not have heard her? He was only a few feet ahead of her. "Bernie!" she called again. "Wait!"

He turned the corner without looking back.

She stood in the church's empty parking lot for a moment, looking at the old stone building, remembering Denise's words: *"Bernie never stepped into that church again, not even for Steven's memorial service."*

What had brought him back tonight? And why hadn't he stopped?

The door to the church stood ajar. On impulse, Grace walked up the steps and went in. The room was empty, dark and smelled of incense. The only light came from a row of candles, their flickering flames casting oddly-shaped shadows on the walls. Pews on each side of the aisle led to the altar, where a tall pillar candle burned.

"Father Donnelly?"

The silence turned oppressive, and the unpleasant sensation she'd had earlier seemed to intensify.

"Father Donnelly? Are you there? It's Grace McKenzie."

Standing in front of the altar, she looked up at the statue of Jesus on the cross. She felt both apprehensive and foolish and didn't know why.

"Are you looking for me, Ms. McKenzie?"

Grace let out a small cry and spun around. Father Donnelly stood a few feet from her, his expression serene, his hands folded across his midriff. "Father." She placed a hand over her heart. "You scared me."

"I'm sorry. Have you been here long?"

"Yes. No. I mean, I called your name several times."

"I just stepped out for a moment. I didn't realized you were here until I walked back in." He smiled. "What can I do for you, Ms. McKenzie?"

Her heartbeat was slowly returning to normal. "I just saw Bernie come out of the church and I was hoping to find out if—"

He frowned. "Bernie Buckman?"

"Yes. I saw him running out of the back door."

He shook his head. "You must have been mistaken. Bernie wasn't here. He hasn't set foot in this church since his mother died."

"I'm not mistaken," she said maybe a little too sharply. "It *was* Bernie. He ran out of that door." She pointed. "The same one I used to come in."

"There was someone in a back pew, praying, but it wasn't Bernie." His smile was gentle, comforting. "What's bothering you, Ms. McKenzie?"

"I don't understand why Bernie didn't stop when I called his name."

"Maybe whoever it was didn't hear you."

"He heard me, Father."

"I don't think Bernie would have ignored you. I'm aware of what you did the other night. I talked to his sister the following day and she told me how grateful she and Bernie were for your heroic action."

He closed the distance that separated them and together, they started walking down the main aisle, toward the front door. "Bernie is a good man. He was once very devoted to the church, and to God. His mother's death changed all that. I tried to help, but…" He lifted both arms and let them drop in a gesture of helplessness. "Sometimes even the best efforts fall short of our expectations. I would like to believe that Bernie was here, that he was ready to make peace with God and with the church, but as I said, I was at the altar for nearly an hour, praying, before I went into the sanctuary. If Bernie had been here, I would have seen him."

How could she doubt him? Men of the cloth didn't lie. Maybe something had spooked Bernie, forcing him to run out before Father Donnelly returned from the sanctuary. "You must be right. I'm sorry to have bothered you, Father."

"No need to apologize." They had reached the door. "However, I am holding you to your promise of attending Sunday mass."

She would have to make the effort now. She owed him. "I'll be there. Good night, Father."

"Good night, Ms. McKenzie."

She walked out onto the parking lot and took a deep, steadying breath. Hands in her pockets, she headed back toward the gallery where she had left her car. Just before Bridge Street, she turned around for one last look at the spot where she had last seen Bernie.

Father Donnelly was still there, standing in the church doorway.

The gentle, comforting smile was gone.

Thirty

Dry leaves swirled around Grace's feet as she walked briskly across the empty parking lot. Although calmer now, she was eager to get far away from the church and Father Donnelly, whom she sensed was still watching her.

The gallery was only a couple of blocks away, but she now regretted not taking her car. Her uneasiness turned into raw fear when her peripheral vision caught a moving shadow. She stopped and turned just in time to see someone duck behind an oak tree. Father Donnelly had vanished, but the thought that *he* could be the one following her was too ridiculous to consider.

She started to run. Born and raised in a big city, with its share of violent crimes, she wasn't about to take a chance with another unknown assailant, no matter how well she may have perfected her kicking technique.

As she burst onto Bridge Street, a car went by. For an instant, she thought of flagging it. But what if the driver didn't stop? She would lose precious seconds and put herself at the mercy of whoever was following her.

Her footsteps resounded loudly on the pavement. She had no idea if her pursuer was still after her. She focused all her attention on reaching her car, praying she'd have enough time to get in and lock the door.

She wasn't that fortunate. As she rounded the corner, she collided with a man. She would have fallen if he hadn't caught her.

"Let me go!" she shouted when he gripped her arms.

"Grace!" The man shook her. "Stop. It's me, Matt."

She went still. "Matt?" Still shaking, she glanced over her shoulder. Except for the headlights of an oncoming car, the street was deserted. Had she imagined her pursuer? "Were you following me just now?"

"No. Why would I do that?"

"I don't know." She waited until the car went by. "What are you doing here?"

"I stopped by the gallery, thinking I might catch you before you closed. Are you okay? You're trembling."

"I'm fine." She took a few shallow breaths. "No, I'm not," she admitted. "Someone was following me."

Matt scrutinized the street. "Where?"

"In the church's parking lot."

"What were you doing there?"

"I went to see Father Donnelly. I wanted to ask him if he would talk to Bernie and try to convince him to go away. It was a long shot, I know, but I had to try. As it turned out, I never got a chance to ask him anything." She told him about seeing Bernie run out of the church, and Father Donnelly's denial that he had been there.

"Are you sure it was Bernie?"

"Not you, too," she said impatiently. "Yes, I'm sure. It was Bernie. Something frightened him in that church, Matt. That's why he ran."

"Maybe he didn't recognized you, or your voice."

"No, he had to know it was me."

Matt took her arm and they started walking at an easy, calming pace. "Why are you so concerned about Bernie?" he asked after a while. "He's a grown man. He's smart and self-sufficient and seems to be getting along just fine."

"I don't know how to answer that question. It's true that I'm being overprotective of him. Maybe it's because he had no friends other than Steven, and now that Steven is dead, he's all alone again. Or maybe it has something to do with what happened at the river the other night. I heard that once you save someone's life, you become responsible for that life forever."

"That saying has been amended." Matt's tone was light and comforting. "The words 'responsible' and 'forever' have been deleted."

"You're making this up."

"I tell you what. You show me where you read *your* saying, and I'll show you where I saw that amendment. Deal?"

"You're crazy."

Still holding her arm, he made a sudden one-hundred-and-eighty-degree turn.

"What are you doing? Where are we going?"

"I don't want you to lose any sleep over Bernie, so we'll do it your way. We'll go and talk to Father Donnelly."

The tension of the last twenty-four hours began to ease off. "Thank you."

The parking lot, still deserted, seemed much less threatening now that Matt was with her. And whoever had been lurking in the shadows was long gone.

"Is this the door you used?" Matt asked as they approached the side entrance.

"Yes. Bernie had left it open and I just walked in."

Matt tried it. "Father Donnelly must have locked it. We'll use the one on Main Street."

The church was as silent as it had been a few minutes ago but no longer felt as oppressive.

"Father!" Matt's voice echoed loudly. "Father, it's Matt Baxter. I need to talk to—"

She stopped him. "He's praying," she said, pointing at Father Donnelly kneeling at the altar. "We probably shouldn't disturb him."

"Stay here." Matt's tone had changed.

"Why? What's wrong?"

"I don't know yet." He pushed her back and started walking toward the praying man.

Ignoring his instructions, Grace followed him, stopping a split second after he did.

Her mouth opened, but no sound came out.

Father Donnelly was on his knees. His head was bent in prayer, his hands joined together.

Sticking out of his back was a knife.

Thirty-One

His face grim, Chief Nader contemplated the motionless body of Father Donnelly. He was still in a praying position, his upper torso supported by a small gilded railing. Two police officers had cordoned off the crime scene while out in the street, Deputy Montgomery tried to calm the growing crowd.

After a few more seconds, the chief walked over to where Grace and Matt stood. Matt had wrapped a protective arm around her shoulders and she was grateful for the comfort and safety that arm provided.

"I understand that you two found him," the chief said, his voice heavy with sarcasm.

"That's right," Matt replied.

The chief turned to his other deputy, a young but surprisingly efficient man Grace had met at the police station the previous day. "Locheck, come here and take some notes." Then to Grace. "You were the last one to see Father Donnelly alive, so you go first."

Matt looked at her. "Do you feel up to it? If you're not, I'm sure Josh won't mind waiting until tomorrow."

"Excuse me, Matt, but I run this investigation, and I do mind. I need to have the facts as Ms. McKenzie remembers them right now, while the details are still fresh in her mind."

Grace laid a hand on Matt's arm. "It's all right, Matt. I can do this."

The coroner had arrived and she turned away so she wouldn't have to look at the body again. In a voice that was more or less steady, she told the chief about seeing Bernie, her talk with Father Donnelly, and his denial that Bernie had been there.

At the mention of Bernie's name, the chief waved two of his officers over. "You two know where Bernie Buckman lives?" he asked.

"Yes, sir. He's up on Windy Bush Road."

"Go get him. Don't give him any details, but be sure to tell him this is not an arrest. I just want to talk to him." As they walked away, the chief turned to Matt. "Your turn."

As Matt gave his version, Grace looked around her. A police photographer was taking pictures of

Father Donnelly from various angles, while two members of the crime scene unit were dusting for fingerprints. A third searched the floor and the pews for any evidence he could find.

She felt light-headed and out of touch, as if she was watching a movie being filmed without being part of it. She kept thinking about Bernie. How would he handle a police interrogation? Had she betrayed him by bringing up his name?

Fifteen minutes after the two officers were dispatched to Bernie's residence, they came back. "He's not home, Chief," one of the officers said. "We stopped by the hospital to talk to his sister. She hasn't seen or heard from him all day. She's on her way here now."

"Good. In the meantime, I want you to keep looking for him. He was last seen on foot, so he couldn't have gone far. Or he could be driving Fred Baxter's Firebird." He rattled off the license plate number.

As he turned to talk to the coroner, Matt put a hand on his arm. "If it's okay with you," he told Josh. "I'd like to take Grace home."

Pleased to have been consulted, Josh nodded. "I have more questions but they can wait until morning."

Grace felt Matt's hand on her back, pushing her gently toward the door. "Come on. Let's get out of here."

* * *

It took all of Matt's persuasion to get the crowd outside the church to let them get through. More than thirty people followed them to the car, hurling questions Matt refused to answer.

"It's not my place to comment about a case under investigation," he said. "However, the chief should be out momentarily to make a statement."

"Grace!" Denise unceremoniously pushed through the crowd and threw herself into Grace's arms. "Thank God, you're all right. Adele Scott rang my bell a minute ago. She said that someone had been killed and you were involved. I was scared out of my wits." She walked with them. "Where are you taking her?" she asked Matt.

"Home."

"She can't stay alone. I'll come and stay with her. Or you could come to my house, Grace. We have plenty of room."

"She won't be alone," Matt said. "I'll stay with her."

Normally, people speaking for her was one of Grace's pet peeves, but for some reason, she didn't mind. It had been a long time since she'd let a man take charge, and it actually felt good.

"I'll call you in the morning," Grace said, giving

Denise a quick hug. "Don't worry, okay? I'm in good hands."

Denise gave Matt a long look before whispering back, "You go, girl."

"Would you like some coffee?" Grace asked as they hung their jackets on the rack in the foyer. "I'm pretty decent with a coffeemaker."

"I'd love some, and while you dazzle me with your coffeemaking skills, I'll start a fire. Is that all right?"

Grace wasn't sure a fire could warm the cold she felt inside, but it couldn't hurt. "That sounds good, thank you."

Ten minutes later, she was curled up in front of a roaring fire, her hands wrapped around a mug of coffee. "I can't get the picture of Father Donnelly out of my mind," she said. "It was so gruesome, and... irreverent. How could someone stab a priest in the back, while he was praying?"

"Twisted minds do strange things, Grace. I'm sorry you had to see that."

"Who would want to kill him? And why?"

"Probably for the same reason Steven was killed. He may have known something about Felicia Newman's abduction. And perhaps Steven's death as well."

It was a valid possibility but not a practical one.

"How could a priest know something about a murder that could clear an innocent man and not come forward?"

"Priests are often called upon to make difficult decisions. Concealing a horrific crime must be one of the hardest."

"What makes you so sure that he knew something?"

"Certain details are beginning to make sense."

"Like what?"

"I went to see Ellie Colburn today—"

"Who is Ellie Colburn?"

"Dusty's mother. Dusty was the man charged with Felicia's abduction. He was later found incompetent to stand trial and was sent into a mental institution for life."

"I remember now. Denise told me about him. He can't talk, therefore he was unable to defend himself. What did you find out from his mother?"

Matt told her about Father Donnelly's uninterrupted weekly visits.

"Actually, that's not so unusual," Grace said. "I come from a Catholic family and one thing I remember about our parish priest is the role he played in the lives of his worshipers. He didn't just perform services for all the important events, he was invited to all the parties—birthdays, weddings, Christmas celebrations, Thanksgiving. He, too, would have continued to visit Dusty, no matter how far he had to travel."

"Would he also have lied about Bernie being there?"

Grace hesitated. "No, I don't believe he would have."

"So what does that tell you about Father Donnelly?" When she didn't answer, he added, "Priests are human, Grace, and not as beyond reproach as we'd like to think. That's a reality the church has had to deal with for the last several years."

"You really believe that he could be involved in a murder?"

"Maybe not directly, but he knew something. He must have, to end up with a knife in his back."

"And now we'll never know," Grace said softly. "Father Donnelly took his secret to the grave."

"Maybe not."

She gave him an inquisitive look.

"We have Bernie. The fact that he went to see Father Donnelly after a twenty-year absence tells me that, somehow, he is involved."

Grace was thoughtful for a moment. "How old was Bernie when Felicia disappeared?"

"Thirteen or fourteen. From what I recall, he was

one of Father Donnelly's most devoted altar boys. He sang in the choir, too."

"He and Father Donnelly must have spent a lot of time together. He could have overheard something."

"Possibly. Everyone in town, including his sister, believes that his sudden withdrawal from the church and society was triggered by the death of his mother, but it could have been for an entirely different reason."

"We have to find him, Matt. Before the killer does."

Her cell phone rang. She picked it up but didn't recognize the number on the display screen. "Hello?"

"Ms. McKenzie?" The voice was so low and shaky, she didn't recognize it.

"Who is this?"

"Me. Bernie."

Thirty-Two

"I can't see a thing," Grace said, peering through the windshield. "Are you sure you're going in the right direction?"

"That's the road to Erwinna. The mill shouldn't be much farther."

Grace's phone conversation with Bernie had been brief. He had talked to his sister and knew that the police wanted him for questioning in connection to Father Donnelly's murder. He didn't want to run anymore. He was ready to talk, but on his terms, and not to the police, not until he'd had a chance to tell his story to someone he trusted. That someone was Grace.

Including Matt in the deal hadn't been easy.

Bernie liked Matt, but didn't know him well enough to entrust him with what he knew.

"I vouch for him completely," Grace had told him. "If you trust me, you can trust him."

Reluctantly, he had agreed.

"I can't believe he walked this entire distance on foot," Grace said. "We must have driven close to ten miles."

"He couldn't take a chance on driving my father's car. He would have been picked up within the hour."

"He sounded so scared, Matt."

"He has every reason to be. The police *and* a killer are looking for him." He slowed down, looking for road signs.

"Is that the mill?" Grace pointed at a tall, narrow stone structure with a single window at the top.

"Looks like it." Matt stopped and flicked his headlights on and off, as Bernie had instructed.

Within a few seconds, a head appeared from behind the building. Matt flicked his lights again. Bernie raised a hand and ran toward them.

Grace climbed in the backseat and opened the door for him. "Are you all right?" She handed him a quilt she had found in Steven's closet.

Bernie wrapped himself into the spread's cottony

warmth and fell back against the seat, eyes closed. "I am now."

"I was worried about you," Grace said.

He reopened his eyes. "Thanks for coming, Ms. McKenzie. You, too, Matt. I know you're taking a big chance."

"Does your sister know that you're here?" Grace asked.

"I wouldn't tell her. I didn't want to get her involved in my mess."

"How much of a mess are you really in?" Matt asked.

Bernie looked down at his hands. They were thick and calloused. The hands of a hard worker, Grace thought. She refused to believe they were also the hands of a killer.

Sitting in the front seat, Matt turned all the way around so he and Bernie faced each other. "Look, Bernie," he said calmly. "I can imagine what you're going through right now, and while I would like to keep what you're about to tell me confidential, if you've committed a crime—"

"What do you mean by 'crime'?" Bernie asked.

"We could start with murder. Did you kill Father Donnelly?"

"No!"

"Do you know who did?"

"No, but I know *why* he was killed."

"Why?"

"He knew who shot Steven."

"He witnessed the murder?"

Grace held her breath.

"No, not exactly." Bernie gazed out the window at the moonless night. "It looks so much like that night," he said as though talking to himself. "No moon. Just the darkness and the bare fields."

Grace and Matt exchanged a glance. "That night?" Matt repeated.

Bernie brought the quilt tighter around his neck. "I can't go to the police," he said again. "The chief would never believe me."

"Why not?" Grace asked.

"Because what I have to say is not going to be easy for the townspeople to accept. They'll say I made it up. They already think I made up the story of that green pickup truck pushing me into the river. Chief Nader told my sister that the green paint could have come from another scrape. As for the dents, he said they could have happened as I rolled down the embankment."

"If you're telling the truth," Matt said, "I'll make sure that the chief believes you."

"Thank you."

"Do you know who killed Steven, Bernie?"

"No, but…" He shrank back in his seat. "I'm pretty sure that it's the same men who kidnapped Felicia."

Matt sat up straight. "Men? How many were there?"

"Two." He took a deep breath. "Maybe I should start at the beginning."

He waited a second or two before dropping his bombshell. "Father Donnelly is a child molester."

Grace drew a quick intake of breath. As Bernie had predicted, her first impulse was to not believe him. There had been many stories about abuse in the church over the last few years, and tons of negative publicity during which priests had had to either resign or stand trial, or both.

But Father Donnelly?

She looked at Matt and could see that he, too, was having difficulties coming to terms with what he had just heard.

"That's a serious accusation, Bernie," he said. "Do you have any proof?"

"Me," he said in a low whisper. "I am the proof. Father Donnelly sexually molested me for months before I finally put a stop to it."

Grace's hands flew to her throat. "Oh, Bernie."

"I was thirteen." He sounded dispirited, but his voice was firm. "My mother was already sick. I knew she was going to die and I felt helpless and lost. Father Donnelly was there for me. He was a great comfort at first. He was kind, he gave me strength and lessened my pain, until one day, when his way of comforting me took a new direction."

Grace felt sick. Matt merely waited.

"When I tried to stop him," Bernie continued, "he told me that it was all right, that he was helping me cope with my mother's illness. 'Just let it happen,' he kept saying. 'Trust me. You trust me, don't you, Bernie?' He kept repeating those words over and over until I believed that everything he was doing was for my own good. At the same time, I felt ashamed and torn. Torn between the need to tell someone and the fear of betraying a man I had always trusted." He bowed his head. "In the end, I decided to keep quiet."

"How long did that go on?" Matt asked.

"Several months."

"Tell me what you saw the night Felicia disappeared."

"I was helping Father Donnelly prepare for the spring festival. The mayor had agreed to let us use the fairgrounds out on the county line. We were inside the concession stand. It was late and I wanted to go home, but Father wanted to show his appreciation for my good work in what he called his 'own special way'. That's when I saw her."

"Felicia?"

He nodded. "I looked out the window, and there she was, carrying a flashlight and walking down the road. Father was standing beside me. He saw her, too."

"Was she alone?"

"Yes, but soon a car went by. For a while, I didn't think it was going to stop, but then it backtracked. One man jumped out of the passenger's seat and grabbed her. She started to scream, but he clamped a hand over her mouth and then the car sped away."

"Did you recognize the man? Or the driver?"

He shook his head. "It happened too fast, and I was too scared. But Father Donnelly recognized them."

"Did he tell you that?"

"No, but I could tell by the shocked look on his face. When I asked him if he knew them, he turned away and didn't answer me."

"And he didn't go to the police?" Grace asked, horrified. "He let a poor, helpless man be put away for life for a crime he didn't commit?"

"We didn't find out about Dusty until several days later. I went to see Father Donnelly then and told him that we had to go to the police. We had to tell them that Dusty was innocent."

Bernie pressed two fingers against his eyes. "He told me that going to the police was out of the question. Both of us would be questioned, and he didn't think that I—an innocent, scared, impressionable thirteen-year-old—could handle a police interrogation. In his persuasive voice, he explained that the public wouldn't understand the special affection he and I had for each other. They would look at our act of love as something dirty and shameful. The church would be disgraced, causing thousands of worshippers to turn away from God.

"'Think of all the people I could no longer help,' he told me. 'The sick, the poor, all those who count on me from day to day.' When I wasn't convinced, he reminded me of what the truth would do to my sick mother, and my sister, who had just begun to work as an R.N. He talked for a long time, painting an ugly picture of what our lives would be if I went to the police."

His voice nearly broke, but he managed to go on. "So I kept quiet. A week later, my mother died. I was devastated, certain that her death was God's way of punishing me for my sins. That's why I left the church. I felt too much like a hypocrite."

"Why didn't you go to the police at that time?"

"I was too ashamed, and worried about jeopardizing Judy's career."

Grace's eyes filled with tears. Twenty years later, Bernie's pain was almost palpable. The thought that a priest, a man an entire community had held in such high esteem, had put that burden on those young shoulders was nothing short of despicable.

Those weekly visits to Dusty made sense now. They were meant to help Father Donnelly deal with his guilt. But what about Bernie? How had *he* dealt with the guilt?

Matt was the one who broke the heavy silence, but his voice was subdued. He, too, had been affected by Bernie's candid confession. "How was Steven involved?" he asked after a while.

Bernie looked down at the quilt's colorful squares. "That was my fault, too. Making a new friend, especially one as nice as Steven, was a new experience for me. I found that I could talk to him about everything, my work at the cemetery, my mother's death, my sister's sacrifices. I hadn't planned on telling him about my relationship with Father Donnelly, but, somehow, I did. As I talked to him, I started feeling better, almost as if a huge weight had been lifted off my shoulders."

"Did you tell him about seeing those two men who had abducted Felicia?"

"Yes."

"That was risky, wasn't it? Steven could have gone to the police."

"I made him swear not to, and he didn't."

"Didn't you wonder why?" Grace asked.

"I knew why," he said simply. "Steven was my friend. Friends don't betray each other."

Or, Grace thought, Steven had realized the potential value of his silence.

In the Jeep's dim light, Grace saw Bernie's expression turn mournful. "Six months later, Steven was killed. I started thinking of all the bad things that happened because of me—Dusty's arrest, my mother's death, my abandonment of the church, Steven's murder and the attempt on my own life. I decided that no matter what happened to me, I had to come forward and tell the truth. That's why I went to see Father Donnelly tonight. I wanted him to know what I was going to do and why."

"How did he take it?"

"Not well. He begged me to reconsider, to think of all the pain I was about to inflict on him, on my sister and on the Catholic church. I was more disappointed than angry. I thought he would understand. I thought he would feel my pain, but all he cared about was the church's reputation. And his."

"What made you run out the way you did?" Grace asked.

"I saw someone step out of the confessional booth. I knew he'd heard me. I got scared and ran."

"Man or woman?" Matt asked sharply.

"A man, I think, but it was too dark to see clearly."

"You were lucky," Grace said.

"I know." He looked from Grace to Matt. "I don't want to run anymore."

"You won't have to," Matt said. "Here's what we're going to do."

Thirty-Three

Persuading Bernie to go along with the plan hadn't been easy. Wrapped in the quilt, his face solemn, he had listened to Matt's idea, or part of it, before he started shaking his head. It had taken Matt another twenty minutes to convince him that the police station was the safest hiding place at the moment, and that turning himself in was the only way to catch the killers.

Josh was a harder sell. Grace watched him closely as Bernie talked. The expression on the chief's face as he learned that Father Donnelly had been a child molester was one of shock and disbelief. To his credit, he didn't interrupt. When Bernie had answered his questions and signed a statement, the chief instructed his deputy to lock him up. Then, he listened to Matt's plan.

When Matt was finished, the chief still didn't look convinced. "You're asking me to believe that a man an entire community has revered for almost a quarter of a century was a *child molester*? Why don't you try convincing me that the moon is made out of green cheese?"

"It's not the first time a priest strays from his vows and it won't be the last."

"But Father Donnelly? Did you see what's going on in front of St. Peter's Church? Two hundred people are holding a candlelight vigil for him. Bernie's lucky if they don't march in here and lynch him."

As if to confirm the chief's words, Deputy Montgomery rushed in. "The press is out there, Chief. They want to talk to you."

"It's ten o'clock at night, for God's sake. I'm going home."

Matt shook his head. "They're not going to leave until you talk to them, Josh. The sooner you deal with them, the sooner they'll be out of your hair."

"What the hell am I supposed to tell them?"

"Give them an abridged version of the truth. Bernie has been arrested on suspicion of murder. The motive is still under investigation."

"What will that do?"

"It will buy you some time, ease the town's anxieties and give the killers a false sense of security. Remember," Matt added, "it's your show, not theirs. Take questions, and only answer those you want to answer. If it gets ugly, leave."

For a moment, Grace thought the chief was going to ask Matt to come out with him, but after a short hesitation, he put his hat on and walked out the door.

"He doesn't look comfortable," Grace said as she went to stand at the window with Matt.

"He's not used to being in the limelight," Matt replied. "Neither was my father, but when push came to shove, he could handle it. Josh surprised me. I had expected a little more guts on his part."

Together, they watched the chief answer one last question, then he turned his back on the crowd and walked back into the station.

Deputy Montgomery had just hung up the phone. "That was Paul Doone," he said to the chief.

"If it's about his neighbor's fence encroaching onto his property again, tell him to get a surveyor to handle the problem. I have no time for that crap now."

"It's not about the fence. He says he saw a pickup tear out of Main Street at about the time Matt and Grace found the body. He thinks the truck was dark green."

Grace stiffened. "That could be the same truck that pushed Bernie into the river."

The chief shook his head. "We don't know that."

"Why else would he tear out of Main Street?" Matt asked.

"Get off my back, okay, Matt? And stop telling me how to do my job."

Matt put his palms up in a gesture of surrender. "Sorry. I was under the impression that you wanted my help."

"I don't."

"In that case, we're out of here." He took Grace's arm. "Take good care of Bernie," he said as they walked out.

"Are you sure that Bernie will be all right in there?" Grace asked when they were in Matt's Jeep.

"I was hoping my father would still be there to keep an eye on him, but they finally transferred him to the county jail." He patted her hand. "Don't worry about Bernie, okay? He's tougher than he looks. Did you see him when Rob took him away? Mr. Calm and Collected."

"Thanks to you. That man-to-man talk you had with him before we left Erwinna did wonders for his self-confidence. What did you tell him anyway?"

Matt put the Jeep in gear. "It wouldn't be a man-to-man-talk if I told you now, would it?"

"True." She leaned against the seat back and stifled a yawn.

Matt threw her a quick glance. "Tired?"

"It's been quite a day."

"Will you be all right at home by yourself? If not, I'd be glad to stay."

Grace laughed. "Do I look that tragic?"

"Are you kidding? You're a rock. I just thought you might want some company."

"If I do, I'll call Denise. She looked a little offended earlier when you told her *you'd* be staying with me."

"I'm afraid I wasn't thinking of her feelings at the time, but you're right. I shouldn't have been so abrupt with her." He pulled into the driveway. "Here you are."

"Thanks, Matt. And thanks for being so patient with Bernie."

He took a fistful of her jacket and gently pulled her to him. "Is that the best you can do to show your gratitude?"

She let out a nervous laugh. How long had it been since she had practiced the complex art of flirting? A year? More? What if she said something stupid? "Now that you mention it—"

"Shh. No more talking." His hands slid behind her neck, drawing her even closer.

She wasn't sure what startled her more, the heat

of the kiss, or the way he moved his mouth, forcing hers open without seeming to force it at all.

Warning bells went off in her head while her old buddy, the Voice of Wisdom, tried to worm its way into her head. *He can't possibly be as fantastic as he seems. Something is wrong with him. You've been there before. Back away before it's too late.*

It would have been so easy. One little push against that hard, comforting, amazing chest and he would be gone. Instead, she found herself leaning into him, responding to his kiss while some distant part of her mind continued to transmit warning signals.

She ignored them all. Overwhelmed by sensations and longings she hadn't experienced in a long time, she shuddered, aware of a delicious ache deep within her.

The alarm bells started ringing frantically.

This time, she listened. Gently, reluctantly, she pushed him away. "Wow."

Wow? Was that all she could say to discourage him?

She half expected him to kiss her again, or to invite himself in now that she seemed more willing, but, being the gentleman that he was, he let her off the hook. "Call you in the morning?" he said lightly.

She picked up her purse from the floor. "I might be a little late. I'm meeting with a couple of artists whose work is presently on consignment. They heard about the forgeries and want to talk to me."

"Do you anticipate problems?"

"I don't know. Maybe they just need reassuring, although I wouldn't blame them if they decide to take their paintings back." She finally felt brave enough to meet his gaze. "What about you? What's on your agenda for tomorrow?"

"Me?" He looked smug. "I'm going shopping for a green pickup truck."

Thirty-Four

Following a hunch that had nagged Matt since his talk with the Badger brothers earlier this week, he drove to their home in Hunterdon County, hoping to come across a green pickup. There was no guarantee he'd find it. Cal and Lou might not be smart enough to think of hiding it, but chances were they worked for someone who had his wits about him. He had to, or he wouldn't have gotten this far without being caught.

Cal and Lou Badger lived in a big rambling house that hadn't been painted in several decades. A motorcycle and a beat-up van were parked on the cracked driveway, and half a dozen circulars no one had bothered to pick up littered the front steps.

The backyard was just as bad, with auto parts and other junk scattered throughout. A path led to a shed, and behind the shed, Matt could see a faded blue tarp over what looked like some sort of vehicle.

"Bingo," he said under his breath.

He walked over to the protective cover and lifted it. Excitement turned into disappointment. The vehicle was nothing more than a John Deere tractor put away for the winter.

He looked around him. The property was small, half an acre at most. He walked over to the four-foot fence and looked into the neighbor's yard. It was a little more orderly, but the only items in the small expanse of grass were a jungle gym and a sandbox.

Before Matt could retrace his steps, the back door opened and a man in his late sixties whom Matt recognized as Horace Badger stepped out. Although a little shorter than his sons, he was just as powerfully built, and just as mean looking.

"What the hell you're doing in my backyard?" the man shouted.

"Mr. Badger?" Matt asked. "Mr. Horace Badger?"

"Who wants to know?"

"I came to look at the pickup truck you have for sale."

Badger came down the steps, resting his hand on a baseball bat propped against the wall. "I ain't got a pickup for sale."

"Are you sure? A *green* pickup? I'd be willing to pay a good price for it."

"Who the hell are you? Who sent you?"

"There was an ad in the paper—"

"Wait a minute." Badger shook a crooked finger at him. "I know who you are. You're that Baxter boy." His voice rose. "Get the hell off my property before I break your knees."

Matt remained calm. "Come on, now, Mr. Badger. You wouldn't want to assault an FBI agent, would you?"

"You're trespassing, boy. That means I can do anything I damn please." He started hitting the tip of the bat against his palm as he advanced toward Matt.

"Matt!"

Matt glanced over his shoulder. Eddie O'Hara was getting out of his dark-blue BMW. "What the hell are you doing here?" Eddie asked, walking toward him.

"Maybe I should ask you the same question." Matt looked around. There was nothing but farmland in these parts. "You're a little far from home, aren't you?"

"I was on my way to the produce market to pick up a few things when I saw your car."

"Your friend was trespassing," Horace said, his tone still belligerent. "And harassing me to boot."

Eddie took Matt's arm. "Come on. This looks like

a scene from a bad western. Let's get out of here before Horace calls the cops."

Matt was beginning to find Eddie's interference annoying. "What are you all of a sudden? My keeper?"

"Maybe I should be. What's wrong with you, man? You know what a nasty old goat Horace is. You don't even need to antagonize him. He sees a face he doesn't like and he starts swinging."

He wrapped an arm around Matt's shoulders. "What did you want with him, anyway?"

"I'm looking for a green pickup truck. Maybe you've seen it around?"

"Ah, that elusive pickup. I've heard of it, but I can't say that I've seen it." He waited until they had reached Matt's Jeep before he asked, "You think Horace pushed Bernie into the river?"

Matt turned around, casting one last glance over his shoulder. Horace was still there. He raised his bat and shook it, as if to discourage him from coming back. "Not him," Matt replied. "His sons."

A call to Buzz Brown found the farmer back from Kansas and happy to hear from him.

"Come on over any time, Matt," Buzz told him on the phone. "You're always welcome here."

A few minutes after Matt left the Badgers'

property, he headed toward Suddenly Farm on Route 232. Buzz stood on the front porch when Matt pulled in. "It's good to see you, son." He pumped Matt's hand. "What do you say we go in and have some coffee?" He was a small, almost frail-looking man who, by virtue of his size, should have been anything but a farmer. After fifty years in the business, he continued to amaze skeptics with his stamina, his strength and his genuine love for the land.

"Coffee sounds great," Matt said. "Do you still make it hot and strong?"

"There ain't no other way to serve it."

"Then make it a mug—a big one."

The farmer chuckled as he led him to a large, immaculate kitchen that had always been the heart of the house, especially in Alma's days. "How was your trip to Kansas?"

"Interesting. I was all set to move out west, but then my brother said he wanted to come back to Pennsylvania, so here I am, making room for him until he finds his own place."

"Something tells me you're happy about his decision."

"Yeah. Jerry and I always got along. And it ain't fun to be alone." He took two large mugs from a cupboard. "How's your dad?"

"Making the best out of a bad situation. He says hi."

"You tell him I'm rooting for him. Josh must have lost his marbles when he put Fred in jail."

"That's why I'm here, Buzz. There seems to be a new angle to Steven Hatfield's murder and I was hoping you could help me."

"Me?" He handed Matt a mug filled with strong, fragrant coffee. "I'll be glad to help you, but how?"

They walked over to a big maple table where a lazy Susan held containers of sugar, salt, pepper and honey. Buzz took a noisy slurp of coffee. "What's on your mind, Matt?"

"I was talking to Duke a few days ago and I got curious about that planning board application that was turned down."

Buzz's face had turned somber. "That's a sore subject, Matt."

"I know, and believe me, I wouldn't be here, rehashing the past, if I didn't think it was important."

Buzz gave a spin to the lazy Susan and watched it whirl around. "Alma loved the farm, as you know. A day didn't go by without this kitchen being filled with friends, or neighbors or kids, enjoying one of Alma's famous pies."

He stopped to take another sip of coffee. "But my Alma was a sick girl. She had bad lungs and every winter, she'd start with her bronchitis and finish off with a nasty case of pneumonia. I almost lost her twice. That second time, the doctor told me she wouldn't last another winter unless we moved to a sunnier climate, like Arizona or New Mexico.

"Now, you know how much I love the land," he continued. "And with God as my witness, I hated the thought of my daddy's farm being turned into a development. Problem is, I never struck it rich. Oh, don't get me wrong, we lived well, but all the money I made went right back into the business. After I had that talk with Alma's doctor, I'd lay awake nights, wondering how in hell I was going to support us in Arizona, without the income from the farm. So, when Gordon Shapley, a developer from Delaware, approached me and told me how much he was willing to give me for the land, I couldn't turn him down. I couldn't let Alma die."

"But the application didn't go through."

His mouth tightened. "No, and all because of Steven Hatfield. That son of a bitch started harping about how a subdivision of that size would destroy the integrity of the area. He started to talk about higher taxes, increased traffic, sewer problems. You should have heard him. Soon, he had the community so damned worked up, residents were campaigning against the project. He convinced most of the board, too, because only a couple of them voted yes." His voice dropped. "That winter, Alma died."

"I'm sorry, Buzz. And I'm sorry to make you relive those difficult times."

"It's all right. Although, I must admit, I don't see the connection."

"I'll explain in a minute. Right now, tell me why Steven was so opposed to developing the farm."

"I told you. He felt that this area of Bucks County—"

"Should remain pristine. Yes, I heard you, but unless my radar's way off, Steven wasn't exactly a tree hugger, was he?"

"He sure wasn't. In fact, there were times when he voted for a project that had no chance of getting through—like that gas station so close to Glenwood Estates."

"Did he have a problem with you in particular?"

"Not that I know of."

"Alma?"

"No." He walked over to the counter, picked up the glass carafe and brought it back. "Refill?"

"Please."

He sat down again. "What I can't understand," he said, "is what caused such a turnaround on Steven's part."

"What do you mean?"

"When that developer first came to town and the word got out that he was looking at my farm as a possible site, Steven came to see me. Seems that a couple of people in town weren't happy about the farm being developed and Steven wanted to know if I knew why."

"Who were the people?"

"He didn't say. Actually, he was kind of vague about it. I couldn't help it, though. I had no idea why anyone would have any objections. My farm is pretty much in the middle of nowhere. It has no historical value, nothing anyone would want to preserve. Hell, the only excitement those woods ever saw was when high school kids came here to neck and I had to chase them with my pitchfork."

Matt slowly put his mug down.

Trying to keep his voice even, he said, "Correct me if I'm wrong—it's been a long time—but didn't a couple of kids show up the night Felicia was abducted?"

"Two of them—both boys. I started going after them, like I always did, but they got scared and ran. A moment later, I heard the sound of a car speeding away."

"Did you tell the police?"

"Of course I did. I see where you're going now, Matt, but it's no good. Your dad and his team searched those woods from one end to the other. Not a single property in the entire county was spared. They found nothing."

Duke's words came back to Matt. *You'd have thought there was gold buried in those woods.*

No, Duke, Matt thought. Not gold. A body.

Buzz was observing him. "What is it, Matt? What's on your mind?"

An idea, a little wilder than most he'd had during his twenty-year career, began to take shape in his head. He looked at Buzz, who, at the present time, was his best bet. "Do you trust me, Buzz?" he asked.

A sly smile curved Buzz's mouth. "Something tells me that I'm going to have to."

Thirty-Five

Less than an hour after Matt left Buzz's home, the news was all over town. For maximum impact, Buzz had made the announcement at Pat's just as the pub was beginning to fill up. He would not be moving to Kansas after all. Instead, his brother was coming here. With his help, Buzz would finally be able to do what he had wanted to do for a long time—farm the other fifty acres on his property.

At the other end of the bar, Matt listened as Buzz followed his script, adlibbing every now and then, but overall, doing a fine job.

"What will you be planting?" Sam Gladstone wanted to know. A farmer since high school, Sam had retired five years ago.

"Soybeans. These days, everybody wants soybeans. I'm going to make a killing."

Sam shook his head. "Preparing those fifty acres for planting is hard work, Buzz. And you ain't getting any younger."

"That's why I've hired a four-man crew. They'll do all the hard work, cut down trees, pull out roots and turn the soil over."

"You've got the equipment to do all that?"

"In place and ready to go. If they work fast, I might have time to plant some rye as a cover crop."

As Matt sipped his beer, he glanced around the pub to see who was leaving, or picking up his cell phone. No one moved. Too bad the Badger brothers weren't here yet, or his bet would have been on them.

He glanced at his watch. Five o'clock. Customers were still coming in, and Buzz was still talking. It was time to put this little plan into action.

He drained the last of his beer, left a ten dollar bill on the table and left.

As Matt talked, Grace found herself growing excited at the thought that he may have found a way to force the killers to reveal themselves.

"That's brilliant, Matt," she said. "Will it work?"

Matt perched a hip on the corner of Grace's desk. "No plan, no matter how well orchestrated, is one-hundred-percent foolproof, but if my hunch is right and Felicia *is* buried in Buzz's woods, the killers will have no choice but to act. Fast."

"Do you think they were there? Listening to Buzz?"

"If they weren't, I hope they heard about it through the grapevine. If my theory is right, they'll wait until dark, drive to the farm and find the spot where they buried Felicia so they can dig her up."

Grace shivered. "That's horrible."

"No more so than putting her there in the first place."

"How will you catch them?"

"I'll be there, watching them from a distance. When they start digging, I'll call the police."

"What if something goes wrong?"

"What can go wrong? I'll be hidden. I'll have my cell phone. And I'll be armed." He smiled. "Does that make you feel better?"

"Yes. Will you call me as soon as it's over?"

"Are you worried about me, Grace?"

She felt her cheeks heat up. "A little," she admitted. "All this cloak-and-dagger stuff may be routine for you, but for me, it's nerve-racking."

"I'll be fine."

"Can I do anything?"

"Just wait for my call. Until then, remember, not a word to anyone. This operation can only succeed if it catches the culprits completely off guard."

"My lips are sealed."

There was a twinkle in his eyes as he came off the desk, but that's as far as he got. The door opened and a young couple walked in.

"I know you'll be closing soon," the woman said. "I promise we won't be long. I just wanted to show my husband that landscape by Bruno Fendi?"

"I'll be right with you," Grace said.

Matt kissed her cheek. "I'll see you soon," he whispered.

She held his arm as a wave of panic gripped her. "Be careful."

"Always."

"Here you go," Matt said, putting Felicia Newman's file on Josh's desk. "Twenty-four hours, as promised."

Josh sat back in his chair. "Found anything helpful?"

"Nothing that I didn't already know."

"Told you." He turned his head. "Montgomery!"

The deputy walked in and shook Matt's hand. "How's it going, Matt?"

"Could be better."

Rob looked at the file on Josh's desk. "Not much in there, huh?"

Matt shook his head. "Your boss warned me but I didn't believe him."

"You can put the file back," Josh told Rob.

He was about to say something more when a commotion in the front room stopped him.

"You can't go in there, Cal!" Officer Duncan shouted. "If you want to see the chief, you'll have to—"

"Get out of my way!"

There was the sound of a crash. Then, as Josh sprang out of his chair and Rob Montgomery drew his gun, Cal Badger burst into the room, Duncan right behind him.

"I tried to stop him, Chief," the officer blurted out, "but—"

Josh waved him off. "What the hell is your problem now, Cal?" he demanded.

Cal ignored him. He moved forward, his finger pointed at Matt. "Won't do you any good to hide in here, bureau man."

Matt stood up. "Who's hiding?"

"Hey, hey!" Josh came to stand between the two men. "You two will have to settle your differences elsewhere. And if there's any violence involved, I'll throw both of you in the cooler. Is that understood?"

"That son of a bitch trespassed on *my* property," Cal barked. "And started to push his weight around, threatening my father and scaring the shit out of him."

Matt laughed. "That scared man you're describing came at me with a baseball bat."

"That's because you wouldn't leave." He turned to Josh. "Are you going to arrest him or not?"

"No, Cal, I'm not going to—"

Cal never gave him a chance to finish. He let out a sound that was something between a growl and a howl. Then, head down, he charged like a bull, knocking Josh down and heading straight for Matt.

Matt quickly stepped to one side. Cal went crashing into Josh's desk. Not giving him time to get back on his feet, Matt grabbed him, spun him around and slammed his fist into the big man's face.

Blood spurted out of Cal's nose. He wiped it off with the back of his hand, but before he could strike again, Josh, Rob and Duncan wrestled him to the ground and held him there until Rob was able to handcuff him.

"He broke my nose!" Cal screamed. "The son of a bitch broke my nose!"

Josh stood up. He was in a foul mood and breathing hard. "Throw him into a cell," he said to Rob. "Him, too," he added, motioning to Matt.

"Now wait a minute," Matt protested.

"No. *You* wait a minute. You've done nothing but cause trouble for this town and this department since you arrived and I'm fed up. Do you hear me? *Fed up!*"

"What the hell was I supposed to do? Let him hit me?"

"You should have let me handle it."

"Well, excuse me, but you haven't done so well in the handling department lately."

Josh took a deep breath and nodded at Rob. "Lock him up."

Rob clamped a hand on Matt's shoulders. "Sorry, Matt."

Matt didn't argue. Rob had a job to do. Any resistance would only delay the inevitable. He thought furiously. Now that his plan was in motion, nothing could stop it. He hated to turn the job over to another party, but he had no choice. Someone had to be there, at the farm, waiting for the killers to show up. He'd call Buzz and ask him to cover for him.

He patted his pocket for his phone.

"Come on, Matt. Let's go." Rob gave him a gentle push.

"Hold it. I can't find my phone. I must have dropped it when Cal attacked me."

"You can look for it later," Josh grunted. "When I authorize you to make your phone call."

"Dammit, Josh, what is wrong with you? I'm entitled to a phone call—right now."

Josh's only answer was to walk out of the room.

Thirty-Six

"Matt's in jail!" Denise said the moment Grace opened the door.

Grace felt her jaw drop. "What do you mean, Matt's in jail? What happened? What did he do?"

Denise walked past her, into the living room and sat down on the sofa. "Rob just called. Apparently, Cal Badger went after Matt at the police station and they had a free-for-all."

"Is Matt hurt?"

"No, but Cal has a broken nose. That's why Matt's in jail."

"For defending himself?"

"The reason doesn't matter. Josh felt like throwing them both in jail and that's what he did."

Grace picked up her cell phone.

"If you're planning on calling Matt, forget it. They took his phone away and won't let him talk to anyone. He can't even call a lawyer, not until Josh says it's okay."

"When will that be?"

Denise's shoulders went up. "Whenever Josh feels like it."

"But it will be tonight, right? It *has* to be tonight."

Denise raised an eyebrow. "Why does it have to be tonight?"

Grace glanced at her watch. Seven-thirty. There was still plenty of time. "We have to get Matt out of jail."

"You're not listening, Grace. Josh locked him up. He's been wanting to do that ever since Matt got into town. Now that he has, he's not about to let him go. Not until he's good and ready."

Grace started to pace the room. "I have to find a way to get him out."

"Okay, you're starting to creep me out. What's going on? Why can't you wait until morning?"

"I can't tell you."

"You don't trust me?"

"This has nothing to do with trust. It's a very sensitive matter and I gave Matt my word that I wouldn't tell anyone." She turned around. "You've got to know someone who can help me. Think, Denise, please. I need someone with clout. Someone Josh will listen to."

Denise jumped out of her chair. "George Renchaw! The mayor," she added, when Grace gave her a blank look. "He's a good friend of Matt's. He has pull with Josh, *and*," she added proudly, "he's an attorney."

"The mayor—of course! Why didn't I think of it? I met him the other day when Matt took me out to lunch." She picked up her red leather jacket. "Where do we find him?"

Denise glanced at her watch. "He could still be at city hall. He sometimes stays until late."

Grace slipped into her jacket as she made a beeline for the door. "Let's go."

Two stops, one at city hall and another at George Renchaw's law office, got them nowhere. The mayor had left his office at six o'clock to get ready for a production of *Mame* at the Bucks County Playhouse.

Grace glanced at her watch. Seven fifty-five. "Come on," she told Denise as they rushed out of the building. "If we hurry, we can get him before the curtain goes up."

Denise ran to keep up with her. "Won't you please tell me what's going on? I swear I won't tell a soul."

They jumped into Denise's Toyota. "I'll tell you later. Drive!"

Denise made a U-turn and headed down on South Main. "There it is." She pointed at a red building across the canal. "It looks packed. Let's hope I can find a parking space."

After circling the parking lot twice, Denise gave up, went back on the street and found a space half a block away.

"My mother used to volunteer here as an attendant," Denise said as they ran across the parking lot. "Maybe someone I know is on duty tonight."

"Denise," a gravelly voice said. "Is that you?"

Denise let out a sigh of relief as a short, rotund woman with short white hair approached them. "Sandra, thank God, you're on duty. I have a small favor to ask."

"Why are you out of breath?"

"It's a long story."

Taking her time, Sandra looked at Grace with a great deal of interest. Apparently, the urgency in Denise's voice hadn't affected her. "Are you Grace McKenzie?"

Grace gave her a nervous smile. "Yes."

"I heard how you saved poor Bernie from that freezing river—"

"I don't mean to be rude, Sandra," Denise interrupted. "But I need to talk to Mayor Renchaw."

"Right now?"

"Right now."

"But the show has already started."

"This is an emergency. Believe me, Sandra, if Mayor Renchaw knew that I tried to see him and couldn't, he'd be very unhappy."

"What kind of emergency?" She looked from Denise to Grace. "And why are *you* here and not someone from his staff?"

"Because it's a private matter." She dropped her voice. "A matter of life and death, Sandra."

Sandra's hand went to her breast. "Oh, my! Why didn't you say so?" Apparently convinced, she nodded. "I'll go get him, you wait here."

"Thank you."

Less than thirty seconds later, the door reopened and George Renchaw walked out, looking annoyed. "My house better be on fire, Denise," he said sharply. "Because that's about the only emergency I would consider serious enough to make me miss the first act."

Grace couldn't let Denise get in trouble. "This is all my doing, Mr. Mayor. Denise came with me practically under duress."

"Somehow I doubt that, but go ahead. What's the emergency?"

"Matt is in jail and the chief won't let him see an

attorney, or make any phone calls. You're the only person who can help."

"What did Matt do?"

"Cal Badger stormed the police station and attacked him. Matt defended himself, and Josh threw both of them in jail."

"Anybody hurt?"

"Cal has a broken nose. Will you call the chief, Mr. Mayor? Please? As I said, Matt was only defending himself."

"Come on now, Ms. McKenzie. You know perfectly well that I can't interfere with the chief's decision. How do you think the voters would feel if they found out that I was doing favors for my friends?"

"Oh, for God's sake, George," Denise said. "Can't you see that Josh is just being stubborn? If you're so worried about the voters, you'd better think twice. The people of New Hope are already unhappy with Fred's arrest. Now the chief arrests his son, *for no good reason*, and you're supporting the decision?" She shook her head. "That's not a smart move."

The mayor seemed to weigh Denise's words for a moment before giving a nod. "Normally, I wouldn't intervene, but you're right. The punishment doesn't seem to fit the crime. And since it seems to mean so much to you, Ms. McKenzie, and this town owes you a favor, I'll try to get Josh to reconsider, but I make no promise."

"Thank you."

He took out his cell phone and walked away.

The conversation lasted much longer than either Denise or Grace had expected. When the mayor returned he looked somber. "I'm sorry, ladies. I tried. Josh feels that both men need to cool off. He won't release them until tomorrow morning."

He slid his phone back into his suit jacket. "Now if you don't mind, I'm going back to my play." He inclined his head. "Denise, Ms. McKenzie. You have a good night."

"What now?" Denise asked after the mayor had disappeared behind the door.

"I guess it's all up to me."

Denise's expression turned suspicious. "What's up to you?"

"To finish the job Matt started."

"And what's that?"

Grace took her arm and together they walked out into the cold night. "It's up to me to catch two killers."

Thirty-Seven

Trying not to be overly dramatic, Grace brought Denise up-to-date, stressing that Matt's hunch was just that, a hunch, and that the next couple of hours would either prove him right and end this ordeal, or send him back to the drawing board.

The thought that her sister's murderers were just within reach almost proved to be too much for Denise. She leaned against the stone wall bordering the canal and took a few deep breaths.

"Are you all right?" Grace asked when she saw her leaning over the water.

"Are you kidding? I'm ecstatic. This is what my parents and I have been waiting for all these years, so yes, I'm all right. I'm just fine." She turned to Grace. "I want in."

"What?"

"I want to help you catch those bastards."

"Absolutely not."

"Don't be silly. You're going to need help."

"I will not put you in—"

"Do you know where Buzz's farm is?"

"I'll find it."

"Do you know where to park the car so it won't be seen from the road?"

"I'm not helpless."

"Neither am I. And we make a good team, don't we? Wouldn't you rather wait with me at your side than all alone?"

"It could get risky."

"You said it wasn't dangerous at all, that all you had to do was wait until the killers start digging and call the police."

"Yes, that's the plan, but something could still go wrong."

"You mean we could get captured, tied to a chair and tortured?" Denise laughed. "Come on, Grace. This is New Hope, Pennsylvania, not the set of *24*."

"Well, you're right about one thing. It would be more interesting with you along."

Denise rubbed her hands together. "Good. Now, what's the plan?"

"Matt didn't go into a lot of details, but common sense tells me that we should arrive at Suddenly Farm early and be prepared for a long wait."

"I'll bring coffee and sandwiches. And a blanket."

Grace's adrenaline kicked in. "Flashlights. We'll need flashlights. And batteries."

"I've got plenty of both."

"We probably should take my car. It's smaller and not too many people will recognize it. How well do you know Buzz's farm?"

"I haven't been there in a while, but I know it well enough to get around."

"Then you'll drive. We'll go to your house to get what we need, then we'll drive to the cottage to pick up my car."

Within moments, they were on their way.

They gathered everything they needed in record time and shoved it all into a large beach bag. Music filtered through from one of the upstairs bedrooms.

"Lucy," Denise said when Grace glanced up at the staircase.

"Shouldn't you tell her that you're going out? To a movie or something?"

"She doesn't like to be disturbed when she's

studying. We said good-night to each other earlier. She'll just assume that I went to bed early."

At the cottage, they transferred the bag into the trunk of the Taurus and waited until a car had driven by before backing out of the driveway.

Denise drove expertly, accelerating as she turned onto Route 232 but respecting the speed limit.

"How much farther?" Grace asked.

"A few miles. We can't miss it. Buzz has a big sign on the side of the road." She glanced at Grace. "Nervous?"

"My mouth is a little dry."

"Me, too. I have to keep telling myself that this crazy caper could get Fred out of jail."

"*If* Matt's theory is right."

"There it is!" Denise pointed at a sign for Suddenly Farm. She left the main road and turned onto an unpaved, rocky path barely wide enough for Grace's Taurus. "Do you see another car?" she asked.

Grace's gaze swept across the heavily wooded area and its surrounding. "No. It's too early."

The car rocked back and forth as Denise slowed down. "This is a good place to stop," she said. "The vegetation is high and thick. The car will be well hidden." She brought the Taurus to a stop and turned off the ignition.

"Where do we go from here?" Grace asked as they both got out of the car.

Denise pointed up. "That crest up there will make a perfect lookout."

"It's a little bare. Won't they see us?"

"I don't know. We'll find out when we get up there." She looked up toward the sky. "Full moon. We might not even need those flashlights. Here, take the blanket. I'll carry the bag."

The climb took only a few minutes. The area Denise had selected wasn't as bare as Grace had thought, but surrounded by shrubbery high enough to hide a sitting person. In the distance, the farmhouse was all lit up, and looked inviting.

"This should be fine," Denise said, stopping behind a wild holly. She spread out the blanket and looked around her. "When do you think they'll show up?"

Grace crossed her legs and sat down, yoga style. "They can't afford to wait too long. They'll need time to locate the exact spot, otherwise they could be digging all night."

Quietly, Denise poured them each a cup of coffee.

"This isn't going to be easy for you," Grace said, looking at her friend. "Are you sure you're going to be all right?"

"I admit that I have mixed feelings. A part of me

dreads what's going to happen, while another feels almost relieved."

A flash caught Grace's gaze. "Showtime," she whispered.

"Are they here? I don't see anything."

"They just turned their lights off." She pointed at a dark form moving along the winding, rocky road.

"I see it, thanks to that moon."

"Do you recognize the car?"

"No."

A cloud drifted over the moon just as the car came to a stop. Two men came out and looked around. After a few seconds, they walked around the car, opened the trunk and took out two shovels.

"One is a little taller than the other," Grace remarked. When Denise raised her head above the holly bush, she yanked her down. "What are you doing? They'll see you."

"We have to know who they are."

"We'll know soon enough."

To calm herself down, Denise began biting her nails. "For God's sake, what are they doing? Why are they standing there like two zombies?"

"They're trying to remember the exact spot." The moon reappeared, large, yellow, a perfect harvest moon.

Suddenly, the shorter man pointed at the house.

Grace followed his gaze. At the farmhouse, the lights were being turned off, one by one.

"Is Buzz supposed to do anything?" Denise asked. "Is he part of this?"

"No. Matt didn't want to risk the chance of him getting hurt. I don't believe he even knows that Matt was planning this ambush tonight."

Another ten minutes went by, then the two men swung their shovels over their shoulders and started walking deep into the woods. Thanks to the moonlight, Grace could follow their progress, step by step.

Her heart was beating like a drum. It wouldn't be long now.

Next to her, Denise let out a small cry.

Grace started to shush her, then stopped when she saw the look on her friend's face. "What is it?"

"Oh, my God," Denise whispered. "Oh my God, oh my God, oh, my God!"

"Denise, for heaven's sake—"

She shook a frantic finger toward one of the figures. "*It's George! It's the mayor!*"

Thirty-Eight

Grace's head snapped back toward the woods. "Are you sure?"

"Yes! Look at his face. He's turning around."

Denise was right. The man in the blue parka was the man she and Denise had talked to a little over two hours ago at the Bucks County Playhouse. The same man they had turned to for help. The town's mayor. Matt's good friend.

Denise sat down. "I can't believe it. He was one of the volunteers who searched the county for my sister, did you know that?"

"No." Grace was still too stunned to make any further comments.

"I voted for that son of a bitch." Denise's voice had turned thin and cold. "I not only voted for him, I *campaigned* for him." She let out a dry laugh. "Mr. Good Guy, always ready to help, like Fred, except that Fred is the real thing and George is a phony. And a murderer," she added, her voice trembling with rage. "God, what I wouldn't give to go down there right now and beat the living shit out of him." She turned to Grace. "Do you suppose he knew about Buzz's new plans when we went to see him at the playhouse?"

"He had to. How long are the plays?"

"Two hours at most."

"He would have gotten out of the Playhouse at ten o'clock, taken his wife home and gone right out again, on some pretext. Or he could have waited until she was asleep."

"I want to kill him," Denise said fiercely. "I want to kill him with my bare hands."

"He'll get what's coming to him, Denise. For now, we have to stay calm. And we have to catch them red-handed."

"You mean, the fact that they're walking through those woods with a shovel on their shoulders isn't proof enough?"

"Matt was planning to wait until they started digging and that's what we'll do."

But Denise was itching to get her hands on her

sister's murderers. "What if they can't remember the spot and can't dig? *What if they leave?*"

"They won't leave. As far as they know, Buzz is planning on putting those bulldozers to work first thing in the morning, remember? They'll stay here all night if they have to, so don't worry about them leaving. They can't afford to."

She moved around, switching her weight from one hip to the other. "Do you recognize the other man?"

"No, but I haven't had a good look at him yet."

The mayor and his mysterious partner were still walking around aimlessly, sometimes turning around in circles or stopping to look at a spot on the ground before resuming their walk.

"They stopped," Grace said.

"Again? At this rate, we *will* be here all night."

"I think they're on to something. See? They're lining some landmark up with the house."

The sound of muffled, excited voices reached them. "This could be it, Denise," Grace said in a hushed voice. "I think they found the grave."

As if on cue, the two men removed their jackets and began to dig.

Grace jammed her hand into her bag and started searching for the phone. Her hands were shaking and her heart beating so fast, she thought it was going to jump out of her chest.

"Hurry!" Denise urged.

"Relax, will you? It's going to take them a while."

"Not at the speed they're going." She grabbed Grace's bag. "Here. Let me. You're shaking like a leaf."

"I have it."

Both reached for the phone at the same time, then watched in dismay as it flew out of their hands and over the edge.

"No!" Grace lunged after it, making a desperate attempt to catch it in midair. She, too, would have gone over the edge if Denise hadn't caught her in time.

"What are you trying to do? Kill yourself?"

Grace watched the phone roll down the rise. She prayed that something would stop its descent, a stone, or a branch, but nothing stood in its way as it rolled farther and farther out of her reach. At the clearing down below, it finally stopped.

The men turned around, momentarily frozen. The taller one turned his head a fraction and said something to his companion who shook his head before he resumed his digging.

"Why did you have to do that?" Grace asked in a furious whisper.

"You were taking forever."

"And I told you that we had plenty of time. Didn't you hear me?"

"You think this is my fault? You think I threw your phone over the edge on purpose?"

Grace took a deep breath. What were they doing? Bickering when they should be uniting. "I'm sorry. I guess I'm more jumpy than I realized."

Denise, who was always quick to forgive, nodded. "And I was overly anxious."

"No harm done. We'll use your phone."

Denise brought her big beach bag onto her lap and started going through it. After a few seconds, the searching became a little more frantic.

"What's wrong?" Grace asked. "You did bring your phone, didn't you?"

"Of course, I brought it. I can't function without my cell phone."

She pulled out a thermos, more foam cups, two sandwiches wrapped in Glad wrap, two cans of orange sodas, her knitting, three flashlights and half a dozen batteries.

"You brought your knitting?"

"No, I didn't bring my knitting. This is where I keep it and I just didn't bother to take it out."

Grace looked at the items spread out on the blanket. "Where's the phone?"

"I don't know." Denise looked miserable. "In my haste, I must have left it in my other bag when I switched from one to the other." She looked up. "I'm sorry, Grace. I ruined everything."

"No, you didn't."

"How are we going to call the police?"

Grace didn't reply. Down below, the men were still shoveling. They had slowed down a little, but were still going at a fairly good pace. How much more they would have to dig depended on the depth of the grave.

"I'll go get my phone," Grace said.

"Are you insane? It's only a few feet from them."

"I'll be quiet. Besides, they're too occupied right now to pay attention to anything that's going on behind them."

"I don't know about that. You saw how they turned around just a second ago."

"Whatever they think they heard, they probably figured it was an animal of some sort."

"You'll be in the open. One glance in that direction and they'll see you."

"I'll crawl, and stay behind cover as much as possible."

Denise let out a low groan, but Grace was already lying on her stomach, pushing herself forward with her elbows. The sound of dry leaves under her seemed to make a racket, but she was the only one who heard it.

As she continued to crawl, she tried to gauge the distance between her and the phone, which she could see clearly. Hopefully, it hadn't gotten damaged in the fall.

She stopped and looked around. The more direct route to the clearing was completely barren, but if she kept to the right, she would remain out of sight.

She made a quarter turn and moved as quietly as the conditions allowed. Pine needles dug into her face and palms, but she ignored the sting. She had no idea what Denise was doing. Probably biting her fingernails.

Hidden by a thicket of mountain laurel, she continued her slow descent, peering through the foliage from time to time. She could hear the sound of the shovels hitting the dirt and the grunt the two men made with each stroke.

She was only a few feet from her phone. She would need something to pull it to her. A stick, or a branch.

From her prone position, she broke a branch off the laurel bush. Then, crawling out in the open, she extended her arm. The tip of the branch touched the phone.

She would have to get a little closer.

She gave one last push. This time she was able to position the branch behind the phone. All she had to do was pull it toward her.

But just as the phone began to move, a booted foot stepped on it.

Grace froze.

"Well, well, Ms. McKenzie," a familiar voice said. "Funny meeting you like this."

Grace looked up into the unemotional eyes of Chief Josh Nader.

Thirty-Nine

"I'll take that," the chief said, bending to pick up the phone. He pressed a button to check Grace's last call, then, satisfied that she hadn't yet gotten through to the authorities, he shut it off and slipped it in his pocket.

Still flat on her stomach, Grace stared up at him in total shock. Unable to utter a single word, she looked from him to the mayor, just behind him, and then back at the chief. She couldn't find the words to express all the emotions she was feeling right now.

The chief glanced around him. "Who's here with you?"

She swallowed past the knot in her throat. "No one. I came alone."

He might have bought it if, at that precise

moment, Denise hadn't lost her footing. She caught herself, but it was too late. Josh had seen her.

"Well, well. If it isn't the mighty duo." He took out his gun and waved it in her direction. "Come and join us, Denise."

Without a word, Denise walked down.

He nodded toward her bag. "I'll take that, too." She started to walk toward him but he stopped her. "Just slide it over. You," he added, pointing the gun at Grace. "Stand up. And no fancy stuff unless you want to find yourself with a hole in your head."

When both women were side by side, the chief went through the bag. "Where's your phone?" he asked, looking up.

"At home. I forgot it."

"Likely story. George, frisk her."

As George approached Denise, she gave him a menacing look. "Don't you dare put your filthy hands on me, you slime. If you do, I'll bite your nose off."

George threw a hesitant look at his partner.

"She's not going to bite your nose off, George. She's just mouthing off. Frisk her." To Denise, he added, "You move one muscle and you're dead."

"Stand still, Denise," George said. "I'll make it fast."

He did. After a thorough check of her pockets, he backed off. "She's clean."

"You plan a stakeout and you forget your phone?" the chief scoffed. "How stupid is that?" Not really expecting an answer, he turned to the mayor. "Go finish filling the grave."

"Why don't *you* go and fill the grave?" George protested. "I'm tired. It's a wonder I didn't already have a heart attack."

"Stop complaining and hurry. We've got to get out of here."

Grumbling, George walked away and the chief returned his attention to Grace and Denise. "How the hell did you two figure this out?" he asked Grace.

As Denise shot her a quick glance, Grace gave an imperceptible shake of her head and hoped the chief wouldn't catch it. Their lives may not be worth much right now, but Matt had to be protected. "Guess we're smarter than you think."

"What you are, Ms. McKenzie, is a pain in the ass, but not for much longer. Who did you tell about your little detective work?"

Grace tried to look sincere. "I was going to tell Matt. I even tried to enlist the help of your good friend here, but you refused to let Matt out."

"Stroke of genius on my part." He turned to Denise. "What about you? You've always had difficulties keeping that big mouth of yours shut."

"I didn't know anything until Grace dragged me up here after we left the Bucks County Playhouse." Unlike Grace, she was unable to contain her anger and indignation. "You miserable bastard," she lashed out as if a spring had been released. "You're a disgrace to that uniform, and to all of humanity."

"Save it, Denise." The chief turned toward the woods, where George had filled a bag with what Grace presumed were Felicia's remains. He had already started to shovel the dirt back into the now-empty grave. "How are you making out?" he asked.

"Almost finished." George sounded out of breath.

"Why didn't you send an anonymous letter to my parents to let them know where Felicia was buried?" Denise was determined to speak her mind. "All we wanted was to give her a proper burial."

"You're getting on my nerves, Denise."

Grace touched her arm. "Not now, Denise."

"Listen to your partner in crime. At least, she's got *some* common sense."

Behind them, George let out a grunt as he dragged a large plastic bag to the car, an old Chrysler. As he heaved it into the backseat, Denise could no longer hold her emotions in check. She covered her face with her hands and started to sob.

George leaned against the car, catching his breath. "What now?" he asked.

"Open the trunk," the chief instructed.

George popped the lid. The chief waved his gun. "Inside. Both of you."

Grace half expected Denise to protest, but she didn't say a word. She climbed in and moved toward the back to make room for Grace.

Grace wasn't as accommodating. Once in that trunk, their fate was sealed. Josh and George would take them to another secluded area and kill them.

"No way," she said as Josh motioned for her to follow Denise. As she talked, she readied herself for the same kick that had served her so well on her first night in New Hope. This time, she would aim for the gun. Hopefully she'd send it flying and would get to it before George could.

"Josh, watch out!"

The warning came just as her foot shot out. Remarkably agile, the chief foiled the blow, turning away from it. Angered by her audacity, he backhanded her, hard enough to take her breath away. "Get in the trunk, dammit." He jammed the barrel of the gun into her stomach and gave her a shove. "Or you're going to find out what a long and painful death a bullet in the gut can bring."

She climbed in next to Denise. Maybe between the two of them, they would come up with some sort of escape plan.

The lid came down. The latch clicked, and darkness engulfed them.

"We're not moving," Denise said.

"They're probably discussing where to take us." As her eyes began to get accustomed to the dark, she saw Denise run her fingers along the lid. "What are you doing?"

"Looking for the release latch. There's got to be one. All cars have one now."

"Only recent models do, and this one is at least twenty years old."

"You're right." Denise let her hand fall.

At that moment, Grace heard the crank of the starter. Then the car began to move, slowly at first as Josh drove along the unpaved path, then faster as he turned onto the open road.

"We've got to come up with a plan," Grace said. "If we don't, they'll kill us."

"What do you have in mind?"

"At the moment, not much. I thought that when Josh opens the trunk again, we could come out kicking and screaming."

"What good will that do?"

"It will catch them off guard."

"Then what?"

"Then we zero in on Josh because he's the one we have to worry about. He's tough, he's ruthless and he's armed."

"You can't discard George. He's not about to stand still while we overpower his partner. *If* we manage to overpower Josh, which is very unlikely."

Grace turned to look at her friend. "Are you giving up, Denise? I didn't think that was your style."

"Who said anything about giving up?" Denise did a few contortions, struggling to reach the cuff of her jeans. "You see, Josh's plan to kill us doesn't really matter because…"

Her hand came up, holding a gun. "I'm going to kill him first."

Forty

"You had a gun? Where was it? How did George miss it?"

"He was looking for a phone, remember? Not a gun. He just checked my pockets. He was too damned scared to go any further." She let out a smug snicker. "Did you see his face? He actually believed I was going to bite his nose off."

"So did I. You looked absolutely fierce out there."

"I can be convincing when I want to."

Grace laughed. "This is rich. Here's the chief, accusing us of being stupid, and it doesn't occur to him to search you for a weapon." She pushed herself up on one elbow. "Tell me one thing, though. Why didn't you use the gun earlier?"

"I thought of it, but the right moment didn't present itself, so I decided to save my ace card until later."

Grace kissed Denise on the cheek. "Denise, you're beautiful."

"Thank you. Should I blast the lock?"

"No! We're going much too fast. We'll wait until they open the trunk."

"And then I'll blast them." She sounded as though she was actually looking forward to the showdown.

"Let's not do anything reckless, Denise. Remember, we're still locked up in a trunk, therefore at a disadvantage. What I'm saying is that we only have one chance."

"You don't think I can do this, do you?" Denise's tone was reproachful.

"Didn't you tell me that you couldn't shoot to save your life?"

"I'll be at point-blank range. How can I miss?"

Grace glanced down at the weapon in Denise's hand. "Is that a .22? Because if it is, it doesn't have much stopping power."

Denise chuckled. "I may not know how to shoot, but I know guns. I would never count on a .22 to save my life." She held the gun up and turned it around. "This baby is called the Grizzly and is one of the most powerful handguns ever made. It's loaded with .357 Magnum bullets. They make new models now, but Fred wouldn't trade his Grizzly for anything."

"How's the recoil?"

"Just what you'd expect in a gun this size."

"Is that going to be a problem?"

"The last time I shot a .357 Magnum the recoil almost knocked me to the ground."

That wasn't too encouraging. "Does the chief know that you can't shoot?"

"Everyone knows, but it doesn't matter. Fred told me once that men are more afraid of women with no shooting skills than vice versa."

"That makes me feel a whole lot better."

"Shh. We're slowing down. Give me some room. I need to face them when they open the trunk."

Grace squeezed herself against the back to allow Denise to get into position. It was a crazy plan, something that only worked in the movies, but she couldn't think of any other option. Either they shot their way out of this car or wait to be executed.

The choice was a no-brainer.

A moment later, the car stopped. A door opened, then the other. Grace heard the muffled sounds of voices, footsteps coming closer. "Are you ready?" she whispered.

"Ready." Denise braced herself against the back of

the trunk and wrapped both hands around the gun handle. "Okay, boys. Come to mamma."

The trunk popped open. Denise jumped out, screaming like a marine, and catching the two men completely off guard. "Hands in the air!" she barked as Grace climbed after her. "Now!"

At the sight of the formidable weapon in her hands, both men jumped three feet backward.

"Guns on the ground!" Denise screamed. She swung the Grizzly back and forth between Josh and George. "Quickly, or I start shooting."

"You crazy broad," Josh shouted. "Put that gun down before you hurt yourself."

Denise fired a shot. It went wild, but it had the desired effect, on George anyway, who turned out to be armed as well. He pulled a revolver from his belt and dropped it to the ground.

Grace quickly scooped it up.

Josh stubbornly hung on to his. "What are you doing, you nitwit?" he told George. "Can't you see that she's fucking with your mind again?"

Denise fired another shot, and this time she hit her target, because the chief cried out in pain. The gun flew out of his hand and he started jumping around on one foot, holding the other with both hands. "That bitch hit me! Jesus Christ, she hit me!"

"There's a full moon out there," Denise said. "Never underestimate an armed woman on a full moon."

"Don't shoot! Please!" George cried. He looked sick, but managed to raise his arms above his head.

"Shut up, George." Denise pointed the gun at the chief. "Josh, kick your gun over to Grace. Nice and easy."

Grace picked up Josh's gun and tucked it into her waistband, cringing at the cold contact. She held George's weapon pointed at the two men, although from the looks of things, all danger seemed to have passed. Josh sat on the ground, moaning and rocking back and forth while holding his injured foot. As for George, he looked petrified.

She walked over to the chief. "Who's stupid now, Chief?" She extended her hand, smiling down at him. "Cell phone, please."

Grimacing, he reached into his pants pocket and handed her the phone. With one hand, Grace dialed the number she had memorized.

"New Hope Police Department."

"This is Grace McKenzie," she said calmly. "Denise Baxter and I are holding Chief Nader and Mayor Renchaw at gunpoint. We need your help."

There was a long silence while the dispatcher tried

to decide what kind of crank caller he was dealing with. "Miss McKenzie? Uh…are you all right?"

"I am, but the chief has been wounded."

She heard commotion at the other end of the line, and hushed voices. A moment later, Deputy Montgomery came on. "Grace? What's going on? Where are you?"

"Denise and I caught Chief Nader and Mayor Renchaw as they were digging Felicia Newman's grave. They killed her and buried her on Buzz's farm. Her remains are in the backseat of an old Chrysler. They were going to kill us, too, but, well, we'll tell you the details later. Talk to Matt if you don't believe me. He had planned on catching the killers himself. When Josh put him in jail, Denise and I decided to ambush them ourselves."

"I already talked to Matt. I'll put him on if you'd like."

"There's no time for that, Rob. Just bring him with you."

"Where are you?"

She looked down at Josh. "Where are we?" she asked.

"Durham Road in Ottsville." He gave her a dirty look. "Just past the Easton Road intersection."

"I got that," Rob said. "Hang tight, Grace."

Forty-One

It was going to be a long night. Grace, Denise and Matt were brought back to the police station, along with George and Josh, the last two in handcuffs. Felicia's remains were taken to the morgue, and although Denise had wanted to go along, Rob had advised against it.

"The contents of that plastic bag is not something you want to see right now," he had told her. "The next few days will be much easier for you if you remember your sister the way she was."

With Grace by her side, Denise had called her parents in Florida. They were taking an early flight and would be here in the morning.

Acting as interim chief of police, Rob had taken down their statements. He had seemed a little overwhelmed at first, by the events that had shaken New Hope and by the sudden responsibility that had fallen upon him. But after a little floundering, he had stepped into his new role with his usual efficiency and good nature.

Once the statements were signed, he rose from the chief's chair. "Okay, people. We're done here. Why don't you all go home? I promise I'll stop by as soon as I have news I can share with you."

"What about Bernie?" Grace asked.

"His sister came to get him. He'll call you in the morning."

Matt pushed his chair back and rose as well. "And my father?"

"I've already talked to the D.A. He'll want to talk to George and Josh, but I've been told that Fred's release will not be a problem. Where will you be?"

"Home," Denise said quickly. "We're all going home, right, Matt?"

Grace looked at Matt and kept her fingers crossed. Denise had proven her love and loyalty for her husband far beyond what anyone had expected. It was time for Matt to recognize that.

"I will come home," Matt replied. "But I need to talk to my father first. I want to break the good news to him in person. You and Grace go on and I'll join you shortly."

Impulsive as always, Denise raised herself on her tiptoes and kissed him on the cheek. "Thank you."

He started to leave, then turned around. "Denise, that pumpkin pie you made for Lucy the other day. Is there any left?"

A wide smile brightened Denise's face. "No, but I'll be glad to make you a fresh one. It'll be ready by the time you get back from the county jail."

Although Fred had already heard bits and pieces of what had taken place at Buzz's farm, he doubled over with laughter when Matt told him about the shooting incident.

"Did she really blow Josh's big toe off?"

"Actually, she only blew off half of it. Rob tells me it's not a pretty sight."

"Oh, man." Fred wiped his eyes. "I would have paid good money to see that." Once the laughter had subsided, he asked, matter-of-factly, "Denise okay?"

"She's fine." Matt let a couple of seconds pass. When it was obvious that his father would make no further comment regarding his wife, Matt took the initiative.

"Look, Pop, I'm the last one to tell you what to do, or God forbid, give you advice in the romance department, but don't you think that Denise has suffered enough? Doesn't she at least deserve to hear from you? Considering all she's done?"

"When did you join her fan club?"

"Let's just say that she came through for this family in ways I didn't expect, and I'm a little humbled by it. She put her life on the line for you, Pop. A little thank-you would be nice."

"I hear she wasn't alone," Fred said, smoothly changing the subject. "Your Ms. McKenzie was there, too, kicking butt and risking her life for a man she's never met."

"I intend to thank her properly, when the time comes. But don't get carried away. She's not *my* Ms. McKenzie."

"That's funny, because I hear that the two of you have become inseparable." His eyes narrowed as he studied Matt's face. "You like this woman?"

More than he should, considering he had no idea where this relationship was going. He shrugged. "She's okay."

Fred threw his head back and let out a hearty laugh. "Don't give me that, Matty. This is me, remember, your daddy, who knows you better than anyone. I might be behind bars but I'm not blind. I can see the look in your eyes when you talk about her.

It's not a look I've seen often, so you understand why I would notice."

"All right, yes, I like her. A lot. The problem is, I'm not sure I should act on that feeling."

"Why the hell not?"

"What do I have to offer her? Months of living alone while I chase terrorists around the world?"

"Weren't you thinking of transferring to another department? Back to profiling, maybe? Or did I imagine that?"

"No, I've been considering it."

"Then do it. After four years with the antiterrorist unit, you deserve a change of pace. That would certainly reduce your traveling."

"She doesn't know anything about me."

"So fix that. Take her somewhere, away from flying bullets, stabbed priests and drowning men. Let her see the side of you we all know and love. Jesus, son, do I have to tell you everything?"

Matt chuckled. "You know, you're showing great aptitude for a whole new career in matchmaking."

"Do you want another piece of advice?"

"No. I can handle it from here."

"I'll give it to you anyway. If you're going to make a move, do it fast, because Rob likes her, too."

That wasn't exactly a surprise, but he appreciated

the heads-up anyway. He and his father shook hands through the bars. "Thanks, Pop. I'll see you at the hearing tomorrow morning."

Matt arrived at the Baxter house an hour later. "My father has a court appearance this morning at ten," he said as Denise handed him a thick slice of freshly baked pumpkin pie. "The D.A. doesn't expect any problem regarding his release."

Grace embraced him warmly. "Oh, Matt, that's wonderful news. Your father must be so relieved."

"Yes," Denise echoed. "It's wonderful news." She looked at Matt expectantly. "Did he say anything about me? Our situation?"

"No. I'm sorry, Denise."

She nodded. "I didn't expect he'd change his mind. I was just hoping, that's all." She looked around the room. "What should I do? Move out?"

"Certainly not," Matt said. "This is your home. Why would you leave?"

"It's been Fred's home longer, and if he's going to file for divorce, then, I should be the one to leave."

"Did your father say anything about a divorce?" Grace asked Matt.

"Nope."

"Then don't do anything rash, Denise. You and Fred

need to talk. If he won't initiate a meeting when he gets out of jail, then you do it. What do you think, Matt?"

"I agree with Grace. My dad is being stubborn. He'll come around, but it might take a little persuasion." He glanced up toward the staircase. "I don't mean to change the subject, but Lucy will be up soon and I wanted to say something about…her affair with Steven."

Denise was instantly on the defensive. "What about it?"

"Since their relationship had no bearing on what happened, I thought it'd be best if we kept that episode of her life between us." He looked directly at Denise. "Do you agree?"

"Oh, God, Matt, yes! Absolutely. Although, she might decide to tell your father herself, not right away, but eventually."

"That will be entirely up to her."

Denise refilled his coffee cup. "Now that we've got that straightened out, why don't you stop playing with that pie crust and tell us what you found out. Grace and I are dying to know what those two weasels are saying. Did they admit to killing my sister? Or are they claiming that it's all a big mistake?"

"They're not denying anything, but it's not a pretty story, Denise."

"I'm sure of that, but finding out what happened to my sister after all these years is the only way I'll be able to find some peace."

"Very well." He leaned forward, hands joined. "First of all, Josh isn't talking until his lawyer arrives. He knows his rights and he's exercising them."

"What about George?"

"Our illustrious mayor, on the other hand, is singing like a canary. He is also swearing high and low that he had nothing to do with Felicia's murder. He's hoping that in exchange for his full cooperation, the D.A. will go easy on him."

"I want them both to burn in hell," Denise said fiercely.

"If the D.A. has his way, they will. The man is out for blood."

Denise sat down on a footstool, close to Grace. "What happened that night, Matt?"

"George confirmed what Bernie told us. He and Josh were driving around and raising hell when they saw Felicia walking down the road. Josh stopped the car and asked her to join them. When she refused, he told George to grab her. She fought him hard, and she fought Josh just as hard later, but in the end, she was no match for them."

"Those bastards raped her, didn't they?" Denise

struggled to hold back her tears. "They raped her, killed her, buried her and never gave her a second thought."

Grace leaned over and touched Denise's hand. "Maybe Matt is right. You shouldn't hear this. It's going to be too painful."

"Not nearly as painful as what Felicia went through." She wiped her eyes. "Go on, Matt. Please."

"According to George, only Josh raped her. He may have another version, but as I said, we won't know his side of the story until he's ready to talk, so for the time being, we'll have to take George's word."

Denise nodded.

"At some point, your sister started screaming and Josh slapped her, hard. The back of her head hit the window's edge, probably killing her instantly. George was standing outside the car, unaware that she was dead until Josh came out and told him."

"That fat rat thinks that because he didn't rape my sister and didn't kill her, he is without blame?" Denise's voice was thin and sharp. "He helped bury her, didn't he? And he sure helped dig her out. I was there. I saw it."

There was a long silence before Grace broke it to ask the question she had been burning to ask. "What about the Badger brothers?"

"They're wanted for questioning, but can't be

found. Just before I left, Rob took a call from a motorist who spotted a green pickup heading south on Route 29. Three patrol cars are on their way. If it's them, they'll be arrested momentarily."

Grace stood up and went to look out the window. "And if it's not, they could be hundreds of miles away by now."

Matt came to stand behind her. "Rob will find them."

"But until he does, Bernie is not safe." She turned around. "Maybe Rob shouldn't have been so quick to release him. What if Cal and Lou come back to finish what they started?"

"You're assuming they're the ones who tried to kill him."

"You do, too. That's why you went to their home, looking for a green pickup."

"Even if the Badger brothers are working for Josh, they're much too busy saving their own hide right now to worry about Bernie."

Grace fell silent. His reasoning made sense. Still, she would feel a lot better once she knew that those two men were behind bars.

Forty-Two

Deputy Montgomery arrived an hour later, the bearer of good news. The pickup sighting on Route 29 had turned out to be a false alert, but soon after that, Cal and Lou Badger had been apprehended at a roadside motel on Route 202. They might have escaped in time if Cal hadn't gotten stuck trying to climb out of the bathroom window.

The anecdote provided some much-needed comic relief. Then Rob sat down and told them what he had learned from George Renchaw.

"As soon as Father Donnelly realized that Felicia was missing, he went to see Josh and George and begged them to turn themselves in. George was the weak link. He would have gone to the police if it hadn't been for Josh, who was tougher, and in a way, smarter. It didn't take him long at all to find out about the priest's dirty little secret and how that secret could benefit them. He was right. Father Donnelly was never a threat. Nor was Bernie, who didn't know the identity of the two men. From that moment on, they never gave Felicia a second thought."

"Until Steven came along," Denise commented.

Rob nodded. "Steven was much smarter than anyone gave him credit for. After hearing about Felicia's disappearance from Denise, he started a little investigation of his own. There's not much doubt now that his interest was motivated by greed and not mere curiosity. His lucky break came when he met Bernie. While I wouldn't swear it on the bible, I'm inclined to believe that his friendship with Bernie was genuine and that he found out about Father Donnelly by accident, as Bernie opened up to him. How could he have known that Bernie held the key to a twenty-year-old murder?

"My theory," Rob continued, "is that when Steven found out where Bernie and the priest were on the night of the abduction, he quickly put two and two together, went to see Father Donnelly, and threatened to expose him if he didn't give him the names of the two men."

"Didn't Father Donnelly realize that Steven was planning to blackmail the killers?" Grace asked.

"I'm sure he did, but what could he do? In order to save his reputation, his job and probably his freedom, he had no choice but to keep quiet."

"How much money did Steven extort?"

"He demanded one million dollars. That was not an outrageous sum for George, who is independently wealthy, but Josh has no money to speak of. Because George's money is tied up in stocks and real estate, he agreed to give Steven two hundred and fifty thousand dollars right away and the rest in installments. At the same time, he expected Josh to pay his share of the balance.

"That's where Steven's luck took a turn for the worse. In order to raise the cash, Josh would have had to sell his hunting cabin in the Poconos and he wasn't about to do that. He told George that Steven would never be happy until he had drained every cent out of them and that the only way to stop him was to kill him.

"Together they masterminded the entire scenario, including framing your father," Rob added, looking at Matt. "Fred's rationale was right on the mark. As his deputy, and later as the new chief, Josh spent a lot of time in your father's house. He knew his habits, his shooting schedule and where he kept his guns and ammo. He knew everything."

"But he didn't know about Steven and me," Denise said. "Who told him?"

"We both found out from one of our officers. He saw you coming out of Steven's cottage one evening as he was going off duty. Out of respect for Fred, Josh and I told him to keep quiet and I'm sure he did. But by telling us, he gave Josh the ammunition he needed to finalize his plan. All he needed was a way to spread the word about Denise and Steven so Fred would find out, in front of witnesses, and react accordingly."

Matt let out a brittle laugh. "And the best he could do was enlist the help of two idiots like Cal and Lou Badger?"

"There aren't many people in this town who would agree to frame your father, Matt. The Badger brothers, on the other hand, had no love lost for him and jumped at the chance to screw him. Surprisingly, though, everything went off just as Josh had intended. The only snag in his otherwise 'perfect' crime was you, Grace."

"Me?"

"George and Josh never felt threatened by Steven and Bernie's friendship, not until it was too late. So, when you showed up, found that tackle box and invited Bernie to the cottage, they started to worry that the two of you might also become friends."

"How did they know he was coming over? Did they tap his phone?"

"They didn't go that far. Bernie is the one who let the cat out of the bag so to speak. He was so excited about that tackle box that he told another worker at the cemetery and, well, you know how quickly news gets around in this town. When the chief heard that Bernie was going to stop at the cottage, he decided not to let it happen."

"Enter a green pickup truck," Denise said.

"We just found out that the truck in question belongs to Horace Badger's brother, who's presently serving time for auto theft."

"Upstanding family," Matt said dryly. "What are those two clowns saying?"

"Not much, but the lab report just came back. The fingerprints found at the church match Cal's, so he had no choice but confess."

"He admitted to killing Father Donnelly?"

"Yes. After the attempt on Bernie's life failed the other night, Josh instructed Cal to back off for the time being, but to keep an eye on him. When Cal saw Bernie go into the church last night, he followed him inside and hid in the confessional booth. From there he heard about Bernie's plan to go to the police with what he knew. He called the chief, who instructed him to kill Bernie. Fortunately for him, Bernie saw Cal, got scared and ran."

Grace felt a sudden chill. "He was still there when I went to see Father Donnelly, wasn't he? Listening to every word he and I were saying."

"I'm afraid so."

"But if the plan was to kill Bernie, why did he kill Father Donnelly?"

"Because Father Donnelly finally decided to do something noble. He realized what Cal was about to do and tried to stop him. He told him that if he didn't leave Bernie alone, he would break his own silence and go to the D.A. Cal killed him on the spot. He didn't even check with Josh. There was no time. He stabbed the priest and placed him at the altar, in the position you and Matt found him."

"Any reason he did that?" Grace asked. "It's a little gruesome."

"He thought it was funny. He got a big kick out of telling me." He spread his hands out. "That's all I know at the moment. In a day or two, when Josh tells us his version, I'll know more. In the meantime, I've taken steps to have Dusty released to his mother." He smiled at Matt. "You're going to have homemade peach jam until the day you die."

"I'll be generous and remember my friends."

"That's what I was waiting to hear." He looked at Grace and for a moment, she thought he was going to say something more, but he didn't. After checking his watch, he stood up. "I'd better go. I'm meeting the D.A. at six."

Matt rose as well and shook the deputy's hand. "Thanks for everything, Rob."

"You're welcome. I'm just sorry that your family had to go through this ordeal. Let's have lunch or something before you leave town, okay?"

"That's a plan."

At the door, Rob turned around. "Oh, and Denise."

"Yes?"

He winked at Grace. "I almost forgot. Fred wants to see you."

"That's good news, don't you think?" Denise asked after Rob left. She started to pace like a caged animal.

"It's terrific news," Grace replied. "Why don't you get going?"

"Because I'm not ready." She touched her hair. "I'm a mess."

"You're not. You're beautiful."

"What should I wear? Grace, would you help me pick out something?"

Under Matt's amused gaze, Grace took Denise's arm and sat her down. "Listen to me. Stop worrying about the way you look. Your husband wants to see you. Concentrate on that and go. Do you want me to drive you?"

"No." She stood up and looked at her reflection in the mirror. "Okay, here goes nothing."

Grace kissed her cheek. "Good luck, honey."

She walked her to the door and came back to sit beside Matt. "I've never seen her so excited."

"She wears her heart on her sleeve, that's for sure."

Grace tilted her head. "You had something to do with all this, didn't you? With your father's decision, I mean."

"I didn't twist his arm."

"No. Force wouldn't work on a Baxter man."

Matt laughed. "Are you becoming an expert on the Baxter men now?"

"Does that frighten you?"

"No. What frightens me is that I might not have the opportunity to become an expert on Grace McKenzie."

"And why is that?"

"Because you'll soon be turning the gallery over to

Sarah, moving back to Boston and before long, New Hope will be nothing but a distant memory."

"Actually." She started playing with the cuff of his sweater, feeling suddenly giddy and full of bravado. "There's been a slight change of plan."

"What sort of change?"

"I won't be turning the gallery over to Sarah after all."

"You've decided to keep it?"

"Yes, but I won't be running it."

"Who will?"

"Bernie. I haven't asked him yet, but I plan to, as soon as I talk to him."

Matt's reaction was exactly as she had predicted. He looked startled. "Bernie?"

"He's perfect, when you think of it. He knows more about art and about the Hatfield Gallery than anyone in town. He is responsible, loyal and totally trustworthy."

"But he's not a businessman."

"He's a quick learner, and I'll come down as often as he needs me to. The rest of the time, I'll be just a phone call away."

"What about his social issues?"

"Now that he's no longer carrying the burden he's carried for the past twenty years, and realizes that no one blames him for what happened, he should be improving quickly. He's already made tremendous progress."

Matt took her hand and brought it to his lips. "That's a wonderful thing you're doing, Grace. I'm not sure Sarah will be thrilled with your decision, though."

"Oh, I don't know. She's no longer the ogre she used to be. And believe it or not, she is beginning to rely on my decisions."

"Will you be delivering the news in person?"

Grace nodded. "I'm taking the noon flight to Boston and will return tonight. I'll try to soften the blow as much as I can, but how do you tell a mother that her son was a blackmailer? That he could have freed an innocent man from a mental institution and didn't?"

"You'll find a way."

"What about you? What are your plans?" She tried to sound matter-of-fact, but wasn't sure she pulled it off. The thought that she might never see him again was clouding any hope she'd had for a relationship.

"I've taken a temporary leave of absence," he said.

"That's understandable. You'll want to spend time with your family." She hoped he wouldn't notice the disappointment in her voice.

He leaned toward her. His warm breath brushed

her face. "What about you, Grace? Would you like to spend some time with me?"

Her heart skipped a beat. "You and all the Baxters?"

"No, just you and me."

The knot in her throat got a little bigger. "What did you have in mind?"

"A long weekend, somewhere warm and exotic."

Don't blow it by telling him that you're allergic to the sun. He'll find out soon enough. "By warm and exotic, you mean sandy beaches, palm trees and piña coladas?"

His lips touched hers. "And teeny little bikinis. You do have a bikini, don't you, Grace?"

"Not with me, but—"

He sank his fingers into her hair. "Forget the bikini."

This time she didn't hear any bells. "I would have to call my father, let him know that there's been another delay."

His cell phone magically appeared in his hand.

Laughing, she wrapped her arms around his neck. "When do we leave?"

CHRISTIANE HEGGAN

32126 THE SEARCH   ___ $6.99 U.S. ___ $8.50 CAN.
32005 SCENT OF A KILLER   ___ $6.50 U.S. ___ $7.99 CAN.
32228 NOW YOU DIE   ___ $6.99 U.S. ___ $8.50 CAN.

(limited quantities available)

TOTAL AMOUNT $ _____
POSTAGE & HANDLING $ _____
($1.00 FOR 1 BOOK, 50¢ for each additional)
APPLICABLE TAXES* $ _____
TOTAL PAYABLE $ _____

(check or money order—please do not send cash)

To order, complete this form and send it, along with a check or money order for the total above, payable to MIRA Books, to: **In the U.S.:** 3010 Walden Avenue, P.O. Box 9077, Buffalo, NY 14269-9077; **In Canada:** P.O. Box 636, Fort Erie, Ontario, L2A 5X3.

Name: _____
Address: _____ City: _____
State/Prov.: _____ Zip/Postal Code: _____
Account Number (if applicable): _____

075 CSAS

*New York residents remit applicable sales taxes.
*Canadian residents remit applicable GST and provincial taxes.

MIRA®

www.MIRABooks.com

MCH0906BL